Dear Reader,

I fell in love with Kate Larimer way back in high school. At the time, she'd have nothing to do with me, and how can I blame her? I was just a scrawny, awkward teenager. I guess when I went off to Hollywood, somewhere in the back of my mind I was thinking—I'll show her.

Now, three wives, one highly sculpted body and a hit TV show later, I find I'm right back where I started—making passes at Kate that fall flat on the ground. She thinks I'm careless, cocky and irresponsible, and—hey!—I am. But what's worse, she thinks I'm false.

Well, there's nothing false about the way I feel for Kate, and there's nothing false about how I keep coming back to Victoria Bend, Mississippi, just to see her.

All I know is, whatever it takes, I've got to make Kate Larimer see the real me.

Kevin Dawson

REBECCA FLANDERS

After the Storm

Mississippi

Harlequin Books

TORONTO • NEW YORK • LONDON
AMSTERDAM • PARIS • SYDNEY • HAMBURG
STOCKHOLM • ATHENS • TOKYO • MILAN
MADRID • WARSAW • BUDAPEST • AUCKLAND

HARLEQUIN ENTERPRISES LTD.
225 Duncan Mill Road, Don Mills,
Ontario, Canada M3B 3K9

AFTER THE STORM

Copyright © 1986 by Donna Ball, Inc.

ISBN: 0-373-45174-1

Published Harlequin Enterprises, Ltd. 1986, 1993, 1994

Chapter One

Katherine Larimer had known Kevin Dawson since the third grade, when he used to consistently con her out of the last Twinkie in her lunch box. He hadn't changed much.

He strolled into her office with his jacket tossed carelessly over his shoulder, his curly brown hair professionally tousled, his sexy, sauntering gait professionally coached and his grin warm enough to melt the coldest heart. "Hello, sweetheart," he greeted her. "How about buying a poor boy dinner?"

Kate restrained the urge to applaud lightly. No one had a way with an entrance like Kevin Dawson. But then, no one had had as much practice.

She feigned innocence. "Why Kevin, what a surprise! I didn't know you were in town."

His grin sparked into something a bit more natural, and he lounged against the doorframe. Every man, woman and child in Victoria Bend had known of Kevin's impending arrival for slightly over a month now. He put on a straight face and inquired politely, "Should I have phoned first?"

She looked at him dryly. "I probably wouldn't have answered."

His eyes twinkled. "Exactly. So I saved myself a quarter."

Kevin Dawson was Victoria Bend's proudest product, the local boy who made good, the favorite son of a small town, which, before Kevin, had been on its last legs. He was Colt Marshall on the prime-time action-adventure series *Code Zero*. He was also incredibly wealthy, and half the women in the United States were in love with him. And that was just for starters.

He was in Victoria Bend to officiate at the ground-breaking ceremony of the new hospital—a project made possible largely through his funding. For all his many faults—and there were plenty—Kate had to give Kevin credit for one thing: he had never forgotten where he came from. A good portion of all his charitable, and business, activities had been funneled back into Victoria Bend, and the contribution to the small town's economy was not to be taken lightly. The hospital was the latest of his benevolent gestures, and though it was desperately needed and greatly appreciated, Kate couldn't help wishing it could have been acquired without her ever having to deal with Kevin Dawson.

So far, it had worked out quite well. She had worked exclusively through Kevin's lawyers and planners and managers, for Kevin Dawson was a busy man and couldn't be bothered with details—fortunately for everyone concerned. On camera he was brilliant; off camera he was hopelessly incompetent. He had simply never learned how to deal with real life.

Feeling some token thanks were called for, Kate said now, "It's a good thing you're doing with the hospital, Kevin. We really need it."

He straightened up, smiling endearingly. "I know. Aren't you impressed?"

"Not as much as you are." Kate lost her own battle with a rueful smile and gestured him toward a chair. "Sit down. I have some work to finish up."

Kevin arranged his long body in the faded orange easy chair before her desk and looked lazily around the familiar surroundings. There was a couch, a desk, another chair, a couple of filing cabinets. Kate's diploma hung on one wall; her medical books lined another. It was a very dull office. He said, "So how's business?"

"Slow, thank goodness."

He lifted an eyebrow. "That attitude will not lead to fame and fortune, Katie. Take it from me."

She got up to file the chart on which she had just made her last notation of the day. "Fame and fortune is not why I became a doctor in Victoria Bend, Mississippi. And in the medical business, it might surprise you to know, a slow day is a good day—it means everybody is healthy."

He shrugged cheerfully. "Well, just wait till we get that hospital finished. You'll be a rich woman in no time, up to your elbows in gallbladders and appendixes."

She rested her arm on the open file drawer, turning to look at him with a mixture of tolerance and dismay. It never ceased to amaze her, the ease with which this thirty-four-year-old man had allowed himself to become trapped in perpetual adolescence—and how little he seemed to care. She said, "What do you want from me, Kevin?"

"Dinner," he replied promptly. "I haven't had a home-cooked meal in so long—"

"I don't have time to cook for you." She closed the drawer.

"Well..." He knotted his brow dubiously. "We could go to Jacksonville, but the fans would drive you crazy."

"I don't want to have dinner with you at all, Kevin," Kate explained patiently, clearing off her desk. "Why don't you make the mayor feed you?"

"Oh, come on, Katie!" He looked pained. "You know everything the mayor's wife cooks comes wrapped in tinfoil. I damn near broke a tooth on it one time."

"Nobody ever broke a tooth on tinfoil."

"Well, it can't be good for the digestion."

"I don't believe there's ever been an adequate study made on that."

"We could pick up a couple of steaks—"

"Cook your own steaks."

"I haven't even opened up my house yet," he insisted. "I'm not even sure the electricity's on, and I know there's nothing in the fridge. Katie..." His eyes took on a hint of hurt. "I came all this way to see you."

She had no intention of falling for it, of course. It was the same whenever Kevin came to town. He would borrow her car and leave it with the gas tank empty. He would invite himself to dinner and tie up her telephone with long-distance calls to people he called "babe." He would keep her up half the night earnestly seeking her advice on some project or another and then do the absolute opposite from what she had suggested. And it didn't matter whether it was the last piece of pie or a bottle of Cabernet Sauvignon she was saving for a special occasion or the package of M&Ms she hid at the back of the cabinet to satisfy a sudden chocolate attack—or the last Twinkie—before Kevin left her house, she could be certain he had helped himself. To the rest of America, Kevin Dawson might be the hottest thing since the Hula-Hoop, but to Katherine Larimer, he was a pest.

She looked at him with as much forbearance as she could muster at six o'clock in the evening of a muggy

Mississippi May. "Why do you keep bothering me, Kevin?"

"Bothering *with* you, you mean."

She repeated firmly, "Bothering me."

He was not in the least offended. He thought about it for a moment and came up with a grin and a shrug. "Because you turn me down with more class than anybody I know."

Kate snorted and picked up her medical bag. "*Nobody* turns you down, Kevin Dawson. That's your trouble."

"You just did," he pointed out.

"So I did," she agreed with satisfaction. Not that she believed for one minute that she had gotten away with it.

"Isn't there something in the Hippocratic oath that keeps you from letting a man starve?"

Kate smiled patiently. "There are almost twelve thousand residents in Victoria Bend, any one of whom would be beside himself at the thought of having Kevin Dawson to dinner. My conscience is utterly clear when it comes to your starvation."

He looked at her with a fair imitation of genuine perplexity. "Why do you always give me such a hard time, Katie dear?"

"It's nothing complicated, Kevin," she told him pleasantly, as she must have told him a dozen times over the course of the years. "It's just that I really don't like you. I've never liked you. Now, I realize that there are millions of people in the United States who disagree with me, but then, that's what makes horse races, isn't it? And please don't call me Katie dear."

His lazily amused brown-eyed gaze didn't waver. "You always were a poor judge of character."

She moved toward the door, stepping carefully over his long legs and half expecting him to trip her.

"It's a little late to look for another date," he suggested, somewhat mournfully.

"It certainly is." There was a note of smugness in her voice. She wasn't proud of it, but Kevin always brought out the worst in her.

He lounged back in the chair, ankles crossed comfortably, hands linked across his flat abdomen, looking as though he had no intention of leaving and gazing at her with patience and confidence. Kate had never considered him a very good-looking man—perhaps because she remembered him with braces and too-short jeans and the occasional outcropping of adolescent acne. He had always been tall, and his arms and legs grew too fast for the rest of his body, so that, from ages twelve to fifteen, she had secretly nicknamed him Lurch—an appellation that had initiated particularly vicious retribution on more than one occasion. Of course, by age sixteen he had filled out quite nicely, and that, in combination with his innate effusive charm, had made him Big Man on Campus in no time at all. That was when Kate had really begun to dislike him.

Even now, however, she couldn't entirely understand what a swooning female population saw in him. His features were too sharp for Kate's taste, and they didn't quite fit with those soft, mischievous brown eyes. He certainly kept himself in good shape, lean and rangy rather than muscle-bound, which she supposed some women would find appealing. The thick, curly chestnut hair made him look younger than he needed to look, and so did that impish grin that he thought was so adorable. All in all, he looked manufactured, put together for effect and not quite real. But thirty-nine percent of the American viewing audience could not be wrong, and Kate could only conclude that he must have something she hadn't discovered yet. And most likely never would.

He said now, reasonably, "Come on, Katie, what's one evening out of your life? A couple of hours at most. Where's that hometown hospitality this part of the country is supposed to be so famous for?"

The corners of Kate's mouth came down dryly, but she didn't bother to point out that his "couple of hours" invariably stretched into marathon sessions that robbed her of sleep, stripped her cupboards bare and eroded her temperament to the jagged edge of civility. Instead, she replied with simple finality, "I'm sorry, Kevin. I have other plans for the evening."

He thought about that for a moment; then his face relaxed into an easy smile. "Oh, right, I forgot; tonight's Monday. You'll be watching my show. No problem; we can watch together."

Kate hoped he couldn't see the guilty truth that backed her irritable scowl. As a matter of fact, she was a closet *Code Zero* addict, a phenomenon she had never been able to explain adequately to herself. Unless it was the fact that Colt Marshall was the ultimate hero—clever, strong, courageous, gallant...everything that Kevin Dawson was not. It was a pity.

She turned back to him with a pleasant smile. "Go home, Kevin," she advised. "Fix yourself a nice TV dinner and watch your reruns by yourself. The solitude will do you good. I'll see you tomorrow at the councilmen's luncheon."

He made a wry expression of resignation that brought the dimple in his cheek to prominence and very reluctantly gathered himself to his feet. "Your final word?"

"My final word." She opened the door.

He sighed. "There's just one problem. I told my driver to pick me up at your place. I don't suppose you'd consider giving me a ride home?"

Kate turned to him, weary incredulity etched on her face. Just when she thought he had finally run out of ploys. "That was rather irresponsible of you, don't you think?"

He looked defensive. "Hey, even the servant class deserves some time off every once in a while." Then he shrugged and grinned, hooking his thumb in the collar of his jacket and flinging it over his shoulder again. "Besides, irresponsibility is one of my trademarks. Isn't that what you're always saying?"

With her hand still on the doorknob, she hesitated, scowling as she battled with herself. He knew as well as she did that she was not going to make him walk the five miles to his place. For one thing, the mayor would never forgive her. For another... She sighed inwardly as she faced the inevitable. As irritating as he was, she owed him a lot. The town owed him a lot. And, she supposed, deep down, beneath all the tax shelters and investment quotients and scatterbrained notions of philanthropy, he did mean well. She only wished he didn't get on her nerves quite so badly or that she could learn to live with it.

"All right," she agreed with considerable ill grace. "How much can one ride cost me? Let's go."

A suspicious light of triumph was in his eyes as he sauntered toward her, politely holding the door as she passed through. Then he grinned and draped a companionable arm around her shoulders. "We've got to stick together, Katie. After all, you and I are the only things worth mentioning that ever came out of this town. It's only right."

She gave him a withering look, and he dropped his arm as they moved through the deserted reception room. He knew when he was pushing his luck.

The evening was sticky and overcast, prematurely twilit because of the low gray sky. The humidity and the barometric pressure were working on Kate's mood, she knew, and this was not the most propitious time for a visit from Kevin Dawson. She had other things on her mind.

Kate had never had any ambition beyond obtaining her medical degree and coming back home to Victoria Bend to join her father's practice. She had no illusions about herself: she was a good doctor, but she did not like challenges. A practice in a big city or a metropolitan hospital ward would have made a wreck of her in no time. The slow-paced, easygoing life-style of the small town was perfect for her, for it allowed her time for the rarest and the finest of the medical arts—compassion. But while the advantages of a small practice in a relatively isolated town were many, the one glaring disadvantage quickly became obvious: the lack of adequate medical facilities.

Kate's office included a small clinic that could handle most emergencies, but major cases had to be transferred to the county hospital twenty miles away. For some of them, the slow trip over poor country roads proved to be too much. The town desperately needed a hospital of its own, and Kate had campaigned for one since she had come here. Her relief at finally winning the battle—even if it was due to an unwelcome benefactor—was overwhelming. But she had not been prepared for the fact that the real challenge had just begun.

Her father, an ex-navy doctor who had kept Victoria Bend healthy with commonsense medicine and house calls for over thirty years, had retired when Kate came home to practice. He still saw a few old-timers who simply would not trust a female doctor—even if she was Doc Larimer's daughter—but for all intents and purposes, Victoria Bend had only one practicing physician. It had therefore been up to Kate to meet with the planning committee, lawyers and consultants in these first stages of organizing the hospital. It was no small task.

The community hospital was designed to grow with the town, beginning with sixty beds, two operating rooms, a fully equipped lab and maternity, cardiac and emergency units. It was Kate's responsibility to consult on design, order equipment, formulate policy and hire a staff, all of which were overwhelming tasks. She had done more traveling in the past year than she had ever done in her life; she had spent at least twice as much time on the phone embroiled in red tape as she had with her patients. She disliked the upheaval in her life and resented the time the project took away from her patients, but it was a necessary evil. And so far the only thing with which she had not been able to cope completely was the hiring of the staff.

It was an awe-inspiring responsibility. Kate had a very protective, almost possessive attitude toward her patients, and it was very difficult to entrust them to some stranger. The plan was to take a surgeon into partnership in her practice immediately, train him until the hospital was open and expand the medical staff from there. Kate had interviewed scores of candidates and had yet to come to a decision. Her father accused her of acting like a mother hen toward her practice, and she was beginning to worry that he was right. Another candidate was due to arrive tomorrow, and the interview weighed heavily on her mind. She couldn't postpone making a decision indefinitely. But how could she entrust the people who had come to depend on her to someone who was no more than a one-page résumé?

She took out her keys as she approached her car, and Kevin immediately snatched them from her hand. "I'll drive," he volunteered cheerfully, and completely missed her glare as he slid behind the wheel. Kate didn't like the way he drove her car. He kept forgetting it was a Buick, not a racing-model Porsche, and that this was Elm Street, not the Santa Monica Freeway.

"You sure have some lousy weather down here," Kevin commented as she got in beside him and slammed the door. He revved the engine. "How come it's always raining whenever I come down?"

Kate smiled sweetly. "Why do you keep coming?"

He grinned and pulled out into the street. "Why, because this is home, sweetheart."

Kevin's parents had moved to Florida some years back, and Kate had thought that would put an end to his constant visits. Not so. He liked the feeling of the conquering hero returning to the place of his origin; he liked being adored but not mobbed. And the people of Victoria Bend did respect his privacy—he never passed through town without fanfare, but neither were there hordes of autograph seekers trailing him. The small lakeside town would have been the perfect place for a harried star to relax and regroup, but Kevin never stayed long enough to do either. He swept through town dispensing favors and gathering accolades and then disappeared for weeks at a time without a backward glance. Kate still wondered why he kept coming back.

Fortunately, there wasn't much traffic. Kevin's foot lay heavily on the accelerator as he turned on the radio. An announcer blasted out something about heavy thunderstorms, and Kevin pushed the button for a hard-rock station. Kate immediately reached over and changed to easy listening and lowered the volume.

"How long are you staying?" she asked, to take her mind off his maniacal driving.

"Just till this business is over with day after tomorrow. I've got a big party to go to Wednesday; then I thought I'd drop in and see my folks."

"Hmm." The sound was noncommittal. Kate winced as the car screeched to a stop at an intersection, drawing the attention of Doug McCall, who was on patrol tonight. The policeman whipped his head around, glaring suspiciously at the car, then recognized Kevin and waved. Kevin waved back. The force of his acceleration pressed Kate back against the seat.

"For heaven's sake, Kevin, the streets are wet! Slow down!"

He lowered his speed fractionally and glanced at her. "A bit wound up tonight, aren't we?"

"You seem to have that effect on me," she muttered.

He lifted an eyebrow. "My notorious sex appeal?" The look she cast him made him chuckle.

When they were younger, Kevin used to come on to her—mostly because, even as an adolescent, he couldn't seem to help making a pass at anything in skirts. Kate had never found him particularly hard to resist, but she let him kiss her once, out of curiosity more than anything else. It was the singularly most disappointing experience in her life, and Kevin had been too embarrassed by his obvious failure ever to try it again. Both were rather relieved to have the experiment out of the way so they could go back to a more comfortable relationship. If, indeed, their relationship could have ever been called comfortable.

"So tell me what's got you so uptight, love," he invited. He stretched his hand over the seat to massage the back of Kate's neck. The gesture made her nervous—not because he was touching her but because he was driving with only one hand.

Kate made a disgruntled sound and deliberately reached up and removed his hand, placing it firmly on the steering wheel. "Since when are you interested in anyone's problems but your own?"

"Since I don't have any."

"What?" She feigned amazement. "No crisis in your love life? No fights with the network? No gruesome contract negotiations, no sudden desperate yearning to know the meaning of life?"

He did not even have the grace to look abashed. He shook his head confidently. "Nope. Everything's rolling along as smooth as silk. Couldn't be happier. Do you want to stop somewhere and get a drink?"

"Are you an alcoholic now?"

"No, just thirsty."

She glanced at him suspiciously. "I don't get it. Why would you want to have a drink with me unless it's to cry out your problems on my shoulder?"

He repressed a long-suffering sigh. "It couldn't be that I'm just being friendly?"

She laughed softly, shaking her head. Kevin, in small doses, could be quite endearing, which was, of course, the only reason she had put up with him as long as she had. She reminded him, "It's a dry county, Dawson. If you want anything to drink, you're going to have to send your driver across the line for it."

He made a sudden sharp left turn into the supermarket. "Never mind. I'd rather eat than drink, anyway."

He pulled up shortly into the fire lane and jerked on the emergency brake. He turned to her persuasively. "You don't mind running in and getting a few things for dinner, do you? I would, but it would take me forever to get out, and I know you're in a hurry."

The warm humor she had felt for him a moment ago dissipated immediately into a more familiar sentiment, and she glared at him. She must have been crazy to think she could evade his manipulation; his technique was flawless. He had to eat, and there were no supplies at his house. And he was right; if he went in, he would be tied up for hours, greeting friends and would-be friends, shaking hands and receiving congratulations and giving little pieces of himself to eager fans who would make him the prime topic of dinner-table conversation tonight. It would have been simpler, Kate realized now, to have invited him home for dinner in the first place, for Kevin Dawson always got what he wanted, one way or another.

He was looking at her, those sweet brown eyes softened with a confident smile, and there was nothing Kate could say. With an impatient, irritated puff of breath, she got out of the car and slammed the door hard behind her, stalking into the store.

Chapter Two

Getting in and out of the store in a hurry was not all that much easier for Kate than it would have been for Kevin. There had been, off and on, speculation over the years that the local doctor and the famous TV star were lovers—which was only natural, considering the way Kevin zeroed in on her whenever he was in town—and despite her best efforts, not everyone remained convinced they were only friends. At any rate, it was only assumed that Kate knew everything there was to know about Kevin, and everyone she saw had some message to pass along to him.

She moved as quickly as she could through the aisles, reaching instinctively for Kevin's favorites and tossing them into the cart. For her own part, she would have been happy to have supplied him with a can of spaghetti and a pint of milk for his dinner, but she knew the gesture would be futile. He would only find a way to maneuver her into a real dinner sooner or later, and she would save herself the trouble by doing it right the first time. There was no winning a battle of wills with Kevin Dawson.

It had begun to drizzle when she came out, and a small crowd had gathered at the car, talking to Kevin through the window. He was leaning back against the seat, laughing and quipping with his adoring fans and basking in the attention. Friends and neighbors greeted Kate as she came up; someone was eager to take Kevin's groceries and put them in the back seat, and it was up to Kate to make the fatal announcement. "Sorry, folks," she said. "We've got to get the ice cream into the freezer before it melts. We'll see you all at the ceremony Wednesday, okay?"

They broke up reluctantly but with goodwill, calling goodbyes to Kevin and conferring among themselves about what a really *nice* person Kevin Dawson was. Kevin waved his final goodbyes and started the engine.

"Don't you ever get tired of it?" Kate asked curiously.

"What?"

"All the attention. Not being able to make a move without a crowd following you. Having to be 'on' all the time."

He laughed, glancing at her in surprise. Kate was relieved to notice he was negotiating the crowded parking lot with a bit more care than he had used on the main roads. "Are you kidding? I love it. Why should I get tired of it?"

Kate was genuinely puzzled. Being an intensely private person herself, she had never understood how anyone could enjoy the type of life Kevin led—but that was only one of the many things she had never understood about him. She said, shrugging a little, "I don't know. The lack of privacy seems to be the biggest complaint among celebrities, but it never seems to bother you. I mean, what happens if you have a bad day and just want to be left alone?"

"I never have bad days," he returned smugly. "That's what makes me so good at what I do."

She looked at him with helplessness mixed with amusement, not knowing why she should have expected any other response. Only people with depth of character experienced identity crises. Kevin barely had any character, much less depth.

She shrugged and leaned back against the seat, commenting, "Well, I'll give you credit—you've certainly stuck with it longer than I ever would have thought. I figured you'd have grown bored with the show long before now and started throwing tantrums for bigger and better things."

"Hell, no," he replied cheerfully, and swung onto the highway. "I never had any ambition; you know that. Besides, I love old Colt—he's my alter ego. Always thinking on his feet, rescuing damsels in distress, brave and smart and as solid as a brick. There's nothing that man can't do. He always has the right change when he has to make a lifesaving phone call, always finds a parking place at the airport when he has three minutes to stop a plane from taking off, can run a mile uphill with crooks dogging his every step and not even get winded.... Who wouldn't like to have a life like that? Like I said, I've got it made."

Kate laughed softly, shaking her head. "Oh, Kevin, won't you ever grow up?"

He cast a twinkling glance at her. "Nope. Did you really get ice cream?"

"No." She extended her hand. "That'll be thirty-two dollars and eighteen cents, by the way."

He managed to look regretful and adorable at the same time. "Sorry, I don't have any cash. Do you take American Express?"

Kate made a bitter face and dropped her hand. Typical.

Kevin had a luxurious lake house in a secluded cove five miles from town, complete with Jacuzzi, sauna, indoor pool and gym. The taxes on it alone had gone a long way toward building the new civic center, and Kevin used it less than a dozen nights a year. The rest of the time the house stood empty, for Kevin did not bother to employ caretakers; the pool grew algae, cobwebs collected, mildew stained the draperies, and hinges rusted. About once a year he took it into his head to replace all the furnishings and oftentimes didn't even have a chance to see what his latest decorator had wrought before it was time to redo everything again. That, too, was typical of the kind of careless extravagance Kate couldn't help but abhor.

He made an abrupt right-hand turn onto a narrow gravel road, and Kate sat up sharply. "What are you doing? Don't take my car down this road—there's been construction here, and there are nails and potholes all over the place!"

"It's a shortcut," he replied easily. "I thought you were in a hurry."

Kate winced as gravel banged against the undercarriage and the wheels bounced wildly over a hidden dip. Kevin didn't slow his speed. "You crazy person!" She had to shout over the sound of rocks and debris destroying her car. "You're going to get us both killed!"

He reached over and patted her leg, smiling at her soothingly. "You're a fussy old maid, Katie dear. Relax. I know this road like the back of my hand."

"Will you watch where you're going?"

The car bounced over a pile of loose boards that had strayed from a nearby house under construction, and

Kevin glanced out his window curiously. "The place is really growing up. Who are my new neighbors?"

Kate groaned and pressed her head against the headrest, closing her eyes.

The three minutes that the car dipped and careened down the twisting makeshift road seemed like three hours as Kate counted every dent and scratch and imagined just how serious the accident they were about to have was likely to be. With a spray of gravel and grinding protest of the sliding back tires, Kevin pulled up in front of his own house and announced cheerfully, "Well, here we are. Thanks for the ride."

Kate gave him a look that could have killed a man twice his size and flung herself out of the car. Kevin followed at a leisurely, mildly curious pace as she stalked around the vehicle, inspecting the damage.

"You're so picky, Katie," he complained. "You always were. I didn't hurt your car. I got us here okay, didn't I?"

"You are the most inconsiderate, self-centered, thoughtless, *careless* excuse for a human being I've ever had the misfortune to know," she grated, restraining more colorful epithets with a great effort. Her tolerance level for Kevin had been reached the moment he ordered her into the grocery store, and now it was long since surpassed. "Didn't your mother ever teach you respect for the property of others?"

"Hey," he objected defensively, "there's no need to bring my mother into this."

"Oh, just shut up and take your groceries into the house, will you? I've done my Christian duty; I've brought you home. Now go away."

Kevin had the good sense to shut up, but he did not go away. He followed her with a modicum of polite concern on her tour around the car. In the darkening twilight she could see very little—a few chips and scratches, a leafy branch pinned between the drive shaft and the chassis, and—

"Oops, a nail in the tire." Kevin bent down. "Gee, I'm sorry, Katie."

"Kevin, don't—"

He worked his fingers under the protruding head of the nail and deftly pulled it out. Kate stared in dismay as air began to hiss from the newly created hole at an alarming rate.

"—pull it out," she finished flatly, and Kevin looked up at her with a weak smile of apology.

Kate compressed her lips tightly and without a word stepped around him and reached inside the driver's door to unlatch the trunk. Kevin got to his feet. "Come on, Katie, don't get mad. It's just a tire. You take life too seriously, you know."

She walked around to the trunk and flung it open, reaching inside for the tools. Kevin followed her. "What's the big deal? We'll go inside and call the garage."

"The garage is closed," she said tightly, and pushed past him.

"Oh." He leaned against the car, watching as she braced her legs and used the tool to pop off the hubcap. The tire was completely flat now. "Well, here..." He pushed away reluctantly. "I'll do it, I guess."

She glared at him. "Do you have any idea how to change a tire?"

He looked a bit disconcerted. "Well, it can't be all that hard. And anyway, you're a doctor. You shouldn't hurt your hands."

Kate drew in her breath sharply and formed a small silent prayer for patience. "Where did you get that line?"

she muttered, and began to work the lugs with a particular vengeance.

He grinned. "From TV."

"Welcome to real life, hotshot." She panted as she twisted the tool against the mechanically tightened bolt and then staggered backward as it abruptly loosened. With a grunt of satisfaction, she attacked the next bolt.

"At least let me help. Don't you have to put the jack on first?"

"Don't help me, Kevin," she warned grimly. The exercise was not dissipating her temper any.

He rummaged around in the trunk. "Where's the jack? Is that it? How does it work, anyway?"

"I said don't help me, Kevin."

He leaned against the trunk again and began absently twisting screws and bolts. Kate looked up just as the jack fell into three neat pieces on the ground. At that moment the sky opened up and rained torrents.

Kate straightened up slowly. Kevin looked in dismay from the broken jack to Kate's darkening features. "It was an accident," he defended quickly.

Cold rain soaked through her clothes, plastered her hair to her head and dripped into her eyes. She weighed the tire tool in her hand; her eyes narrowed grimly. "No jury in the world would convict me."

Kevin smiled uncertainly. "I wonder what Colt Marshall would do now."

She took a step toward him. "Run like hell, if he had any sense."

He threw up a hand in half surrender, half defense. "Temper, temper, Katie."

And temper was exactly what she allowed herself as she threw the tool into the trunk and snapped at him, "Well, are you just going to stand there in the rain like an idiot? Pick up that jack and let's get inside!''

Kevin hurriedly gathered up the pieces of the jack and tossed them into the trunk, barely getting his fingers out of the way before she slammed the lid. He paused only long enough to get the groceries out of the car before following her up the steps at a run.

Kate stood shivering in the eaves as he fumbled for his keys. She was quite certain that if he told her now he had forgotten his keys, homicide would not be out of the question. At last, with a smirk of triumph, he came up with the right key, and shifting the soggy grocery bag to his other hip, swung the door open.

Kate squeezed past him, glaring, as he stood in the doorway, feeling for the light switch. He found it at last and pressed the button. Nothing happened. Impatiently, Kate brushed his hand out of the way and tried it herself. Nothing.

She looked at him in the grainy darkness for a long time. "You didn't have the electricity turned on," she accused flatly.

"Sure I did. At least I think I did. I mean, I'm pretty sure I told someone to have it done.... Well, hell, Katie, I told you this afternoon I wasn't sure—"

"Do you have a match?"

"Wh-what?" He blinked, and the tone of his voice was suspicious, as though, in her present frame of mind, a match was far too dangerous a weapon to put in her hands.

Kate whirled and picked her way across the unfamiliar room toward the shadow of the fireplace. Running her hand along the top of the mantel, she upset a pair of candles and a piece of bric-a-brac before reaching an ornamental matchstick holder.

A three-foot circle of yellow light sprang to life around her as she struck the match, and then diffused into a wider glow as she righted the two candles and lit them. Kevin looked relieved as he came toward her. "Well, that's not too bad, is it? At least we can change our clothes and wait for the storm to stop. I'll call somebody about the electricity right now."

He set the bag of groceries on a sheet-covered table and reached for the telephone. One look at his face told Kate what she had expected. He quietly replaced the receiver, glancing at her hesitantly. "I guess I forgot to have the phone reconnected, too."

"I always said you needed a keeper."

Kevin missed the sarcasm; instead, he shrugged, running a hand through his dripping curls. "At least we're out of the rain. My luggage is still in the limo, but I probably have some dry clothes around here somewhere. Do you want me to try to find something for you?"

The corners of Kate's mouth tightened threateningly. Her silk blouse clung transparently to her skin, and she did not need the way Kevin's interested gaze wandered to her chest to remind her that her lace bra—as well as a good deal of flesh—was perfectly visible through the material. "I'm not particularly fond of standing around in wet clothes, no," she retorted. "And stop staring at me. You've seen me without a shirt before."

"Not since you developed breasts," he informed her frankly, and stepped past her to pick up a candle. "Why don't you put the groceries away while I see what we have? It'll only take a minute."

Kate was on the verge of inquiring what good he thought that would do, since his refrigerator wasn't working, but decided not to waste the breath. He was already disappearing around a corner.

Fortunately there was a supply of dry wood in the basket by the fireplace, and Kate had a nice little blaze going by the time Kevin returned. He had taken the time to change his own clothes before looking for something for her to wear, and he came in wearing a pair of snug white jeans and a soft maroon sweater, rubbing a towel through his hair. A blue terry-cloth robe was draped over his arm. Kate took it, and the candle, from him without comment.

"There are clean towels in the bathroom," he told her. "Do you know your way around?"

"I'll find it," she told him shortly, and strode from the room without looking back.

Kate had been in Kevin's house a couple of times before, for parties and such, and knew the general layout. She had never been in his bedroom, and the only thing that identified it as such now was the pile of his wet clothes, which were making a damp stain in the middle of the dusty hardwood floor. The furniture was shrouded in dust covers, the draperies closed on the large window that overlooked the lake. In the flickering glow of the candle the spacious, shadowed room reminded her of a scene from *The Phantom of the Opera*.

She resisted the maternal impulse that made her bend to pick up Kevin's discarded clothes and with a grimace of self-reproach straightened up and stepped over them. She set the candle on the sheet-draped nightstand; shivering, she began to peel off her wet clothes.

Kate did not have the disposition to maintain a high level of anger for long. By the time she had dried off with the towels she found in Kevin's bathroom and wrapped herself in the warm, knee-length robe, she was feeling, if not exactly benevolent toward Kevin, at least more equanimous. Perhaps tolerance came with exposure, for over the years she had learned to expect nothing but the worst from any encounter with Kevin Dawson and that rage was a waste of energy he did not deserve.

The wind had begun to lash rain against the windows in furious waves as she picked up her wet clothes and the candle and returned to the living room. Kevin was digging through the grocery sack as she came in.

"If Colt Marshall were here," he said over his shoulder, "he would no doubt find a way to barbecue steaks over the open fire. But since he's not, it looks like we're going to have to make do with crackers and cheese."

"Why do you keep this place, Kevin?" Kate couldn't keep the note of exasperation out of her voice as she knelt to spread her clothes on the hearth to dry. "What a waste. All this room, the beautiful furniture—you never use it. You just leave it here to rot."

"But I like knowing it's here. Move back." He snapped a cloth off the sofa and spread it on the floor before the fire, like a picnic cloth. "I found a bottle of Grand Marnier in the kitchen; I poured you a glass."

"Thanks." She took the glass he brought down from the mantel and sank to the sheet-covered floor, warming herself by the fire. Being trapped in a deserted house with Kevin Dawson in the middle of a storm was not precisely the way she had wanted to spend the evening, but she curbed the instinct to rail against the elements and chafe against the unavoidable. Trapped she was, at least until the weather let up enough for her to change her tire, and the Grand Marnier would make the whole situation go down a lot easier. She took a healthy sip.

He sank cross-legged on the floor across from her, dumping a box of crackers, two kinds of cheese and a package of cookies into the center of the cloth. "When I built the place," he continued, glancing around at the flickering shadows cast on the shrouded furnishings, "I thought I'd spend more time here than I do. I still plan to, every year, but it never works out. You're right, though. It does look kind of sad, all wrapped up like this."

"Spooky is the word."

He looked around thoughtfully. "No. Lonely, I think. Anyway..." He shrugged, and turned back to her, taking up his glass. "I keep the place because it reminds me of things—permanency, security, a sense of belonging. Important things."

Kate looked at him in surprise. That was one of the few perceptive things she had ever heard him say.

In the flickering firelight his eyes looked entrancingly luminous, his face gently planed, his body all lean angles and shadows. The V of his sweater dipped over a strong collarbone, and candlelight cast a reddish gleam to the light pattern of hair there. In this atmosphere and this lighting, Kate could understand, however briefly, why women wanted to swoon at his feet.

He smiled at her over the rim of his glass. "You look very sexy in that robe," he said.

That caught her off guard, but only for a minute. She scowled her dismissal and took another sip of the rich liqueur. It spread through her limbs like honeyed fire. "Give me a break, Dawson."

"No, I mean it." His expression was sincere but easy. He set his glass on the floor and began to open a package of crackers. "I bet you never thought I noticed all these years, but I did. You're a good-looking woman."

Kate was an average-looking woman. She was of medium height, ordinary shape, correct weight. Her breasts were full but not voluptuous, her hips firm; her waist was not very small. Her legs, slim and femininely shaped, were her best feature, but she usually wore pants. Her honey-blond hair was straight, cut short and styled simply, parted on the side and swept across her forehead in razor-cut bangs. She had nondescript hazel eyes and a pretty, if unmemorable, face that required little makeup. She was passably attractive but hardly beautiful, and her looks had always been the least of her concerns.

Kate could not help wondering where this line of conversation was leading. Kevin never flattered her unless he wanted something, and experience had trained her to be suspicious. She said, watching him carefully, "And what brought that up?"

He glanced at her and for a moment looked disconcerted, even shy. "Nothing. I just thought you might like to hear it, that's all. I get the feeling people don't tell you that often enough."

And that, perhaps, was the most irritating thing about Kevin. Just when she had made up her mind he was a totally lost cause and not worth the effort it took to despise him, he did or said something so unexpectedly and heart-touchingly sweet like that. But then, quite predictably, he spoiled it all by glancing up from the cracker he was spreading with cheese and inquiring casually, "You sleeping with anybody?"

Kate repressed an exasperated sigh. One thing about Kevin: he never disappointed her. "No." She reached for a cracker herself. "Is that an invitation?"

His laugh was startled. "No, ma'am. Masochism is not one of my vices."

She was not at all certain she liked the way he put that, and with a scowl she started to call him on it. But then he continued smoothly, "As a matter of fact, I have almost no vices at the moment. I've recently taken a vow of chastity.''

She almost choked on the cracker she had started to swallow, her eyes brimming with laughter and amazement. "You? Good Lord, what's the world coming to? The last of the living legends, wiped out just like that!" Then, suspiciously, she asked, "You haven't come down with something, have you?"

His own eyes twinkled back at her. "Come, come, Doctor, you know me better than that. I'm very careful. Actually, I find a little abstinence very restful on occasion. Rejuvenating, as it were."

She laughed softly, shaking her head over her glass. "Kevin, you are incorrigible."

"Right," he agreed cheerfully. "And you're not mad at me about the car anymore, are you?"

Her laughter fought with a reproving scowl and finally lost to a helpless grin. He was right again. She couldn't like him, but she could never stay mad at him, either.

A sudden gust of wind roared down the chimney, spitting sparks and sizzling drops of rain on the wet logs. Kate quickly got up and put the screen in place, and Kevin commented with raised brows, "Some storm. Maybe we'll be trapped here all night."

Kate settled back down with a grimace of exaggerated horror. "Please, don't even think such a thing. I'll walk first."

He pretended surprise. "What? You'd turn down a chance to spend the night in an abandoned house with America's hottest sex symbol?"

"In a heartbeat."

"Flickering fire, a bottle of wine—"

"Grand Marnier," she corrected.

"—a raging storm...and me." His eyes twinkled. "Every woman's fantasy, Katie."

"I can hardly control myself," she murmured dryly.

"Try," he advised, and grinned, lifting his glass. "My vow, remember?"

She couldn't help chuckling, softly.

They sat for a time, eating crackers and sipping the liqueur, listening to the storm ebb and flow. Kate's silk blouse and linen slacks were drying well in the heat from the fire, and when she checked her watch, it was only a little after seven. That wasn't too bad. She certainly didn't intend to waste her whole evening on Kevin, but a short time in front of the cozy fire with him going out of his way to be charming was proving to be surprisingly relaxing. There were too few moments like this in Kate's life, when, by circumstances or choice, she could sit and do exactly nothing.

He stretched out lazily on one elbow beside her, his head near her hip, one hand cradling his glass. He gazed up at her with mild interest. "So tell me, Katie, why don't you like me?"

She stretched a little against the wonderful languor that had stolen over her with the hypnotic glow of the fire and the lulling effects of the drink, wriggling her toes and resting her weight on her palms behind her. She was amused by the way Kevin's eyes followed the curve of her legs.

"Do you mean," she answered, "other than the fact that you're selfish, irresponsible, manipulative and shallow?"

He returned his gaze to her face. "Right. Besides that."

"I don't suppose you've ever noticed that whenever you come into my life you bring catastrophe?"

"Now wait a minute," he protested, raising himself a little. "You can blame me for the tire, but I had absolutely nothing to do with the weather."

She shook her head helplessly. "Do you see what I mean? You're such a child. Take away the perfect body, the sexy grin and the phony charm and what have you got left?"

He flashed his sexy grin at her. "What more would you need?"

"Maturity," she informed him. "Sincerity, depth—"

"Boring," he scoffed, and made a short, dismissive gesture with his hand. "Then I'd be just as dull as you are."

She lifted an eyebrow, not in the least offended. "If I'm so dull, why do you keep hanging around me?"

He appeared to consider this. His slim tanned fingers toyed with the shape of his glass. "Maybe," he decided at last, "for the same reason I keep this house. Because you remind me of things." And then he glanced up at her, eyes sparkling. "Boring things, granted, but things I need to be reminded of, anyway. And also—" his sudden switch to sincerity caught her so unprepared that she almost did not recognize it for what it was "—because you're the only friend I've got."

She stared at him, momentarily nonplussed. Self-pity was a rarity from Kevin, commonly indulged in only when he was very drunk and had run out of conversation or when he needed a favor badly and had exhausted all other approaches. Neither was the case tonight, and it did not sound like self-pity at all. It sounded like a simple statement of fact.

She said, her words sounding clipped because of her surprise, "That's ridiculous, Kevin. You've got people hanging on you everywhere you go."

"Bloodsuckers and fans," he corrected simply. "People who are paid to make me happy and people I'm paid to make happy. A friend is somebody who'll tell you you're a jerk when you need to be told it."

That made her feel strange. She had never spent much energy trying to analyze Kevin or crediting him with three-dimensional characteristics; Kevin was just Kevin, irritating when he was present, easily forgotten when he was not. Knowing that he needed her, for whatever convoluted reason, made her see him for one very uncomfortable moment as more than a stick figure who occasionally passed through her life. It made her wonder whether she, in some bizarre way, did not need him, as well.

"Not," he qualified thoughtfully, "that I could take it in very large doses. Friendship is something that works best in your spare time, I think. Would you hit me if I put my head on your lap?"

"Yes." The answer was decisive, accented by a frown that mingled frustration and amused resignation. Three-dimensional indeed. She quickly remembered why she never exhausted herself trying to analyze Kevin—there was nothing there to understand.

He sighed. "Too bad. I could really go for a nap right now."

She sipped the last of her Grand Marnier with luxury. "You're being a jerk, Kevin."

He glanced up at her, mischief and firelight dancing in his eyes. "You know what you need, Katie? To get married. Best thing in the world for a rotten disposition."

"You should know."

Kevin had been married three times, the longest of which had lasted almost eight months. Those mistakes had occurred early in his career, and if Kate had been disposed to analyze his motivations, she would easily have seen that the short-lived marriages were the manifestation of a rising star's desperate attempt to make sense of a life that was fast moving out of his control. Someone—his lawyer, perhaps—had finally convinced him that there were safer outlets for his naturally affectionate nature than marriage, and for the past six years he had lived the life of the contented bachelor, on-screen and off.

"I loved being married," he said, defending himself now. "It's just that I have a short attention span."

"Or maybe," she suggested, a spark of bland mischief creeping into her own eyes, "your ex-wives just had a low tolerance level."

That explanation, apparently, was not even worth his consideration. He sat up, reaching for a cookie. "So why haven't you, Katie? Ever gotten married, I mean."

She shrugged. "No one ever asked me."

He looked surprised. "Are you kidding?"

"Not since you, that is," she qualified. He looked blank, and she reminded him, "Remember the night of the senior prom?"

"I never took you to the senior prom."

"No, you were with someone else. I told you you were a jerk."

"Was I drunk?"

"No, you were trying to get me to go to bed with you."

"I was?" He looked impressed. "What happened?"

"You kissed me."

He winced, deflated. "Oh, yeah. I remember now. It was pretty awful. You had braces."

"And you couldn't figure out what to do with your hands."

He grinned at her companionably. "I don't have that problem anymore." Then, laughing a little at the memory, he added, "You scared me to death. I don't know how I ever worked up the courage to try it with you, anyway."

She made a derisive sound. "Self-confidence has never been one of your problems, Dawson."

"You were very intimidating," he told her frankly. "Even back then. So," he teased, "you got one marriage proposal and you blew it, huh? Sorry now?"

"I sob into my pillow every night."

She was thoughtful for a moment, turning her empty glass to catch the colors of the fire. She had never consciously made a decision between her career and a family life; it had just worked out that way. For the most part, there were no regrets. Sometimes she missed the company of a man, both the physical and emotional comforts, and she envied her contemporaries who had good marriages. But her career filled her time and most of her emotional needs, and she was satisfied with her life—most of the time.

She said, "You know how it is in a small town, Kevin—not a lot to choose from. And I've never met a man who could keep me interested for more than a few weeks. I'd like my marriage—" she looked at him pointedly "—to last longer than that."

"Too bad," he mused aloud. "Marriage is a great institution." And he winked at her. "But best taken in small doses . . . like you."

She laughed softly and stretched again, then reluctantly got to her feet. The rain had stopped, as abruptly as it had begun, some time ago, and as anxious as she was to get home, she was a little sorry to see the pleasant interlude end. "The storm has stopped," she said, reaching for her clothes, now dry. "I'd better see what I can do about that tire."

For a moment he looked as reluctant as she felt, and she thought he would voice some objection. She was surprised when he didn't, and perhaps just the least bit disappointed.

He got lazily to his feet, and his smile seemed to linger in his eyes with a note of regret. But all he said was "Sure. I guess you'd better."

She went into the other room to change her clothes with the oddest feeling—as though if he had asked her to stay longer, she might have said yes. And she would have enjoyed it.

Chapter Three

The atmosphere outside was very still. A graveyard fog rose up from the lake and lay heavily atop the ground; the temperature felt as though it had risen ten degrees. There was an odd light to the sky, yellowish green and phosphorescently reflective; for a moment, both Kate and Kevin were fascinated by the effect.

"Spooky," Kevin said at last, speaking softly, as though not to disturb the spirits that lurked nearby.

"Atmospheric pressure," asserted Kate, but she, too, was uneasy.

"I've never known it to get *hotter* after a rainstorm, have you?"

"You've been away from this part of the country too long, Kevin." She reached inside the glove compartment of her car and took out a flashlight, although the supernatural color of the sky shed so much light they hardly needed it.

She worked quickly and efficiently, suddenly anxious to be away from this isolated spot and back to the comforts of her own home. Kevin held the flashlight for her and stayed out of her way, and after she had fixed the broken jack, everything went smoothly.

"Bang-up job," Kevin complimented her, and gave the newly installed front tire an experimental kick. She frowned at him in a warning and put the tools back in the trunk, slamming the lid. "You're going to let me ride home with you and use the phone, aren't you?"

She released an impatient breath, knowing there was no point in arguing but compelled to give it a try. "There's no point in that, Kevin. No one's going to come out and turn on your utilities tonight."

He looked at her archly. "My dear, you forget who you're talking to. I've got this town wrapped around my little finger. They'll come out if I ask them to."

The worst of it was, they probably would. "Oh, all right," she grumbled. "But let's get going. I have a feeling that storm isn't completely over yet." She held out her hand for the keys determinedly. "And I'm driving."

She saw debate form in his eyes and then dissolve. He handed over the keys without argument and went around to the passenger seat.

Kate was right. Rain began to splatter on the windshield in huge sporadic drops as she turned into her block, and the angry gusts of wind began to play with the tops of the trees. At least they had missed the worst of it, and she would be safely inside her house before the rain started again in earnest.

Kevin had his arm stretched out along the back of the seat, and as she pulled into her driveway, he rested his hand lightly on her shoulder. "Just in case I can't get my electricity turned on," he suggested, "I don't suppose you'd consider letting me spend the night with you?"

"No chance, loverboy." She jerked on the emergency brake.

His eyebrows shot up innocently. "Hey, you're safe with me. Remember—"

"Your vow, I know." Her voice was dry as she opened the door. "One phone call, Dawson," she reminded him firmly, "and then out you go."

"As soon as my driver comes," he amended confidently, and got out of the car.

The streetlights, reflecting off wet asphalt, guided the way to the front porch of Kate's small, imitation-Tudor-style house. The wind had a cold bite to it now, and she hurried to open the door, expecting another soaking rain any moment.

The house into which they stepped was a brilliant contrast to the one they had just left. Kate touched the light switch, and three table lamps glowed softly, illuminating warm peach and russet furnishings, polished fruitwood tables, gleaming hardwood floors accented by small hooked rugs in assorted shapes and patterns. The ceilings and upper walls were artificially beamed against a white paint that was textured to look like plaster, and a collection of paintings by unknown but talented artists endowed the room with character and warmth. Kate's personality was imbedded deeply in this room, and whenever Kevin thought of her, he imagined her here.

"I've always loved your house," he commented now, looking around appreciatively. "It's so cheery. It looks as if someone really lives here."

Kate supposed that was a compliment. She paused to place her medical bag in the closet and responded only with "At least it has electricity. And a phone." She pointed meaningfully to the telephone on the table near the fireplace.

Kevin ignored her, wandering into the kitchen. "Too bad we left the steaks back at my house. We could have them done in half an hour. Look at that—you've got an open gas grill. When did you have that put in? I've always wanted one.''

"Kevin—"

He opened a cabinet. "What are you having for dinner? Those crackers were okay, but I'm really starving." He took out a couple of cookies and opened the refrigerator. "Say, is your dad home? Let's give him a call and have him over, okay? You know that goulash he makes—"

Kate strode past him and pushed the refrigerator door closed. "No, we're not calling my father to cook for you; *I'm* not cooking for you. Just make your phone call and go home. That was the deal."

He shrugged, unconcerned, and popped a cookie into his mouth. "There's no hurry. My driver won't be here until eleven."

Kate spared him one condemning look and then swung away back to the living room. She snapped on the television set, intent on ignoring him.

That was easier said than done, however. She hadn't realized it was eight o'clock, and the familiar theme song of *Code Zero* provided the background for Kevin's winning grin, Kevin's long legs, Kevin's bare chest, Kevin looking intent and determined with his fists wrapped around the butt of a revolver. With a smothered groan, Kate turned away.

The music stopped abruptly. Far in the distance, above the faint rustle of the rising wind outside, she heard a dim and unfamiliar whining. It took her several seconds to realize that what she was hearing was the civil-defense siren.

She glanced back at the television screen just as the sharp, piercing tone of the high-frequency warning began. The screen now was a brilliant blue; written against it in stark white letters were the words EMERGENCY BROADCAST SYSTEM.

It was the single most terrifying moment in Kate's life. She had been raised during the Kennedy years, in an era where civil-defense drills and emergency broadcast tests were weekly affairs, grim reminders of an uncertain age in which bomb shelters were part of every school and hospital, as well as of many homes, and that siren, that piercing whine, had been developed to announce only one specific event: first strike.

Her reaction was deep and primal and completely paralyzing. Everything within her seemed to freeze; the entire world seemed to come to a standstill in a single second that would be etched on her memory forever. The familiar, cozily lit room of her own house, with its patterned draperies, white beamed walls, brick fireplace, was branded in every detail on her brain with stark clarity. And she herself, in the middle of it, stood helplessly staring, transfixed, at the blue screen and the words EMERGENCY BROADCAST SYSTEM.

Kevin was standing in front of the big bay window in the kitchen; he had pulled back the curtains and was gazing out curiously. Dimly Kate was aware of another noise above the sirens, a sound she couldn't identify— something strange...deep and rumbling and totally alien, like an approaching train or a low-flying jet....

"God, Katie, you should see what the wind is doing to those trees. They're whipping around in circles."

Suddenly it all snapped together for her, more from instinct than reason, and she screamed, "Kevin get away from that window!"

As if in slow motion, he turned toward her, his face surprised and curious, and she remembered thinking what a beautiful face he had, after all, and how she would miss it, how horribly she would miss it, as she had a sudden, terrifyingly clear vision of glass exploding inward, sharp projectiles flying through the air and Kevin standing just inches away.

Kate launched herself at him. She grabbed his arm and pulled him away. The lights went out as she dragged him, stumbling, through the room, and she heard the crashing of glass just as she pushed him down onto the floor in the hallway and flung herself on top of him. It had seemed like hours, but barely ten seconds had passed since she had first heard the sirens.

Kate would never be able to describe adequately what happened next, and neither would any of the other twelve thousand residents of Victoria Bend who lived through the disaster. The roar was deafening. The house shook; supports cracked and creaked and screamed like something dying. The air smelled of wet dust and fear. A lash of cold, piercing rain cut through her clothes and stung her thigh, suddenly, briefly, like the rake of fingernails, and was gone.

She heard the sounds of crashing, of walls falling, of trees splitting. Something hit her hard in the center of her back. Kevin was facedown on the floor beneath her, and she was clutching him, her face buried in his shoulder, her arms, for some reason, covering his head and not her own. She felt Kevin grab her hand and hold it hard. She thought he was shouting at her, and then he was trying to shift away from her, to push her down on the floor and arrange himself to protect her, but with supernatural strength she fought him and kept him still. She might have been screaming or sobbing; she didn't know which. She couldn't hear anything over the shrieking, clamoring, roaring sounds of the world coming to an end.

And suddenly everything was still. So horribly still. Kate heard the echo of rain splattering against her kitchen tiles—she knew it was her kitchen tiles because once she had had a broken pipe and it sounded just like that. A branch fell with an anticlimactic rustle outside. She could hear Kevin's harsh breathing, and his heart-beat—or was it her own?—shook his entire body. The fingers of one of her hands were wound fiercely and almost inextricably into the wool of his sweater, and her other hand was caught in his bone-crushing grip. He gasped, "Katie, my God! What the hell?"

He shifted; she rolled off him and collapsed against the rubble of plaster and wet insulation on the floor. Her own breath sounded like sobs. His face was a white and shiny blur of fear and shock in the dark; his hands were cold as they gripped her shoulders. "What was it? My God, Katie—"

"Tornado." Her words came out in broken syllables between dragged-in breaths. "Had to be. Are you all right? Are you hurt?"

Kevin went limp and his hands fell away. He sank back against the wall and stared at her. For a long time they said nothing, just breathing, just trying to get used to the fact that they were alive.

The moment spun out in a dark kaleidoscope of horrors, a hundred nightmares demanding her attention at once. She thought about her house, her beautiful house, in pieces around her, and her mind darted in ridiculous directions, wondering if this memento or that favorite item had been spared. At the same time, a deep and awful panic rose up inside her while she wondered about her father—if he was all right—and her neighbors, her patients, and how extensive the damage had been. She could imagine in that moment that the entire town lay leveled

around them, that she and Kevin were the only two people left alive in the entire city, perhaps the entire world....

She couldn't believe it. It was like living out a scene in
a movie or a book; surely such things did not happen in
real life. Her father. She had to find her father. People
might be hurt. How could it have happened so quickly,
without warning? How could it have happened to her?

She knew she had to move, to get up and at least inspect the damage. She tried to think like a professional,
to remember everything she had ever learned in disaster
training, to remind herself that people needed her. But
inside she was a small and terrified child, and all she
wanted to do was to crawl into Kevin's strong arms and
hold him tight and cry.

It was the sound of fire engines that pushed away the
fog of encroaching shock. Abruptly, her attention shifted
from personal tragedy to her responsibility to others, and
she pushed shakily to her feet. Every muscle in her body
ached. "I've got to see how bad it is," she said hoarsely,
and extended her hand to Kevin. "Can you stand up?"

He nodded, but he took her hand, and she saw him
wince as he pressed against the wall to stand up. "Are you
all right?" she demanded quickly, and was certain she
must have asked him that before.

"Yeah." He rubbed his arm absently. His face was
shadowed, and he was breathing hard. "Must have pulled
a muscle. God Almighty, Katie, will you look at this?"

His voice had taken on a note of low wonder, reverberating with the kind of hollow shock she felt inside, as
they made their way cautiously out of the protective
hallway. Kate stumbled up against something in the dark,
and he bumped into her; she bent to push the obstacle
aside and realized that it was the lamp table that used to

be on the far side of the living room. The lamp on top of it had not even fallen off.

The filtered darkness showed them a scene of wanton destruction worthy of any screenwriter's imagination. The entire bay window had been torn away; the floor was littered with glass, and a gentle rain pattered on the countertops. Her appliances were completely upended, but her dishes were still on the drainboard. In the living room, beams hung crookedly from the ceiling, and the furniture was gathered in a random pile in the center of the room, as though some playful giant had scooped it all up, tossed it about and let it fall again. Every window was blown out, but the draperies were still hanging. The fireplace poker was embedded like a spear in the wall across from the fireplace.

It was to this amazing phenomenon that Kevin was drawn, murmuring exclamations as he examined it. Kate stood where she was, staring dumbly at the light sheet of silvery rain that was screening her open front door. She could hear voices outside, crying and shouting, and now more fire engines. The sound of others in need broke through the last of her shock; adrenaline began pumping in waves and propelled her forward toward the open door.

Kevin began to sort quickly through the rubble, tossing aside sofa cushions, scrambling through bits of Sheetrock and torn magazines.

Kate stared at him. "What?" she demanded. "What are you looking for?"

"The telephone," he explained patiently, without looking up. "We've got to—"

Kate didn't know whether Kevin was speaking from shock or from habit. Never in his life had he been faced with a situation a single phone call couldn't fix. "Are you crazy?" she said, a little shrilly. "Half the damn town's been wiped out. Who the hell do you think you're going to call?"

He stared at her, his eyes dark and not entirely comprehending in a very white face. One of the artificial beams, which had been hanging by a thread, tumbled to the floor on the other side of the room, and she grabbed his arm, wrenching him forward. "Come on; it's not safe in here."

The scene outside was even more devastating than what Kate had seen inside. The sheer magnificence of it overwhelmed her. Huge trees and power poles blocked the street. From where she was standing, she could see two houses reduced to matchsticks. She tried frantically to remember whether those houses had basements, who lived there, whether anyone had been at home when the storm struck. The roof had blown off the house next door, and pieces of it lay in the street; her neighbors stood on the front lawn, staring at it, and the sound of a woman's soft sobbing seemed anticlimactic. There were other people moving around through the rain, calling out to each other or just crying, looking with unbelieving eyes at what nature had wrought.

In the few seconds Kate stood there, her mind ticked off an urgent list of priorities and possibilities. She had never imagined anything this catastrophic; she had never in her wildest moments imagined how to deal with something like this. There would be injuries. She had to get to the clinic. *Please, God, let the clinic be standing.* She thought of the drugs and instruments that would be so desperately needed, and she thought surely God would have been merciful and spared some of them. She had to find her father. He lived three blocks away; perhaps the damage had not been so extensive in his part of town. *Please let him be all right.*

Kevin said lowly, "God, Katie, look at your car."

Her car was flattened and buried beneath the seventy-five-year-old oak that once had shaded her house. She looked at the car, and all she thought was *Well, I guess we won't be driving to the clinic.*

Someone called shrilly, "Dr. Larimer! Dr. Larimer, thank God you're here! Come quick, please."

She said over her shoulder to Kevin, "See if you can get in the hall closet and get my medical bag. Hurry!" And she began to climb over the broken trees and scattered debris that separated her from her patients.

In the next few minutes she treated a broken arm, a minor head injury, some nasty scrapes and contusions, and one case of shock. It quickly became apparent that this was only the beginning.

"It was worse on the west side of town," someone was saying excitedly. "I saw it touch down there; barely got to the basement—"

"I heard there was more than one—"

"Does anyone have a radio?"

"Won't do any good; the transmitter's out."

"We need some men to help search those houses over there. There must be people inside."

"Dr. Larimer, what are we going to do?"

The voices were babbling around her and blurring together, and Kate was thinking dully, mechanically, *I can't deal with this. I wasn't trained to deal with this.*

And then she looked at Kevin, kneeling beside her in the rain, watching her and waiting for her answer, and she suddenly became aware of two things. The first was that for the only time in their lives the crowd was turning to her and not the luminescent Kevin Dawson. The second was that *she* had to deal with it.

She snapped her medical bag closed and got to her feet. Her words were clipped and decisive. "Stay out of your houses. We'll have the disaster plan in operation as soon as we can get organized." She wasn't even sure the town had a disaster plan. "Meanwhile, form search parties to locate the injured and get them to the clinic if you can. That's where I'm going now. And use flashlights, not candles—there may be broken gas pipes." She couldn't think of anything else. There was too much to think of.

Those few words, issued with authority and confidence, were all it took to galvanize her neighbors into action. The human spirit was an amazing thing, and tonight she would see it at its best and its worst. She took off at a semirun across the slippery grass and broken streets toward the clinic, her mind working in rhythm with her steps.

She would need help. They had two trained paramedics and one fairly well equipped emergency unit—she had worked so hard to establish an emergency service when she first came here, but she'd never imagined the fruits of her labors would be needed to such an extent—and her own nurse, but God, if only they had a hospital! The police force was small and ill trained in first aid, but perhaps it could be of some help in transporting the injured. And surely the damage couldn't be this extensive all over town....

She was not even aware that Kevin was still with her until she stumbled and almost fell over someone's birdbath, which was now half buried in the ground. His strong arm jerked her upright again. She stared at him, panting and somewhat confused. She wanted to tell him to go someplace safe, but she couldn't think of any such place. She hadn't even considered asking him to join one of the search teams; he would have been of no use to them. And strangely, it was good to look up and find him there, to feel his fingers, strong and steady, on her arm. In moments like this a familiar face, any face, was a gift to be treasured.

She said, breathing hard, "We can cut across the park and avoid the streets. I think most of them are blocked, anyway." All those beautiful hardwoods that lined the lazy streets of Victoria Bend, the pride and joy of a sleepy little town, were now the authors of its destruction.

His face was grim as he nodded and urged her on. He did not let go of her arm.

The damage was random. Trees had crashed through roofs, and automobiles had been tossed into the air; walls were caved in and windows torn out. At one house the garage had been reduced to rubble, but the main house was untouched; at another a doghouse floated complacently in the swimming pool with the stunned and whining pooch still safe inside. There were sporadic fires, and a broken hydrant flooded the street in one place. People were everywhere, crowding the streets, shouting confused information and instructions, crying and moaning. Kate stopped as often as she could to check for serious injuries, but it was an overwhelming task, and she had to get to the clinic, to her supplies. She quickly instructed harried volunteers in first aid and shouted orders to bring the injured to the clinic. And she prayed that the clinic was still standing.

As they approached downtown, the scene became more chaotic, though the damage didn't seem to be quite as extensive there. Plate-glass windows littered the streets, and signs had been blown down. The roads were clogged with cars whose drivers, in the insanity of the moment, were apparently intent upon evacuating the area. Frantic pedestrians added to the confusion, and a small fire engine and a police car were inching through the melee. Kate lurched forward to flag one of the police cars down, but Kevin held her back.

"You'll never get through that crowd," he gasped. "I've got to rest a minute."

The brief run had completely exhausted him, and Kate felt a sharp twinge of impatience for his artificially sculpted body, the hours he spent keeping trim instead of keeping in shape. He might look like Adonis, but he had the stamina of a fifty-year-old man.

"For heaven's sake, Kevin," she returned shortly, shaking his arm off, "I can't wait for you to—"

And then she heard a voice through the crowd. "Katie! Katie, here!" Only two people in the world called her Katie—Kevin and her father.

She whirled and saw her father pushing his way through the crowd, a big man in a green golf sweater and a red baseball cap. She ran toward him; he swept her in his arms, hugging her hard. "Good for you, girl, I knew you'd be okay!" he exclaimed into her ear. But, of course, he hadn't known any more than she had known about him, and so their arms tightened briefly around each other as their intense fear gave way to relief, the only luxury of personal feelings they would be able to allow themselves for many hours to come.

He pushed her away and looked down at her intently. His eyes were bright, and his face was flushed as he demanded, "Have you been to the clinic?"

This was a man who had served in two wars and a police action; he was in his element now, utterly unfazed. He would know what to do. Katie didn't realize how terrified she had been until she saw her father and knew everything was going to be all right.

She shook her head. "We're on our way."

He glanced then at Kevin and gave him a companionable slap on the shoulder. "Well, my boy, welcome home!" He had always liked Kevin; Kate never understood why. "Not much like you remembered it, huh?"

Kevin shook his head a little dazedly, still concentrating on regaining his breath. "I keep thinking it's all just a set and I'm waiting for someone to yell, 'Cut!'"

Jason Larimer laughed briefly, and it was an encouraging, if bizarrely out-of-place, sound. He turned back to Kate, now serious. "They say the damage was pretty bad on the west side. I'm trying to get there now. But the clinic is standing, and so's the church across from it, so the best thing is to do triage at the clinic and set up beds in the church. God only knows when the Red Cross will get here—it's beginning to sound like half the county got a touch of this and the roads are shot to hell—so we're on our own for a while. And we've got another problem." He looked grim. "The power is out indefinitely. We're gathering up as many flashlights as we can, but that's going to be precious little help with the kind of injuries we're likely to be treating tonight. Ever do surgery by candlelight, my girl?"

Kate felt a sudden hysterical urge to laugh. Except for the most minor procedures, she had never done surgery at all; she wasn't certified in surgery or even very well qualified, but she knew he was right—every fraction of her skill would be tested tonight, and under the worst of circumstances. She said frantically, "But we've got to have some kind of emergency power system—"

Kevin interrupted, "What about car headlights?"

Kate whirled on him. "For God's sake, Kevin, this is not a movie! We can't drive cars into the clinic!"

"Wait a minute," her father said thoughtfully. "He may have something. Not the cars themselves, but the batteries. It may work! That old generator is still in the clinic storage room, isn't it? The one you used to say belonged in a museum?"

"Daddy, that won't work! It's not even strong enough to light a light bulb. You told me so yourself!"

"Just goes to show what you know about mechanics, girlie!" he retorted. "It can be rigged to run on car batteries with more than enough power to spare. Good for you, Kev!" He slapped him quickly and affectionately on the shoulder again and turned away. "I'm going to put our boys in blue to work on it top priority. You should have lights by the time you need them. Go on ahead and start triage. I'll be there as quick as I can."

A sudden bolt of panic shot through her as she realized he was leaving—leaving her alone, leaving her in charge. An overwhelming sense of inadequacy gripped her, born of too many years of cookbook medicine and safety from challenges, as the full scope of her burden struck her. They were completely cut off; help from the outside world would be slow in coming, if at all. Their medical facilities were limited and their medical needs enormous, and everything depended on Kate.

She cried urgently, "Daddy, wait!" and took a step toward him.

He paused, and his eyes swept the chaotic scene with bitter amazement. "By damn, it's a mess, isn't it? Reminds me of one time in Guam— Ah, well, that's another story! You get to work, Katie. I'll take care of your lights for you!"

And he was gone.

Instinctively, Katie started after him, but Kevin held her back. She looked up at him with all her insecurity and fear written in her eyes, and it was the strangest thing.... She looked at him, and suddenly she didn't feel quite so panicked anymore. He looked so strong, standing beside her, with the rotating blue lights from a passing cruiser dancing off his face, his dark eyes quiet and calm; it may have only been a trick of the light, but she thought for a moment that he knew exactly what she was feeling, his Katie with the feet of clay, and he understood. It probably was nothing more than her imagination, but seeing him there, believing that he understood and supported her, helped the irrational moment of terror and self-doubt to pass.

Then he smiled a little and put his arm around her shoulders, squeezing briefly. "Come on," he said. "We'd better go do what the man said."

They started off toward the clinic again.

Chapter Four

"I hope you're not blaming me for this," Kevin said. He was still a little short of breath as Kate led him around a corner and through the mostly empty parking lots that ran behind the downtown shops and businesses.

She spared him a harried, distressed glance, and he explained, "You said every time I come into your life I bring catastrophe. But this is one even I couldn't have managed."

"Oh, Kevin for—" A gasp robbed the rest of her words, and she drew up short.

A utility pole had fallen across a car, blocking their path where the parking lot narrowed into a alleyway that ran between two buildings. Snapping live wires festooned the air above the automobile and writhed on the ground, hissing and spitting sparks. Frantically, she turned back, but Kevin grabbed her arm hard.

"There's someone in that car!" he said hoarsely.

There was only so much the mind could stand, and comprehension was slow in dawning. Kate stared in shocked disbelief at Kevin, then at the car, where now she could see the shadow of a woman and hear the faint cries for help. And even as she looked, there was something else—the faint gleam of an oily blue stain creeping from beneath the car. Gasoline. And live sparks only inches away.

No, she thought. *No, this can't be happening. Things like this don't happen in real life.* But it was far too bizarre to be a nightmare. And Kate was far too frightened to have imagined any of this.

She turned quickly. "We've got to get that power shut off."

But Kevin had seen the gasoline stain, too, and now the sobs reached them clearly. "Help me, someone! My legs—I can't get out!"

"Katie, there's no time," he said tersely and started forward.

"Are you crazy?" It was instinct that caused her to pull him back and sharpen her voice to a wild hiss. "You'll be electrocuted! If one of those wires touches that car—"

He looked at her with impatience mixed with incredulity, as though she were the one who had lost her mind, not he. "Let me go, Kate! What's the matter with you? That car is going to go up like a bomb if we don't—"

"For God's sake, Kevin, use your head!" she shouted at him, and tried to draw him back, but he broke away from her. "This is not a set, and you're not Colt Marshall!"

He looked at her for a moment with such a turmoil of sharp, twisting emotions in his eyes that she actually stepped back under the force of it. There was hurt there, and disgust and cold anger and violent determination. And then, to her horror, he turned and ran toward the car.

"Kevin, damn you!" It was a scream, hoarse and helpless and much too late. He didn't even look back.

She had thought there was a limit to the amount of terror she could endure. Watching Kevin negotiate the

dancing, humming wires of death and consciously avert-
ing her eyes from the steady drip of gasoline from the
automobile, she realized she had not even scraped the
surface of fear before. She wanted to call out to him, to
bring him back, to tell him she would go for help, she
would rescue the woman herself.... But she couldn't
make her voice work, and she knew her attempt to stop
him would be futile. There was no one but Kevin to rescue the trapped woman. Kate wasn't strong enough to
drag her from the car, and there wasn't time to go for
help, so it was up to Kevin—Kevin, who had never had to
deal with a real crisis in his life; Kevin, who had played
the role of the hero so long he couldn't tell the difference
between a set and real life; Kevin, who was about to get
himself killed.

He had managed to open the door. Kate could hear the
woman's weak sobs of relief; she could hear Kevin murmuring something to her. Just then, a gust of wind
caught one of the dangling wires and swayed it within
inches of the metal frame of the car. A scream, powerful
and breathless, caught like bile in Kate's throat. Her
hands were clenched so tightly around her medical bag
that she couldn't even feel her fingers anymore. Every
nerve was strung to its finest extension; she was frozen in
horror, yet her nerves were straining and pulsing like the
wires on the ground before her. She wanted to scream,
wanted to help, wanted to close her eyes and pretend none
of this was happening.

It was taking too long. She cried out, "What's wrong?
Kevin, for God's sake, hurry!"

Then he was straightening up, backing away from the
car. A plump middle-aged woman in a flowered sun-
dress was in his arms, clinging to his neck as he carefully

negotiated the obstacle course of live wires to make his way back to Kate.

Kate was almost sobbing with relief as he set the woman on her feet. Quickly she checked her for injuries, demanding, "Are you hurt? Can you walk?"

"Just a little shaky," the woman replied tremulously, clinging to Kate for support. She smiled faintly at Kevin. "I always dreamed of being rescued by Colt Marshall, but I never thought it would be like this!"

Quickly Kevin returned her smile. It seemed strained. "I think we'd better get out of here," he said with a backward glance at the car. He took the woman's arm. "Do you want me to carry you?"

"Oh, no, dear, I can walk!" And suddenly her pale, plump face crumpled with tears, and she said, "I have to get home! My house... I have to see if my house... Oh, it's the end of the world, I know it is!"

Between the two of them, they managed to urge the nearly hysterical woman out of the area of danger and back to the street, where an anxious friend or neighbor immediately spotted her and rushed toward her, enveloping her in an embrace that spoke of relief and concern and quick reassurances.

Kate and Kevin watched as the woman disappeared into the crowd. There was a sudden, muffled explosion of the ignited automobile. Curious, excited heads turned, and a few people began to run toward the sound, eager to investigate. The owner of the car was not among them.

It suddenly shot through Kate, what incredible danger Kevin had faced and what a price he had almost paid for his foolish heroics. Even though rationally she knew he had had no choice and that the woman might well have been dead had they not come along when they did, logic had no part in the emotions that assailed her now. She looked at him—white and damp faced, yet so much calmer than he had any right to be—and intense, conflicting shafts of pride and anger speared through her: he was alive, and she wanted to hug him, to hold him in her arms and crush him to her; he had almost died, and she wanted to hit him.

As she stood there, impotent with seething emotions, he gave her a faint impression of his old cocky grin and lifted his hand to push his hair away from his eyes. "There, you see?" he challenged her with gentle mockery that was wonderfully familiar and horribly inappropriate. "Old Colt finally came in handy, after all."

Then she thought she would indeed hit him—either that or kiss him. And almost before she could recognize—much less reconcile herself to—that shocking and totally unexpected impulse, she noticed a trickle of blood on the back of his hand. Now back in her sphere and swiftly competent, she grabbed his hand. "You're hurt," she said. "You idiot, what have you done to yourself?"

He shrugged and pulled away. "A scratch, I guess. It doesn't hurt."

She looked at him, a swell of anxiety and confusion and helplessness and something strangely like tenderness filling her, and she wanted to curse him or shake him. She said in a low voice, surprised to hear it shaking slightly, "Don't you ever do a fool thing like that again, do you understand me? This is not Code Zero, and nobody's going to call in a stuntman when you get in over your head! This is real life!"

The look of wry amusement he cast around made her feel very small and petty. Sirens were wailing and headlights flashing, people were jostling one another in the streets, and the smell of panic was thick. He said, "So I noticed."

Oh, God, Kevin... Despair and a strange sort of understanding filled her eyes with the aftermath of terror, and she knew she didn't want to hit him at all. She wanted to hold him. Not because he was a hero but because he was Kevin. Because he was hers.

"Were you scared?" she asked shakily.

He looked at her soberly. "To death."

She tried to smile. "Me, too." Her voice was barely a whisper. There was a moment as she looked at him when something stirred in his eyes and was answered deep inside her—something too fragile and important to be analyzed in the midst of a crowded, terror-filled street, but something that she wanted to hold on to and treasure... and knew she could not.

"Just don't ever do that to me again," she said roughly, and she pushed through the crowd toward the clinic across the street. Kevin was close behind.

THE SCENE AT THE CLINIC would have done justice to any artist's representation of Dante's *Inferno*. The lights were on as promised, but the relief Kate felt was mitigated by the extent of what she saw. The emergency medical unit had somehow made it through, and the ambulance lights flashed eerily on the crowd that was gathered around the front of the building. Some of the people were injured and in need of attention, but some of them were merely curiosity seekers or frightened persons gravitating toward what looked like a place of refuge. A policeman was trying to sort out the injured from the others, and Kate briefly thanked God for him as she made her way over to the stretcher the paramedics were lifting out of the ambulance.

"Compound fracture, right femur," Tony, the senior EMT told her. "His vitals are stable. You've got worse inside."

The patient was semiconscious but did not seem to be in shock. Kate quickly lifted the blanket and checked the injury, then glanced at the paper on which Tony had written the pertinent information. "Good for you, guys," she said curtly. "Let's get him inside. Have you seen my father?"

"We left him on Macon Street," Tony called over his shoulder. "He's treating them on the site. Said to tell you he'd be in as soon as the worst are transported."

Kate should have known her father wouldn't leave the scene of the crisis until he was absolutely certain his help was no longer needed, but she wondered if he knew what a crisis they had here. And as she quickly followed the paramedics inside, she only hoped he would hurry.

The impact of what she saw inside was enough to freeze Kate momentarily where she stood. Her quiet, routinely run little clinic was now an emergency room that would have rivaled that of any big-city hospital. The reception room and the hallways were filled with people, all of them injured, some of them badly hurt. Many of them had been laid on the floor, others on makeshift beds of tables and chairs. Every available sitting place was filled, and several persons rested against the walls, submitting to first aid by volunteers. The presence of so much pain—and not a small amount of blood—was enough to affect even a seasoned professional, and when Kate felt Kevin lightly touch her back, she knew that his brief stint with heroism had completely faded.

In this light his face had a greenish tint; his eyes were dark and shadowed with shock. He looked as though he were desperately trying to will himself anywhere else. He said, "Katie, I think I'd better—"

"Dr. Larimer!"

It was Iris, Kate's nurse, and Kate whirled gratefully toward the voice. But there was no time for the amenities. Iris called, "You'd better get over here. I need some help with this man!"

The patient to whom she referred was thrashing about and yelling wildly, fighting Iris's attempts to hold him down on the sofa, which was his makeshift bed. Kate made an instantaneous search of the room and found no available volunteers, then grabbed Kevin's hand and dragged him behind her as she quickly crossed toward Iris.

"Fractured ribs and collarbone, some bad lacerations, no artery damage," Iris recited rapidly, struggling to hold her patient still.

"Kevin, hold him down," Kate snapped, opening her bag.

"Katie, I don't think—"

"What have you given him?" Kate took out a syringe and broke open an ampoule. "Kevin, for goodness' sake, hold his arms!"

Iris looked horrified. "You know I wouldn't dispense medications without your permission, Doctor!"

Iris Davison was twenty years Kate's senior; she had been her father's nurse, and Kate couldn't have asked for a stronger, cooler, more competent assistant. But she realized in the brief moment she stared at the other woman that even Iris did not fully realize what they were facing. She was trying to run this disaster the way she ran the office, pretending that all the rules still applied.

Iris was trying to wind a rubber catheter around the man's wildly flailing arm while Kate drew up the medication. Kevin stood by helplessly, watching in transfixed horror at the huge amount of blood that was staining the bandages on the injured man's leg. He said weakly, "Katie, I'm not kidding. I don't feel—"

"Hold him down, damn it!"

The man tried to rise, frantically waving his arms, and the back of his hand caught Iris on the side of her face, knocking her glasses askew. That, at last, galvanized Kevin into action, and he caught the man's arms, making an ineffectual attempt to keep him still.

In other circumstances, Kate's natural compassion for her fellow beings would have allowed her to understand, to sympathize. Kevin had narrowly escaped death twice in the space of an hour; he had witnessed more horror and destruction tonight than he had envisioned in a lifetime of acting out drama for television, and he, of all people, was least prepared to cope with this. Shock was normal. Confusion, disorientation, even hysteria, would not have been unusual. Under normal circumstances, Kate would have expected nothing more of him.

But these were not normal circumstances, and Kate had no sympathy, and little understanding, to spare. Kevin looked as though he might be sick at any moment—he was white and shaky and perspiring profusely—and though Kate had felt the same way more than once tonight, she simply couldn't afford to have him fold up on her now.

As she struggled to fight off the excited patient while holding on to her syringe, she warned Kevin sharply, "If you pass out on me now, I'll leave you where you fall. I swear to God I will! You're going to see worse than this tonight—people might *die* here tonight—so you'd better get a hold on yourself and hold this man down!"

Kevin's dark, stunned eyes met hers for a moment, and then he seemed to focus his energy. His tightly compressed lips went a shade whiter as he applied his strength to bringing the patient under control.

The injection took effect almost immediately, and that was the last thought Kate gave to Kevin Dawson for the next fifteen minutes. People were calling for her, tugging at her clothes, demanding her attention, and each one needed her more than the last. She tried to set up a rough form of triage on this first quick tour of inspection, removing the more serious cases to the examining rooms for treatment, dispensing analgesics and first aid to the rest. And all the while she could feel the panic rising in her, low and certain. One doctor could not cope with all these casualties. Where was her father?

"This looks bad," she told Iris tautly, examining a compound fracture, the most urgent case she had seen so far. The broken bone was exerting pressure on the femoral artery, and if the fracture was not reduced soon, permanent damage could result. But reduction of the fracture required major surgery, the kind she was neither equipped nor qualified to perform. "Get me a hematocrit," she commanded Iris. "I need to know how much blood he's losing."

"Katie..." It was Kevin's voice, sounding very weak and rather hesitant behind her. She had almost forgotten about him; she thought surely he had left for safer ground by now. "Have you got a minute?"

"No, I don't have a minute," she said without turning. She quickly examined her patient's pupils. He was unconscious and beginning to show signs of shock. She didn't know how much longer she could wait.

"I just needed—"

Iris rushed off with the blood sample for the hematocrit, and someone called, "Dr. Larimer, I couldn't find those towels—"

"Dr. Larimer, the mayor is here; he needs to see you."

"Katie..."

"Oh, for heaven's sake, Kevin, what is it?" She turned sharply and almost bumped into a tall blond man in a raincoat. She didn't know him, and he didn't look hurt, so she started to push past him. Someone else was calling her, and she forgot about Kevin again.

The man said, "Excuse me, Dr. Larimer?"

She looked past him impatiently. "Yes, what is it?"

He extended his hand. "I'm Dr. Brandon. I just got in tonight and—"

The name meant nothing to her, but the title was an answer to a prayer. She said quickly, "You wouldn't be a surgeon, would you?"

"As a matter of fact, yes."

"Are you licensed to practice in the state of Mississippi?"

He looked at her with calm gray eyes. "At this point, would it matter?"

Once again she was reminded of a world gone mad, of the shattered rules of predictability and permanence, and did not think about it twice. She said curtly, decisively, "You'd better scrub. I've got a case here—"

And then she saw Kevin. He was leaning against the wall; his face, which had once been merely pale, was now deathly white. He was cradling his arm against his chest, and his fingers were dripping blood.

Of all that she had seen tonight, of all that she had endured, this was the worst. She felt her veins go cold; something tight closed about her chest and squeezed away her breath. She pushed past Dr. Brandon and caught Kevin's shoulders. He looked as though he might collapse at any moment. "Kevin, my God! What—"

"I don't know," he answered simply. And the weakness in his voice, the faint attempt to smile through stiff white lips, went through Kate like a knife.

She cast a frantic look over her shoulder. "Dr. Brandon, can you handle that?"

He was already examining the patient, not even having taken time to remove his coat, and he answered her with a quick, dismissive gesture of his hand. "I'll call you when I need you. What have you got for anesthesia?"

"Ether."

He grimaced. "Not good, but it'll have to do. Okay, I'll cross-match him and round up some donors. Are you in this by yourself?"

"Yes," Kate breathed, and she missed the doctor's incredulous glance of disbelief. She wrapped her arm around Kevin's waist and led him out into the hall, toward her office.

The room was empty; narcotics were stored here, and Iris would not consider even the present shortage of bed space adequate cause to leave patients unattended in Kate's office. Kate helped Kevin to the sofa, where he sat down heavily. "Did you ever have one of those days," he murmured with a gallant attempt at humor, "where nothing seemed to go your way?"

"Oh, Kevin, why didn't you tell me you were hurt?" She couldn't keep the despair out of her voice as she grabbed a suture tray from the storage shelf and came back to him.

He tried to shrug and then grimaced. "It didn't really hurt until I saw all the blood. I thought it was just bruised."

Kate snatched a pair of scissors from the tray and cut away his sweater at the shoulder as he protested jokingly, "Hey, watch it! This sweater is handmade—and imported!" Kate pushed aside the material and caught her breath.

A shard—it looked like glass—had entered Kevin's shoulder just below the collarbone, proximal to his shoulder. It had apparently been embedded quite deeply and only began to work loose as he moved, which explained his unusual pallor and weakness. A stab of remorse, so deep it was physically painful, went through Kate as she remembered how she had berated him and pushed him throughout the night, making him the victim of her temper and her impatience, and all the while he had been hurting and bleeding, and she hadn't even noticed.

Her eyes were filled with pain and regret, and her voice was a little shaky as she looked up at him. "Oh, Kevin, I'm so sorry."

He looked genuinely puzzled. "For what?"

Oh, Kevin, she thought, and the surge of emotion that engulfed her was so great that she couldn't even define it. She could only think again, *Oh, Kevin...*

And because Kevin was sure to begin to read things in her expression she didn't want to reveal—nor did she even understand what it was she felt—she quickly averted her gaze, beginning to swab off his arm.

"So what's the verdict?" Kevin asked after a moment. "Am I going to live?" He kept his face averted, for which Kate was grateful. She had seen patients who had been perfectly calm and composed collapse at the first glimpse of their own torn flesh, and Kevin's wound was not a pretty one. Though his tone was deliberately casual, she could see the tension working in the muscles of his jaw, and she hastened to reassure him.

"Only if you give up sex, alcohol and cholesterol."

"One out of three isn't bad."

She was relieved to notice, as she hastily cleaned off the wound, that her immediate assessment had not been too accurate. The injury was clean and not nearly as bad as it looked. She covered the wound with a gauze pad and went quickly to the narcotics cabinet. "It must have happened when the storm first struck," she explained, wanting to keep him distracted. "You were so hyped up with adrenaline you didn't even feel it. It's not unusual. We would have noticed the bleeding much sooner if you hadn't worn that stupid red sweater."

"Next time I'll know," he murmured dryly, and Kate smiled at him as she filled the syringe.

"What's that?" he asked as she knelt beside him and pushed up the other sleeve of his sweater.

"Morphine." She swabbed his muscled arm with alcohol. "It might make you a little woozy."

"Great. Could you wrap some up for me to take home? I could make a fortune selling it at parties. Ouch!"

Kate managed a smirk for him as she withdrew the needle, and he pretended to glare. "What are you planning here, major surgery?"

"Just a few stitches. I don't know how to tell you this, hotshot, but you may have to keep your shirt on for a few episodes. You're going to have a nasty little scar."

"Maybe I can tell them it's a bullet wound. They can work it right into the script."

"Never at a loss, are you? You can lie down if you feel dizzy. Or just lean your head back and relax. This is going to take a while." As she spoke, she was using the forceps to remove the glass carefully, and she felt a little catch in her throat as she saw how large it was. A few inches lower and it might have penetrated the lung; a few inches higher, the carotid artery....

Kevin said, "No, I'm okay." Until this point her distraction technique had worked. He didn't seem to notice what she was doing until he heard the clink of the glass as it hit the basin into which she tossed it. He winced but did not look around. "I'm not even going to ask what that was."

"Good for you."

"You have a really gory job, Kate. And to think I used to be jealous of you."

She looked up at him in surprise. "You were jealous of me?"

"Sure. You were always so smart, so on top of things. There was nothing you couldn't do."

She laughed a little and turned back to her work. "That's funny. I was always jealous of you."

Now it was his turn to look surprised. "What for? You had the brains, the talent, the grades—"

"And you had everything else."

His eyes took on a distant, slightly sad expression. "We've come a long way since then, haven't we, Katie?"

Yes, she thought, and felt that little catch in her throat again. *A long way... together.* And because that sentiment was making her feel strangely weak and vulnerable, she quickly concentrated her attention on her task, not on the man who was the cause of her confusion.

As she began to suture the fascia, he grew tense and lost his inclination to talk. She asked once, gently, "Are you okay?"

He gathered himself enough to reply, "I've had more fun dates in my time, darlin'. Are you sure that wasn't water you put in that hypo?"

"You wouldn't feel a thing if you didn't think about what I was doing."

"Small comfort."

He fell silent again, and she finished as quickly as she could. "There you go," she pronounced at last, the relief more evident in her voice than she would have liked. "None of your fancy Beverly Hills surgeons could have done a better job."

She applied the last piece of tape to his bandage, and he smiled crookedly, relaxing visibly now that it was over.

"I'll give you this: none of them would be half as pretty to look at while they were doing it," he said.

"Fie, Mr. Dawson, that's just the morphine talking." But she felt a surge of happiness so sweet it made her feel guilty just to hear him use that old teasing tone of voice again, just to know he was going to be all right. And she couldn't help smiling back as she knelt beside him on the couch, using a gauze pad to blot the faint dampness from his face.

He watched her with eyes that were unnervingly alert for the amount of morphine she had given him, thoughtful and perceptive and for some strange reason, unsettling. She found herself growing nervous under the gentle intensity of his quiet gaze, and she said, "I'll try to find you a sling for that arm. You should keep it immobile for a few days, and right now I want you to just rest. You can lie down here, in my office."

He surprised her by reaching up and lightly smoothing away the damp bangs from her forehead. His touch lingered against her face; her own hand fell slowly away from his. And she couldn't seem to move her eyes away from the gentle caress of his gaze.

"Do you remember when you asked me why I kept coming back here?" he said.

She nodded. It seemed like a lifetime ago that they had sat in front of his fireplace surrounded by shrouded furniture and tossed half-serious banter back and forth. And in a way it was a lifetime, for both of them had grown and changed in the past few hours in ways they had yet to realize, and there was still more to come.

His fingertips lightly traced the curve of her eye, and he was looking at her in the deep, abstracted way of a man who has just made a discovery he doesn't fully understand yet. "I always used to think it was because this was the only place I knew where I could escape from the insanity. But now, when the whole world has gone crazy and there's no place to escape anymore, now I realize that it had nothing to do, really, with this place, this town. It was you. The one thing I could depend on, my lifeline to the real world, never changing, never wavering. You're my sanity."

She felt a soft, warm choking sensation in the center of her throat; she didn't know what she would have answered even if she could have made herself speak. His fingers brushed lightly down her face, to the corner of her lips, so warm, so gentle. His eyes followed the course of his fingers, and her breath quickened; she turned her face a little to his touch. She knew he was going to kiss her, and she wanted it, she welcomed it, this little fragment of tenderness in the midst of suffering and chaos. She lifted her face as his hand spread against the side of her throat; she felt his breath brush across her skin. She could almost taste his softness and his warmth.

Kate was to wonder later, in odd, brief moments, what had come over her, and him, and whether she had imagined the entire episode or whether it was all some stress-induced dream. Whether he would have really kissed her, whether she would have responded, or whether one or both of them would have broken away in embarrassment and confusion... and if he had kissed her, what it would have been like. But she was not to know. The door burst open, and the precious moment of half fantasy was completely shattered.

"Kate, I've been looking all over this place for you!"

Kate got quickly to her feet and turned to meet the mayor, whose expression of harried impatience was quickly replaced by a look of alarm. "Kevin! Kevin, my boy, what happened to you?" He came forward quickly. "You're not hurt? Nobody told me you were here. I hadn't heard..."

Kevin smiled, though it was a rather strained smile, very different from the one he had given Kate only a minute ago. "You've got to admit, though," he responded with forced humor, "it took a tornado to upstage me." Then, gesturing to the bandage on his arm, he said, "It's just a scratch. The doc here fixed me right up."

Mayor Brackin looked distractedly from Kevin to Kate, obviously torn between his solicitous duty to the town's most famous—and most benevolent—citizen and the urgency of grander crisis. The mayor was a good politician, a competent administrator and a fairly conscientious servant of the town, but he was no more prepared to deal with disaster than anyone else. He, like everyone else, was rising to the occasion as best he could.

He turned to Kate. "What kind of casualties are we looking at here? How's your medical situation?"

"So far it looks worse than it is," Kate answered. "Mostly minor cuts and bruises and hysteria. We've got a couple of bad cases that need hospitalization—"

He nodded, anticipating her. "I've been on the shortwave with neighboring hospitals. Some of them can take our overflow, but we've got a transportation problem. Most of the streets in town are blocked, and some of the roads leading out aren't much better. If we sent for ambulances now, I'm afraid of how long it would take them to get here."

"What about helicopters?" Kevin asked.

The mayor nodded. "I've contacted the National Guard, but it's going to be daybreak before they can send us any help. We weren't the only place that was hit, and they've got their own ways of deploying their helicopters."

Damn, Kate thought, and her hands tightened unconsciously into fists. They already had one emergency surgery scheduled, and Dr. Brandon was a miracle, but how many more miracles could she count on? They had neither the equipment nor the supplies to handle major cases, and it could get a lot worse before it got better.

Suddenly Kevin said, "I know where we can get some choppers."

The major looked at him with the astonished caution usually reserved for deities; Kate was a bit more skeptical. "Kevin..."

He got energetically to his feet, his eyes alive with determination. "Come on. Let me have a crack at that shortwave."

Kate reached for him in quick alarm. "Kevin, wait, your shoulder—you shouldn't be running around."

He gave her a quick backward wave. "I'm fine, Katie." And he was pushing through the door, the mayor eagerly in tow, just as Dr. Brandon poked his head in.

"I could use an assistant, Doctor."

With the opening of the door came the noise and confusion of crisis and urgency, a swelling tide of demands that clamored for Kate's attention, and then she was certain that the few tender moments alone with Kevin had been nothing more than the product of her overwrought imagination. Kate looked anxiously from the waiting surgeon to Kevin, who was disappearing around the corner. She wanted to call out to him again, to reach for him again, and she had one brief flash of dim puzzlement as to why, with all that waited for her, all those who needed her, it should be only concern for Kevin that was uppermost in her mind.

But Dr. Brandon was watching her with patient, slightly puzzled eyes, and she couldn't hesitate any longer. She said brusquely, "Yes, of course." And hurried to join him.

Chapter Five

Kate occasionally assisted in surgery; it comforted her patients to know she was with them in the operating room. But OR at the county hospital had never been like this. Under normal conditions, it was filled with confident experts, the most modern lifesaving equipment, the highest technology. Irreverent banter and ribald jokes were tossed casually back and forth, usually to the beat of a rock-and-roll radio station playing softly in the background. Everything was routine, relaxed and easy.

The atmosphere in Examining Room Three was taut and silent, broken only occasionally by Dr. Brandon's requests or instructions and Kate's terse replies. Iris carefully administered ether through a gauze pad and anxiously monitored the patient's vital signs; Kate assisted the surgeon and prayed intensely. They had neither the time nor the environment to attend to detail, and what they performed amounted to field surgery—a quick patch-up job that would see the patient safely to a proper hospital. What would have been a routine operation for any moderately qualified orthopedic surgeon was complicated tenfold by the use of the unstable anesthetic, the lack of proper equipment and the appalling conditions under which they worked. Kate tried not to think about the patients who waited for her while three-fourths of Victoria Bend's medical staff was otherwise occupied. She tried not to think about what might happen on this makeshift operating table if even the slightest complication developed, if even one of them made the smallest error in judgment. She tried not to think about Kevin and the look in his eyes when he had touched her face.

After a time, Dr. Brandon said, breaking the tense silence with his matter-of-fact tone, "My name is Jeff, by the way."

Kate concentrated on the retraction she was holding. She did not look up. "It's nice to meet you. I'm Kate."

"Hell of a get-acquainted party you throw, Kate. I think this gentleman is going to be all right. I wouldn't have wanted to wait much longer, though. What are the chances of getting him to a real hospital before these bones start to knit?"

His calm, quiet manner was reassuring, and his work, for the circumstances, was remarkable. He was a godsend. "We're working on it now," she replied. "Hopefully, we'll be able to transport by morning."

"Ah, yes. That young fellow that was rushing out with the mayor. He looked familiar, somehow."

Kate glanced at him. "Kevin Dawson. From *Code Zero*."

His eyebrows arched above the mask. But he murmured only, "I'll be damned," and concentrated again on his work.

"You do good work, Doctor," Kate said after a time. "Orthopedic specialty?"

"No. I spent a few years in emergency services, though. See a bit of everything there. What about you?"

Kate released a long, not entirely steady breath through her mask. "I think I've seen enough tonight to last a lifetime. How's his pressure, Iris?"

Iris's eyes were encouraging. "Holding."

Kate concentrated on trying not to keep telling herself that this couldn't be happening, that she couldn't be performing surgery with a virtual stranger in the examining room of her own clinic, relying on nothing but ether and luck. The last emergency this place had seen had been when Mary Hobbs had given birth two weeks early; before that, one would have to go back to the time Mike Kelly had accidentally shot himself in the foot with his father's hunting rifle. She tried instead to count her blessings, to remind herself that if it weren't for a long tradition of self-reliance, the medical facilities of Victoria Bend would have been unequipped to handle even the crudest of surgeries, that they were lucky the clinic itself was still standing, and that, thanks to Kevin and her father, they had electricity.

It wasn't until the last stitch was in place and relief had strengthened her voice that she said, "Well, Dr. Brandon, are you going to tell me?"

His eyes met hers calmly. "Tell you what?"

"Whether or not you're licensed to perform surgery in Mississippi."

She heard Iris's soft gasp behind her, and Jeff's eyes crinkled above his mask. "Why don't you check my résumé? It's been sitting on your desk for over a month."

Of course. Her interview for tomorrow. How odd to think of her calendar sitting complacently on her desk with a space of time marked off for one more applicant, a name that before tonight had meant nothing but another decision to agonize over and postpone. How unsettling to realize how drastically the future could change in a span of only a few moments and how even more peculiar to know that she had changed, too, somehow.

There was no more time for hesitation, no more room for the luxury of dreading the decision that before tonight had been the biggest one of her life. She smiled at him and extended her hand. "Well, Dr. Brandon," she said simply, "I think you've got yourself a job."

A DAY AGO—even an hour ago—Kate would never have considered leaving one of her patients to recover from such a traumatic experience under the supervision of a doctor she barely knew. She would have sat by his bedside, holding his hand, monitoring his response, reassuring him with the sound of her voice until he was fully conscious, and then she would have moved heaven and earth to make sure he was transported safely to the nearest hospital, and she would have stayed, if necessary, another day and night, until she was certain there was nothing more she could do for him that others could not do just as well. But tonight was a night of firsts for her in more ways than she could count.

The faces, the voices, the demands all became a blur for her. Everyone needed something from her, and everyone needed it now. After a while she stopped wondering where her father was and why he wasn't here when she needed him; she stopped reminding herself that one doctor couldn't possibly be expected to handle all this by herself. She sutured cuts, dispatched patients to X ray for broken limbs and directed those not in immediate need to the church across the street, where a temporary shelter had been set up. She received periodic reports on the situation, one of which was that helicopter service had been arranged to transfer the most needy to local hospitals. She didn't question how.

By ten o'clock a brief lull was in the making, and Kate took advantage of it to rest a moment. Her back ached magnificently, and she was light-headed from hunger. She took a Coke from the refrigerator and a candy bar from Iris's private cache and sat down in the lab, dull with exhaustion and almost too tired to eat the high-energy junk food.

She leaned forward and rested her head for a moment in her crossed arms on the counter. When a warm hand fell on her shoulder, she jerked upright and turned. It was only Kevin.

He had changed his torn sweater for a shirt of soft India cotton and had fashioned a sling for his arm out of a nylon jacket. He was hollow-eyed and rumpled, but he smiled at her, and he looked a lot better than she felt. "Sorry," he said. "You look like you could've used that nap. I just didn't want you to fall off the stool."

She blinked and made a tired sound low in her throat, then took a sip of her Coke. In the melee of the last hours, she had almost forgotten about him. "How's the arm?" she asked with an effort.

He grimaced. "Hurts like hell."

"Do you need another shot?"

"Are you trying to turn me into an addict?"

Kate forced herself to take a bite of the candy bar. It tasted like sawdust. "Find Iris and make her give you some Percodan. That should get you through the night." She broke off the bottom half of the candy bar and offered it to him. "You should really try to find a place to lie down and rest."

"Look who's talking." He took the candy from her and pulled up a stool. "And stop pushing the dope. I'm okay."

They sat in silence for a while, eating the candy and sharing the Coke, and Kate tried to empty her mind, waiting for the sugar to metabolize into the energy she so badly needed. After a while she asked, for it simply had not occurred to her to question before, "How did you swing the helicopters?"

"There's a celebrity limo service in Jacksonville. They were more than happy to put a few of their choppers at the disposal of Colt Marshall."

Kate tried to smile but was simply too tired. "Name-dropper."

He lifted his good shoulder lightly, dismissively. "If you've got it, flaunt it."

"Crazy world, isn't it," Kate commented without rancor, "when hundreds of injured people are put on hold but a celebrity can snap his fingers and have whatever he wants."

Kevin looked at her soberly and made no reply. She hadn't the energy to try to imagine what he was thinking.

"Where did you get the clothes?" She took a final sip of the Coke and passed the can to him, indicating the change of shirt.

He chuckled. "My driver. The fool fought off the highway patrol to get back to me."

She lifted an eyebrow. "Loyal fellow."

"Well paid," corrected Kevin. "And also terrified that he would have to report to his boss that he'd lost Kevin Dawson in a tornado." He finished off the Coke and tossed the empty can into the trash. "So I thanked him very much, took my luggage and sent him off to report to the world that the living legend is safe and sound."

Kate stretched and winced, rubbing the pain in the center of her back. "I'm surprised you didn't go with him."

He lifted an eyebrow. "And leave you in your time of need? Does your back hurt? Here, put your head down." She hesitated, but he stood up, his long fingers already moving soothingly along her spine. "Go on, relax for a minute. I owe you something for interrupting your nap, anyway."

Kate sighed and crossed her arms on the counter again, lowering her head to rest upon them. "I've got to get back to work."

"How bad is it, Katie?" he asked seriously. His fingers, gently pressing the fabric of her blouse against her skin in a long rubbing motion, were already beginning to draw the tension from her back.

"Not as bad as it could be. No one is critical, thank God. And now that we can move some of them to the hospital, I think the biggest danger is past. There's just so much—"

"I know." His voice was heavy. "You wouldn't think in a town this size there could be so much damage."

"That's just the point. We're so small, we feel it a lot more than a bigger town would have."

"At least they've gotten emergency power and telephone crews out. We should be in contact with the rest of the world before too much longer. Don't hit me; I'm going to put my hand under your shirt."

Deftly, his fingers plucked her blouse from the waistband of her pants, and his fingers slid against her skin. Kate let her eyes drift closed. "I don't have the energy to swat a fly," she murmured. "Have your way with me."

He chuckled. "If only you knew how long I've waited to hear that."

Kate moaned in half pain, half pleasure, as his fingers dug into the taut muscles of her back, massaging, loosening, stimulating. "You have strong fingers."

"I'm even better with two hands," he replied smugly.

"I'll bet. Ow!" She bit her lip as those fingers pressed sharply into the tender flesh at the small of her back, gathering and kneading. "That hurts!"

"No pain, no gain."

She groaned out loud. "You can torture my body, Dawson, but have mercy with the clichés."

His hand swept up her back, brushing over the clasp of her bra, working a gently rotating pressure against her shoulder blades, then gathering and releasing the hard muscles at her neck. He *was* good. He was, in fact, wonderful. She felt guilty, allowing herself this luxury while there were people who needed her and things that should be done, and she gathered herself enough to object. "I should be doing this for you. You're the one who's hurt, after all."

"That's the trouble with you, Katie. You're always so busy doing things for other people you don't give anyone a chance to do anything for you."

"I never noticed you objecting before."

"You never noticed a lot of things." There was a strange note to his voice with that, and she wanted to turn her head to look at him, but just then his fingers closed around her neck muscles again and made moving impossible. And with his next words he sounded more like himself. "Anyway, I'll take a rain check on the massage. And you know I'll collect."

She smiled a little to herself. "You always do."

The long, sweeping motions of his strong fingers against her skin were a gentle soporific, a vaguely intoxicating stimulant. He drew warmth to the surface, he stroked away fatigue, and his touch was one moment as deft as that of a professional masseur, the next as sensuous as a lover's caress. Kate had been half drugged with fatigue before he came in; now it was all she could do to keep her eyes open. She let herself drift, pushing aside the nightmare that surrounded her, the demands that awaited her, connected to this time and this place only by the sensation of Kevin's fingers, delicate now and caressing, stroking her skin in slow, soothing, up-and-down motions.

She murmured, half smiling into her crossed arms, "Kevin, if I tell you something, will you promise never to repeat it, not even to me?"

"Hmm. Sounds like a secret worth promising for. What?"

"I dream about you sometimes," she said drowsily. "Not you, exactly, but Colt Marshall."

Only the slightest hesitation in the movement of his fingers registered his surprise. But his tone was mild, hiding a smile of delight or a hint of laughter. "Erotic dreams?"

"Hmm . . . sort of. Not exactly. Romantic dreams. It's not unusual. All women have fantasies. You probably account for a good eighty percent of them."

"I'm flattered." It was becoming harder for him to keep the surprised laughter out of his voice, but his fingers felt so wonderful, moving now with a sensual rhythm along the side of her ribs and downward to her waistband, that she hardly noticed.

"It's funny though." And it was she who smiled, drowsily, to herself. "You told me a while ago that I was your sanity. And you're my fantasy."

There was a tender, rueful chuckle in his voice, and his fingers slipped around to the soft flesh of her waist. She didn't mind. "God, Katie, are you going to regret telling me this in the morning."

"You promised," she reminded him, trying to force sternness into her voice and reaching for alarm she didn't feel. She didn't feel anything but his fingers, now moving gently, caressingly, over the naked flesh of her waist and her ribs. He was closer, too. She could feel his thigh pressing lightly against her hip and the warmth of his chest near her back. He was embracing her, and it felt right and natural.

He said softly, "Katie..."

And the moment he said her name, she realized what was happening. The tone of his voice, the awareness of his hand beneath her clothing and closing lightly on her waist, then the warmth and gentleness of his touch, reminded her that this of all times was no place for fantasy and brought her to an abrupt—however reluctant—recognition of the effect stress and shock can have on an otherwise perfectly rational mind. She straightened up quickly, and he seemed to come to a realization of what was happening at the same time she did. He grinned, half defensive, half embarrassed, and stepped away. He drew a breath to make some teasing comment, but just then Jeff Brandon looked in.

"I'm ready to ship our fracture, Kate," he said. "Do you want to check him over one more time? And the ambulance just got in with the second wave. The patient is asking—" he made a dry face "—no, demanding, to see you."

Kate pushed herself to her feet. "On my way," she said briskly and much more efficiently than she felt. She left the room without glancing back at Kevin.

Across the brightly lit reception room crowded with mattresses and makeshift litters, Kate saw Iris kneeling over the patient on the ambulance gurney. At her approach, Iris looked around and called urgently, "Kate!"

Iris had not called Kate by her first name since she graduated from medical school. That, in combination with the alarm on her face, assured Kate that what she was about to find on the stretcher would not be pleasant. Her heart began to pound adrenaline, preparing herself for renewal of crisis.

"All right, Iris, what have we—" Her voice was calm, reassuring and pleasant until she looked into the face of the patient on the stretcher, and then the air left her lungs in a single painful stab. "Daddy!"

Her father looked up at her, his face grim with impatience and pain. "Get hold of yourself, Katie. I'm not dying. Damn stupid concrete block tipped over on me, cracked at least three bones in my foot and might have chipped the tibia. Just slap some plaster on it and I'll be up hobbling around in no time." He scowled. "Who was that young fool who was trying to push Demerol on me when I came in? You recruiting off the streets?"

"No." Her throat was dry, and her pulse was pounding so frantically she couldn't even get an accurate count on her father's pulse. He pushed her hand away impatiently.

"Pulse one twenty, respiration twenty-five—what do you expect? I'm in pain, here. And my blood pressure's soaring with every minute you make me lie here."

"You should have taken the Demerol," she responded automatically. Her mind was screaming, *No, not this, too. I need you; this can't be happening to me....* "That was Jeff Brandon, my new partner." She whipped her head around and shouted, "Tony—Joel! Give me some help getting this patient into X ray, please!"

"New partner, huh?" Surprise or admiration registered in her father's tone. "So it took something like this to finally get you to make a commitment. It's about damn time." He tried to chuckle, but the sound was cut off with a grimace of pain. Kate's heart wrenched.

She shouted again, "Tony!" and the two paramedics appeared just as her father reprimanded, "No need to make a damn production out of this. Just get me in a cast so I can get up. I've got patients to see."

"You'll do no such thing," Kate responded, gesturing to the paramedics to move the stretcher into X ray. "You've done quite enough for one evening, thank you. Be careful," she ordered, just as though the paramedics had not been personally trained by her and had no idea how to handle a fractured limb. "Don't jostle his leg—"

Her father frowned at her intensely as she urged the stretcher along. "Now you wait just a minute—you're not going to mother me through this thing. I'll set it myself before I'll let you follow me around like a wet nurse. You've got other patients to see. Get busy!"

Iris looked up quickly. "I'll stay with him, Kate," she said a little breathlessly. That was the first time Kate noticed that Iris was holding her father's hand and had been all along—and that he hadn't objected.

At any rate, there was little time to make a decision, for the stretcher was moving quickly toward X ray, and Jeff was calling her name, and with only one last look of despair and confusion at her father, she turned toward the more urgent need.

The night went on forever. It wasn't just the demands of the patients that kept Kate in constant motion, but outside the clinic there was a world trying to right itself, and it did not seem to be able to do so without her assistance. She helped the Red Cross set up, organized local volunteers, located temporary shelters and ordered emergency supplies and medications. She supervised the transportation of patients and received half-hourly reports from the highway patrol and the power crews. She set her father's leg and left him dozing under the influence of Demerol, mumbling that he would be up to help her in an hour or so.

At midnight, an emergency telephone line was hooked up to the clinic, connecting them with the hospitals in the area. At one in the morning they were able to switch from the emergency generator to regular power. Kate felt a dim and distant twinge of admiration for how well they were coping with disaster. And when all was said and done, there were less than a half-dozen patients whose injuries were serious enough to require a transfer to the hospital.

At one forty-five Kate turned away from directing her last patient to the nearest shelter and found no one waiting for her but Dr. Brandon. "Where did everybody go?" she asked in weary surprise.

He was bending over the reception desk, making a notation on a chart. "Here, there and the other place. I've got a laceration in One; it needs a couple of stitches but nothing I can't handle. Looks like the worst is over."

Kate leaned against the wall, smiling at him tiredly and gratefully. "You're really something, you know that? You walked in cold in the middle of a disaster and went to work like you've been doing it all your life. I don't know what we would have done without you tonight."

He inclined his head modestly. "I was born to serve. But..." He looked at her with mock gravity. "After this is over, we've really got to discuss salary."

She laughed. It was a weak, trailing sound, but it felt good nonetheless. "You name it. After tonight it wouldn't take much to talk me into turning over the whole practice.''

''After tonight I'm not sure I'd accept.'' His eyes smiled at her warmly, and Kate relaxed in the knowledge that she had not only acquired the perfect partner but a new friend, as well.

Then he flipped the chart closed and tossed it on the pile waiting to be filed. ''I suggest we take the rest of the night in two-hour shifts. I think I know my way around well enough to be left on my own, and it looks pretty quiet. You go ahead and catch some sleep. If I get into any trouble, I'll give you a call.''

Sleep. She could hardly imagine it. Her body felt like a wind-up toy, but responsibility and anxiety made the concept of sleep an alien one. ''Good idea,'' she agreed. ''But you go first. There's a sofa in my office you can use, and I'll see if I can round up an extra blanket and pillow.''

''Dr. Larimer...'' There was sternness in his eyes despite his rueful tone. ''There's one thing about me you have yet to learn. Behind those skilled surgeon's fingers beats the heart of an incurable chauvinist. And for no other reason than the fact that you are a member of the weaker sex—'' he took her elbow in a firm grip and turned her toward her office ''—I'm convinced you need the rest more than I do. I'll wake you in two hours.''

Kate was simply too tired to argue with him. She managed a half-dry smile and conceded, ''Maybe I will just put my feet up for a minute. Two hours,'' she reminded him firmly, and he gave her a dismissive wave as he turned toward the examining room.

Kate was thinking rather bemusedly of Dr. Brandon and the incredible good fortune that had sent him to her as she walked into her office and turned on the desk lamp. Someone had made a pot of coffee, and she started toward it instinctively, knowing that while she might rest for a few minutes, she would never be able to relax enough to sleep. Jeff Brandon might be used to snatching moments of sleep during emergencies, but Kate's nervous system was tuned to a more sedate life-style, and she could not train herself to turn off the adrenaline once it started, although she wished desperately now she could.

She heard a movement behind her and turned. Kevin sat up from the sofa on which he had been lying, passing a hand through his hair and looking at her sleepily. "Kevin." She came to him quickly. "What is it—are you feeling worse?"

"No, I just needed to lie down for a minute."

"Are you dizzy?" She felt his forehead; it was cool. She touched his eyelid to examine his pupils, and he frowned at her, brushing her hand away.

"Just tired. For Pete's sake, Katie, are you always a doctor?"

She looked at him with as much forbearance as she could muster. "As a matter of fact, yes. How's your shoulder?"

"Not bad. I took one of Iris's pills; that's probably what made me sleepy." He looked at her frankly. "You, on the other hand, look like you could use a transfusion. How is it out there?"

"Quieter." Satisfied that he was, indeed, suffering from nothing more complicated than exhaustion, she got up and returned to the coffeepot. "I just came in here for a little rest."

He gave her a drowsy half grin as she filled her cup and turned. "I'll share the sofa with you," he offered.

Her own lips turned down in a dry imitation of a smile. "Thanks. Maybe another time." She grimaced as she sipped the coffee. "This is awful. Did you make it?"

"Uh-huh. That's why I'm not drinking it." He slid down until his head rested against the back of the sofa, his long, lean legs comfortably sprawled before him. He watched her with gentle interest. "How's your dad?"

"He made me put a walking cast on. He's going to be all right." Her reply was absent as she tried to subdue an unfamiliar sensation of fear deep within her abdomen. She couldn't understand it. The worst was over. But thinking about her father lying broken and helpless in a makeshift hospital bed, thinking about herself, left alone and completely in charge in the midst of a disaster, brought on a wave of retrospective panic she didn't seem to be able to control. She said quickly, turning to place her coffee cup on the desk, "Which reminds me; I should go check on him."

"He was fine fifteen minutes ago," Kevin informed her calmly. "He was sleeping, and Iris was sitting with him."

Kate didn't know whether she was more puzzled because Kevin had been thoughtful enough to look in on her father or because someone other than herself was sitting up with her father while he was ill. She said, "Iris? But I told her to go home and get some rest. Why would she want to sit up with Dad?"

Kevin's laugh was low and amused, and it annoyed her, because he seemed to be laughing at something she didn't understand. "Katie, you are so blind sometimes. It must come from keeping your head buried in all those medical journals."

She frowned at him, too tired to try to figure out what he was talking about. "How did you hear about Dad, anyway? Where've you been the past few hours?"

"Right behind you, mostly."

She stared at him. "I didn't know that. I thought you'd gone."

He chuckled again, shaking his head. "Good old Katie. At least that hasn't changed. You're still the only person in the world to whom I'm completely invisible."

She was certain that wasn't a compliment, and it made her feel guilty, both because it was true and it was unkind. How many times through the night had she looked up to find Kevin there just when she needed him? With his contacts and his power he could have been out of this town within an hour after the storm struck, and Katie was still confused as to why he had chosen to stay. Yet he had been here, catching her when she stumbled, coming up with the answers when she was at an impasse, performing feats of superhuman strength and endurance. When she thought about it, Kevin Dawson's behavior through the night had been among the most bizarre elements of a totally incredible experience. When she needed him, he had been there, supporting, encouraging, helping, yet between those moments of crisis she had completely forgotten about him. That realization made her ashamed.

She said, somewhat uncomfortably, "Listen, go back to sleep. I'm just going to stay long enough to—" she picked up her coffee cup again and made a face "—drink some of this garbage; then I've got to get back to work."

"Nope." He stretched out his legs and crossed them at the ankles on the coffee table. "I feel too guilty about taking your bed. You're the one who needs to sleep."

She shrugged and took her coffee over to the window. She pulled back the curtain and looked out into a black, unreadable night, glad that the darkness hid from her the evidence of what they had lived through this evening.

Kevin's silence was comfortable and undemanding behind her, and once again she was glad of his presence.

"It's stopped raining," she said after a time.

"A few hours ago."

Kate took a deep breath and was surprised to find it
hurt her chest. She placed her cup on the windowsill and
leaned her head against the wall, staring blankly out the
window. For some reason she was thinking of the yellow
roses that had just begun to bloom on the trellis at the
side of her house. That only made her chest tighter, and
she said with dull humor, "At six o'clock this evening,
what was the biggest problem in your life, Kevin?"

"How to get you to take me to dinner," he responded
promptly.

She tried to smile, but it fell short. "And mine was how
to get rid of you."

It swept over her in sudden, unexpected waves of horror—the sounds, the sights, the madness that had in a
space of minutes transformed an ordinary evening in an
ordinary little town into a scene from hell. She gripped
the window ledge, steeling herself against it, and she was
shocked to feel her shoulders shaking, then a wetness on
her face, and then an awful choked noise that sounded
like a sob came from her throat.

Swiftly, Kevin was beside her. She felt his warm hand
on her shoulder, a gentle turning pressure, and then her
face was pressed against his chest, her fists bunched
against his shirt, and she gave herself over to the sobs that
fought their way up from deep within the center of her
and came more rapidly than she could take a breath. It
was primal, it was unpreventable, it was the aftermath of
shock and fear and loss, and she couldn't have controlled it if she had wanted to. She thought about her
house, her rose trellis, her car; she thought about her fa-

ther and all her patients—the pain, the terror, the loss. She thought about that nerve-racking hour in surgery, and the chances they had taken made her weak. And then she thought about sitting before the fire with Kevin, drinking Grand Marnier and tossing light insults back and forth, and she cried harder and clung to him more desperately.

Kevin's arm tightened around her shoulders, and his face touched her hair. "It's okay, sweetheart; it's all over. It's okay now; take it easy."

But the tears wouldn't stop; they soaked her face and his shirt, and her fingers tightened on the material that covered his chest as she pressed herself closer. It wasn't over; it was a nightmare that was never ending. Tomorrow it would begin all over again—the demands, the horror, sorting through the wreckage, assessing the loss, people who needed her and people she couldn't help. Even now it waited for her, and she didn't know how much more she could take. She was afraid she wasn't strong enough; she *knew* she wasn't strong enough.

"Oh, Kevin, I can't deal with this. I wasn't meant to deal with this. I—I'm so afraid. People could have died."

"Hush." Swiftly, his arm tightened, and she felt his lips brush her hair. "No one died. No one's going to. Because of you. You did fine, Katie. It's all over."

"No, no..." The sobs were making her voice unintelligible, muffled in his chest. Turmoil and panic and rage were all twisted inside her, making her helpless and robbing her of reason. "You don't understand."

"Yes, I do, love. It's okay; I promise."

"No, I can't—I don't... I didn't ask for this! I only want—everything to be normal...and quiet.... I want to go home.... Oh, Kevin, I'm so afraid, and I want to go home, but there's—no home to go to! Kevin, hold me, hold me . . .''

"I'm holding you, love." She could feel his arm, long muscled and lean, pressing her close, and his whisper, calm and intense, and his breath, warm on her face. Her arms went around his waist, and she held him tightly as the sobs of panic and hysteria and devastation choked in her throat. She was so afraid, and Kevin was so strong— Kevin who had always been there; Kevin, whom she needed so badly. She lifted her face and saw the blur of his eyes, dark and calm and filled with tenderness, so close to hers. She felt his fingers on the back of her neck, beneath the ruffle of her hair, and then her mouth was on his, and she was drinking from him, deeply.

She tasted the salt of her own tears and the moisture that bathed her throat. She felt need, deep and raw, rising up from within her, and his strength, his energy, infusing her, and his mouth, opening on hers, claiming hers, blotting out all else with a great, powerful urgency that was met and fueled by her own. His fingers threaded through her hair, hard against her scalp, holding her head and turning it to accommodate the mind-stripping demand of his kiss. And then, with sudden gentleness, his tongue entered her mouth, tasting her and exploring her, and it was no longer strength that filled her but a glorious weakness, a flood of heat that swept downward to ache between her thighs in a definitive, unquestioning need.

The tears were gone, consumed by the flare of desire that was rising within her. The tightening in her stomach that once had been panic was now unmistakably arousal; the sound that formed in her throat was a whimper of wanting, not a sob. Her fingers spread along the hard musculature of his back, pressing him closer. She tasted him, she opened herself to him, she let him fill her and draw from her, for as much as he took from her, she wanted to give more; the more he gave of himself, the more she wanted. And all she could think was, helplessly, intensely, *Kevin...yes...yes...*

But she did not say it, and he left her with pulses pounding and muscles quivering, her senses stripped and open and waiting for him. She looked up at him, breathless and shocked and questioning, and through the haze of her own uncertainty and need she saw his face.

He looked as stunned as she felt, confused and disbelieving and strangely hesitant. She could see the sheen of moisture on his parted lips that came from her own and the flush of arousal on his skin. His breath was not quite steady, and his eyes were bright and dark with an inner fire. Those eyes swept her face and her throat and her breasts, and everywhere his gaze touched, a new spark of eagerness and need awoke.

But when his eyes returned to hers, there was something within them that Kate had never expected to see from him, something that found no answer within her. There was strength there, and decision, and even as she drew a confused breath to question he said softly, "No, Katie, it's okay. I understand."

He reached behind his waist and took her hand, freeing it from contact with him, and even as his fingers closed around hers, he was stepping away. He brought her fingers to his lips and kissed them lightly; then he smiled. It was a stiff, forced expression. "It's forgotten, okay?" he said gently. "Now come over here and sit down. All you need is a little rest."

She let him put his arm around her shoulders and lead her to the sofa, and her head was reeling with confusion and sudden deprivation, but she lacked the coherency to put any of her thoughts into words. It was as though she were moving through a mist where nothing was supposed to make sense and answers didn't matter. And because this sudden helplessness was so strange, so unprecedented, it seemed only natural that Kevin should take control, should smile at her in such a quiet, calming manner as he sat beside her and drew her head onto his shoulder. His fingers stroked her hair, and his voice sounded easy and natural as he said, "I'll bet if you were to close your eyes you'd be asleep in two minutes."

"I don't want to sleep." Her voice sounded hoarse and raspy, and she knew she should get up, but she couldn't remember why.

"Sure you do. You're exhausted. So am I. Close your eyes."

She wanted him to kiss her again, and she wanted it with the single-minded demand of a thwarted child. She thought how crazy it was that he should be sitting here, stroking her hair and telling her to go to sleep after what they had just shared, what he had made her feel. And that was when some dim and vaguely conscious part of her mind wondered just how great a part exhaustion had played in what had just happened between them. Exhaustion and hysteria.

She should have been embarrassed. She wanted to get up, to move away from him, to recover. But the motions of his fingers on her hair were soothing, the gentle rise and fall of his chest hypnotic, and without her even being aware of it, her eyes drifted closed.

Her last thought before a deep and dreamless sleep claimed her was that he was wrong; he didn't understand at all.

Chapter Six

Kate awoke feeling stiff and cramped, and orientation to time and place was slow in coming. The room was dim, and her first inclination was to find a more comfortable position and go back to sleep. Her legs moved against the lumpy upholstery of the sofa, and when she turned her head, her cheek brushed against rough denim. That was when she realized that the hard pillow beneath her head was Kevin's thigh and the warm weight across her ribs, just beneath her breasts, was Kevin's hand.

She blinked slowly and looked up at him. "Your lap is very uncomfortable."

His eyes crinkled with a lazy smile. "Sorry. It's the only one I've got."

She sighed and stretched her legs slowly. Someone had taken off her shoes. His hand across her ribs felt comfortable and natural, like an embrace, and his leg, however hard beneath her neck, felt good. She knew she should get up, but her body was heavy, and it was hard to move. She wanted to lie there in Kevin's embrace and just think nothing for a few moments longer.

She murmured, after a while, "Did you sleep, too?"

"Hmm. Off and on." He moved his hand then, upward to brush away a strand of hair that was tickling her eyelash. "That fellow—what's his name?—Brandon—looked in once, but you were dead to the world."

She remembered. She tried to gather herself to sit up. "We're supposed to be sleeping in shifts. What time is it?"

"A little after eight."

"In the morning?" She sat up abruptly, the sudden movement and the shaft of alarm piercing her head with a thud. "I was only supposed to sleep two hours! Why didn't you wake me?"

The anger in her tone registered with surprise in his, and the warm and drowsy moment between them shattered and was forgotten. "You were tired," he protested. "You needed the sleep."

"Damn it, Kevin, *I* know what I need, not you!" She swung her legs over the side of the sofa and searched for her shoes. "I've got people depending on me, things to do! What did you do with my shoes?"

"Will you just calm down? What's the big deal?"

He bent and retrieved her shoes from his own side of the sofa, and she snatched them from him, glaring. In a rush of jumbled memories she recalled the moment of abandoned passion in his arms, and the surge of embarrassment and confusion that accompanied the recollection did nothing to improve her temper. His clothes were rumpled and damp from her having slept against them, there was a stubble of reddish-brown beard on his face and the drowsy early-morning intimacy of a shared night in his eyes, and to her chagrin she felt her cheeks flush just looking at him.

She said shortly, tugging on her shoes, "The big deal is I've got responsibilities! I realize that's an alien concept to you—"

"Responsibilities, hell." His tone was clipped and derisive as he got to his feet. "You just can't accept the fact that the world might have gone on quite nicely for six whole hours without you!"

The jagged edges of temper grated at her; hostility crackled between them and made her head ache. It wasn't natural that she and Kevin should be facing each other with such anger in their eyes; it wasn't right that their words should be harsh and cutting and deliberately hurtful. And a dimension of sadness was added to the other layers of entangled emotions as she brushed past him. "Go back to sleep, Kevin," she said shortly. "I've got things to do."

He opened the door for her but blocked her exit with his arm. "Well, I must say, Dr. Larimer," he drawled, "our first night together has been a very enlightening experience." His tone was lightly mocking, but his eyes were very cool. "If you're like this every morning, no wonder you sleep alone."

She stared at him, seething, until he stepped politely away from the door. She stalked past him and did not look back, dreading, after a start like this, what the day held in store.

As it turned out, nothing was waiting for her but breakfast. A Red Cross volunteer was supervising the clinic and pleasantly informed her, after a brief consultation, that everything was under control and that Dr. Brandon might be found at the church, where a hot meal was being set up for the injured and homeless. Kevin had been right: the world had gone on just fine without her for six hours, and the discovery was disconcerting.

She regretted her loss of temper with him, and she couldn't understand it. She hadn't wanted to snap at him or argue with him. What she wanted was to curl up in his arms and take comfort in his familiar presence, to feel his hard muscles against her weak and aching body, to lean on him and let him quiet her tumultuous mind. And she was honest enough with herself to realize that it was those needs, those impulses, that had caused her to lash out at him this morning in confusion and defense.

The very thought of taking strength from Kevin was absurd. She took care of him; he didn't take care of her. He depended on her, not the other way around. Their sudden, brief and unaccounted for role reversal last night was confusing, at the very least. Kevin was ephemeral, shallow, superfluous in her life, but last night he had somehow taken on a real and solid shape to her; he had become important. Too much had changed too fast, and she didn't know how to deal with it.

She felt low and guilty and uncomfortable with herself as she went into the clinic bathroom to refresh herself before facing the demands of the morning. She was further distressed to look into the mirror and discover she looked even worse than she felt.

Her skin was pasty and puffy, fatigue and stress emphasizing every wrinkle and sag in her complexion. Her eyes were circled in mauve and bloodshot, her lips colorless and cracked. Her hair was limp and tangled in spiky clumps, and her clothes looked the way only wet silk can look after it had been slept in. She groaned out loud and pressed her hands to her face, thinking miserably, *God, I look like a hag as well as acting like one. It's a wonder Kevin didn't push me onto the floor the minute he woke up and run as fast as he could in the other direction.*

Resolutely, she splashed cold water onto her face until some of the color was restored, then brushed her teeth and used the mouthwash she kept in the medicine cabinet for just such contingencies. She brushed away the worst of the tangles from her hair but could do nothing about its lifeless shape. Judicious use of lip gloss and a light blusher would prevent giving the impression she was a patient rather than a doctor, and she covered her wrinkled clothing with a crisp white lab coat she kept hanging on the back of the door. It wasn't exactly a transformation, but it was the best she could do.

A weak sun fought to make its way through a pale gray sky as she walked outside. She had expected devastation and desolation; what she found was the enormously uplifting signs of a town busily rebuilding itself. Heavy equipment and work crews labored to clear the streets of rubble; uniformed National Guardsmen manned recovery details and patrolled the streets for looters. Kate was struck by the need to examine her own house in the daylight, to inspect the damage and make plans for rebuilding, and now she thought she had the strength to do it. But she had to see to the needs of others before taking care of herself.

The concrete-block recreation hall of the church had been transformed into a dining and sleeping room. Mattresses were spread out against the walls, and people slept or rested or just sat and talked; steam tables near the front of the building offered hot oatmeal and powdered eggs and toast, and long tables in the center of the room were filled with diners. The room echoed with clatter and conversation and a battery-operated television and a radio, both of which were tuned to the morning news. The sounds were comforting and invigorating, and as Kate stopped to speak with her patients, checking bandages and dispensing encouragement, she found the atmosphere much more optimistic than she would have expected.

To her surprise, she found her father sitting at one of the tables with Iris and Dr. Brandon, enjoying a hearty breakfast, and he cheerfully waved her over. "What are you doing up?" she began to scold as soon as she reached him, and he cut her off with an authoritative scowl.

"Now, before you start with that tone of voice with me, young lady," he asserted, "I suggest you remember I was practicing medicine before you were even a notion in the back of my mind. And I'll have you know," he concluded airily, "that your new partner and I have already made rounds this morning and there's nothing for you to do but sit down and have some breakfast."

Kate turned apologetically to Jeff. "I'm so sorry I overslept. Why didn't you wake me?"

His eyes were twinkling. "You have some very protective men in your life." Kate felt a tingle of embarrassment that made her irritable, imagining how it must have looked to Jeff when he found her sleeping in Kevin's arms last night. And Kevin refusing to wake her. Damn him, anyway.

As though sensing her discomfort, Jeff turned back to his breakfast, adding easily, "No hardship for me, I assure you. Right after breakfast I'm going back to the motel and sleep for about twelve hours. I'm not officially on staff here," he reminding her with a smile, "so I think I can afford the luxury."

Once again Kate felt an intense surge of gratitude and admiration for him, and the warmth of her smile showed it. She said, "You never did tell me how you happened to show up here just when we needed you most."

"Dr. Larimer, here, sit down," Iris urged. "I'll go fix you a tray."

It was an offer Kate was happy to accept, and she took the chair beside Jeff as he answered, "It was a matter of being in the wrong place at the right time more than anything else. I dropped my things off at the motel and decided to have a look at the town, maybe even catch you in your office. The weather wasn't too bad when I started out. I was in the middle of it before I knew it."

Kate felt a residual shudder sweep through her with the memory. "Well, thank God you were," she murmured, and then looked up, startled at the sound of Kevin's voice.

"Morning, folks." He pulled a chair up to the head of the table and sat down near Kate's father. He glanced at Kate, and their eyes skated away from each other, as though from embarrassment or guilt. They had never behaved that way around each other before, and the fact prickled at Kate in annoyance. She knew she owed him an apology for her skittish behavior this morning, and she fully intended to deliver it. She simply hadn't expected to meet him in a room filled with people before she had mended her fences with him.

Jason Larimer said, "Kev, have you met our new doctor? Dr. Brandon, do you know Kevin Dawson?"

The two men's eyes met, and there was a prickle of hostility Kate couldn't understand. Jeff's reply was a polite "I know him, of course, but we've never actually met. How do you do?" Kevin merely grunted and nodded in what seemed to Kate a very rude way.

Jason gestured to Kevin's Styrofoam cup of coffee. "Is that all you're having?"

Kevin grimaced a little. "I don't have much of an appetite this morning."

"Kevin's tastes run a bit more toward imported strawberries and eggs Benedict than oatmeal," Kate elucidated, perfectly aware that it made him sound like a snob. With the patter of laughter that went around the table, she immediately regretted the statement, and her only justification was that he needed to be put in his place for his rude treatment of Dr. Brandon.

She knew that Kevin looked at her and that his eyes were not friendly, but fortunately she didn't have to meet his gaze. Their attention was distracted at that moment by a television report on the tornado.

The rumors they had heard through the night about county-wide devastation were confirmed by the news broadcast. In terms of property damage and injuries, it was considered the largest natural disaster to strike the county in the century, and as Kate watched the camera pan over scenes of grim destruction, she felt both sickened and fortunate—Victoria Bend had suffered, but there were other places where the damage was much worse.

As the news moved on, there was a brief silence while everyone recovered from the sobering evidence of what they had survived. And then Jason Larimer turned to Kevin. "The press has already descended on the mayor's office," he informed him. "They'll be honing in on you within the hour, if I don't miss my guess."

Kevin looked disturbed as he sipped his coffee. "I hadn't thought of that." Then his eyes swept the table briefly. "Listen, I'd appreciate it if you would all kind of steer them away from me, if you get a chance. No sense turning this place into more of a circus than it has to be."

Iris set a tray before Kate, and Kate thanked her absently, looking at Kevin. She seemed to be the only one who didn't understand his motivations, but she had to ask, rather testily, "Since when did you get so publicity shy?"

Everything she said to him came out like an attack this morning, and the cool distance in his eyes did not make her feel any more pleased with herself. He replied simply, "Don't you think we all have enough to worry about without turning the whole thing into a Movie of the Week? It just seems inappropriate somehow, Doctor."

Both Iris and Jason had known Kevin long enough to sense the strain between him and Kate, and even Jeff was not blind. The unnatural tension was palpable, and it was Iris who broke the awkward moment by pointing out mildly, "People will be worried about you, Kevin. You have to issue some sort of statement."

But Kate hardly heard what she said, because she couldn't help but notice that as Iris resumed her seat beside Jason again, her hand brushed affectionately—almost possessively—down the length of his arm. And all Jason did in reaction to the most unusual gesture was to meet Iris's eyes with a brief, warm smile, as though it were the most natural thing in the world.

With difficulty, Kate focused on what Kevin was saying. "I guess I should call my folks and my agent," he admitted reluctantly. "They're the only ones who really need to know. Then I'd better get over to the mayor's office and see what we need to get this place back on its feet again." He turned to Jason. "You never did tell me how bad the damage was on your side of town. Did you lose much?"

That prompted a discussion all around of experiences during the storm, and Kate listened with only half her attention, feeling as though she had stumbled into a conversation in which she did not belong and not knowing exactly why. Her father reported that he had lost no more than a few windows, and Iris's neighborhood was almost damage-free. Kevin inquired about water damage and broken gas pipes, and that was when Kate knew what was strange about this conversation.

Kevin was asking intelligent questions and expressing concern for someone other than himself, becoming involved in a situation that, in actual fact, had nothing to do with him at all. It hardly made sense. The excitement was over, the heady rush of his first real-life adventure had passed and there was nothing left now but the cleaning up. There was nothing in the aftermath of the disaster to appeal to Kevin's sense of glamour, and surely he would be leaving now.

Kate's father was saying, "Well, in that case, Katie, you'll be needing some transportation." She realized they had been talking about her crushed car. "Allow me to put my car at your disposal." He gestured ruefully at the cast on his leg. "I guess I won't be needing it for a while."

"Thanks," she agreed, and pushed away her empty oatmeal bowl. It had been tasteless but filling. "I do need to make the rounds of the hospitals today."

Her father's attention sharpened. "Serious cases?"

"Well, no," she admitted. "Routine care, mostly. But—"

"But you don't have enough to keep you busy around here?" Her father's tone was faintly sarcastic. "You couldn't consider calling in your orders and taking care of business at home for one day?"

Kate bristled. "Those people have been traumatized, both emotionally and physically. I need to be there for them. And I can take care of business here and at the hospitals, thank you very much."

Her father released a long-suffering sigh and directed his gaze to Jeff. "Try to tell this woman anything," he advised, shaking his head. "She never has learned the difference between dedication and psychotic compulsion. Maybe you'll be able to do something with her. I always did say all she needed was a man to take her in hand and straighten her out."

Kate made a face at her father, and Jeff laughed, looping his arm over the back of his chair and regarding Kate easily. "This is beginning to sound more like a marriage proposal than a partnership."

"Nothing would make my father happier, I'm sure," Kate responded dryly.

"And why not?" her father asserted without a trace of shame. "If ever there was a woman who needed to get married, it's my Katie."

Kate lifted an eyebrow. "That's the second time in twenty-four hours I've heard that," she said, remembering Kevin's teasing comment of the day before. "I don't see how I can fight odds like that." She turned to Jeff, keeping a straight face with difficulty. "So, how about it, Dr. Brandon? Are you available?"

His eyes twinkled. "For anything. I've always liked impulsive women. Just name the date."

"Give me a few hours," she suggested, enjoying the easy rapport that had been established so quickly and so effortlessly between them. "I might hire a partner without references, but I make it a policy never to take a husband without reading his résumé first."

No one noticed that Kevin was the only one not laughing. He excused himself abruptly to refill his coffee cup, and he didn't come back. Kate tried not to let his precipitous departure spoil the first break in the gloom she had experienced since the beginning of the nightmare. And it must have been her guilt working again, because her good humor evaporated like smoke as she watched Kevin walk away.

Jeff followed her eyes as Kevin made his way through the crowd and out of the building. Under the cover of Iris and Jason's conversation with the minister, who had joined their table, he asked mildly, "What is a guy like that doing here, anyway?"

Instantly and unpreventably, Kate sprang to Kevin's defense, surprising herself as much as she did Jeff. "For the past eighteen hours," she responded shortly, "he's been saving lives, fighting a tornado and trying to put the pieces of this town back together."

She saw a flash of startled confusion in his eyes, and she realized immediately how curt—and uncalled for—her tone had been. Jeff murmured, "Just curious," and turned his attention to his coffee cup as he lifted it for a final sip.

Kate sighed, passing a hand over her rumpled bangs, disordering them further. "I'm sorry. I didn't mean to snap." She ventured an uncertain glance at him. "Kevin and I are old friends," she explained by way of further apology. "I'm used to taking care of him."

"Oh, really?" His mild gray eyes registered no surprise, but instead held a measure of perception that Kate found unsettling. "I would have thought it was the other way around."

But before she could question or refute, he pushed away his tray and smiled, changing the subject. "This creates an awkward professional situation, I realize, but I'm sure you understand that when I came down for the interview I wasn't prepared for anything like this." He glanced around the room with a rueful twist of his lips. "I don't like leaving you in the lurch, but I really have to get back to my own patients in the morning."

"Of course," Kate agreed at once, and she smiled. "And please believe me, I didn't stage all this just to see how you cope with pressure. I'm fairly exacting, I'll admit, but I usually settle for a more orthodox interview."

"Which we haven't even gotten to yet," he reminded her.

"Why don't you go get some sleep now," she suggested, "and meet me back at the clinic about three o'clock this afternoon. We can get the formalities over with then."

"Be glad to. But all of this is a bit like having the wedding night before the wedding, isn't it?"

Kate laughed. "There are advantages to that, too, of course."

"So there are." His smile was warm as he got to his feet and extended his hand. "I'll see you this afternoon. If you need me before then, I left the number of the motel with Iris."

Kate stayed a few more minutes, talking with Iris and her father; then she collected her father's car keys and left the table to search for Kevin. There was no point in putting it off any longer.

She found Kevin sitting outside on the steps that overlooked the west parking lot, sipping his coffee and observing the workings of a lineman in a treetop across the way. He heard her approach but did not look around, and Kate felt a strange tingling sensation in her stomach as she looked at him.

Bits of sunlight were diffused against his tousled hair, emphasizing its sheen and giving it a rakish bedroom look as it curled over his collar and brushed his temples. The scrub of a morning beard added a degree of ruggedness to his face that was unfairly appealing, and even his rumpled clothes and the improvised sling on his arm enhanced an image that was masculine and subtly exciting. On anyone else the ravages of the night would have looked haggard and unkempt; on Kevin they simply looked sexy.

She came up beside him and sat down. "How's your shoulder this morning?"

"Stiff." He sipped his coffee, and there was no hostility in his tone. "Not bad."

She lifted his fingers in the sling, examining his fingertips for signs of impaired circulation. They were pink and healthy and warm. He had lovely slim fingers, soft and uncallused. She held them lightly between hers for a moment longer, and then said briskly, "Would you unbutton your shirt for me, please?"

His eyes sparked with a semblance of his old teasing. "Is that by way of a proposition?"

"If it were a proposition," she returned tartly, and began to work the buttons herself, "I'd ask you to drop your pants. That's just about the only part of you I haven't seen on television, anyway." It was only a light comment, similar to dozens she had made to him before, but it didn't sound right this morning. There was an awkwardness between them—or perhaps simply an awareness—that made everything double-edged, and the innocent remark sounded more sexually motivated than it was meant. She even found herself unable to meet his eyes as she explained, a bit too efficiently, "I need to check your dressing."

"That's the trouble with you, Katie," he murmured. "The only way you know how to relate to people is as a doctor." That remark, too, had a bite to it, and one she wasn't at all sure she wanted to understand. So she said nothing.

She pushed the material away from his shoulder and found the dressing to be clean and dry. She could feel Kevin's eyes on her as she hastily rearranged his shirt and closed the buttons, but she didn't look at him. "Stop by later and I'll change it for you," she said. "But it looks good. The stitches should come out by the end of the week."

He took another sip of his coffee.

Kate drew a breath, gathering her courage, and finally was able to look at him. His profile in the filtered morning sunlight looked strong, yet at the same time vulnerable, wonderfully familiar and yet different. Remembering the comfort she had taken in his arms last night, remembering the sensation of his mouth on hers, brought back a swift rush of tangled emotions—confusion and anxiety and warmth, a yearning kind of warmth that made her want to lay her head against his shoulder and have him tell her that everything was all right. And then shame—not for the events of the night but for her behavior of the morning.

She said softly, "Kevin . . . I'm sorry I snapped at you this morning."

He glanced at her, and there was a moment of hesitance in which she held her breath. Then he smiled faintly, and everything was all right. "That's okay. I wasn't in such a great mood myself."

She smiled back, and the relief was wonderful. She had never realized before what a desolate feeling it could be to have Kevin angry at her, perhaps because it had never mattered before. She moved her arm, and her instinct was to put it around his waist, to embrace him briefly, and then to lie against him and enjoy the sensation of being close to him, of being friends. But a moment of awkwardness interrupted the movement, and she didn't know why. Perhaps it was because she was remembering the last time she had been in his arms and the memory made so simple a gesture as a friendly hug seem uncertain, even dangerous.

So she merely rested her weight on her palm behind him and hoped he didn't notice anything awkward in the motion. They sat in silence for a while, listening to the sounds of hammering and chain saws, of heavy equipment and foremen shouting faint and distant orders.

Kevin said, half glancing at her, "That Brandon fellow—do you like him?"

She was a little surprised. "Well . . . yes. Don't you?"

He shrugged, staring at his coffee. "Sure. I mean, if he's a good doctor...and you needed a partner. I'm glad you've got someone to take some of the load off you. It will give you more time for yourself, you know."

She laughed somewhat stiffly. "I don't know about that. I never thought about needing free time. What would I do with it?"

There was no mistaking the slyness in his glance this time. "You might have an affair. With your new partner, perhaps?"

She stared at him, torn between an urge to laugh and the very unsettling notion that Kevin might be serious. "Why in the world would I want to do that?"

"Don't you think he's good-looking?"

"Is he?" She tried to match her casual tone to Kevin's. "Why? This doesn't have anything to do with that stupid conversation at breakfast, does it?"

He looked uncomfortable, and he pretended a great interest in the work of the lineman in the distance. "Maybe. I've just never seen you flirt before. And I guess I never thought of you with another man."

Another man... She almost said it out loud. But it was all too confusing, and she wasn't certain how deep she wanted to get into this conversation when she understood so little of it. But one thing was clear, and it registered with a little thrill of pleasure and cautious disbelief that surprised her. Kevin was jealous.

Kevin chose that moment to offer his coffee cup to her, almost as though to distract her, and she shook her head. Silence fell, and it seemed there were a dozen things to be said between them and both of them were holding back. That had never happened between Kevin and her before.

She thought again about slipping her arm around his waist just to reestablish the old rapport. Except that the old rapport had not included a great deal of touching, at least not in the way she wanted to touch him now. Because when she imagined the two of them sitting here together, with her arm around him, she also imagined her hand slipping beneath his untucked shirt, along the smooth, lean muscles of his back, feeling his skin and his strength, touching and caressing him just for the pleasure of it. Thinking about it made her heart beat faster.

It had been Kevin who backed away last night, not her. If he hadn't stopped, she would have made love with him on the floor of her office without a second thought.

The admission was shocking, but she couldn't deny it no matter how much she tried. A caldron of twisting, jumbled emotions tipped over inside her, scattering reason to the wind. She wondered if Kevin knew how she had felt last night, how far she would have gone, and if that was why he stopped. She wondered whether, if he had known, he would have stopped at all.

It was crazy. It was stress, high-anxiety instincts for comfort and reassurance, and yes, even sex, but no more. There was nothing between Kevin and her; there never had been, and there never could be. It was just the moment, the situation, an escapist fantasy. But even now her pulse was more rapid than it should be. Her skin felt heated, and there was a flutter of question, of eagerness, in her stomach when she thought about him. He seemed so different this morning. Everything seemed different this morning.

Trying to keep the conversation on a rational level, she said, "I guess you'll be glad to get home." She was pleased to find that her voice sounded normal. Casual and friendly and hardly breathless at all.

He made a wry sound low in his throat. "If it's still standing."

It took her a moment to realize he was talking about his home here, in Victoria Bend. "No, I meant to Los Angeles."

He turned to her, and the look in his eyes was slowly surprised, as though he had, in fact, forgotten such a place existed. And then he smiled, though it was a vague and distant expression. "Right." His eyes moved away, a puzzled, faintly reminiscent expression crossing his face. "It won't seem the same somehow. I guess maybe nothing will ever seem the same after this."

Silence fell, long and sweet. It was a shared moment, like so many they had had before, yet with a poignancy and a depth they had never known before. Nothing would ever be the same, because the two of them would never be the same. It was both a sad and an exhilarating realization.

And then Kevin tossed out the remainder of his coffee and got to his feet. "Well," he said, "I've got things to do. So do you."

"Yes." She stood beside him, and for a moment they looked at each other. His eyes were slightly crinkled with the rays of a cloudy sun, dark burnished mirrors in which she could see a faint reflection of herself. Once again she felt the powerful instinct to touch him, to lift her hand

and stroke his cheek, to feel the soft bristled texture under her palm, to trace the strong profile, and then perhaps to lean forward and kiss him lightly on the lips.

Because he was watching her so intently, almost as though he could read her thoughts or as though he were waiting for her to make a move, she felt a slight twinge of embarrassment, or shyness, and she dropped her eyes. He took the cue.

"I'll see you later, then, Katie." His voice was casual.

"Right."

She wanted to call out to him as he turned and walked away, but she didn't know what to say. So she simply watched until he was gone, and then she took out the keys and went in search of her father's car.

Chapter Seven

On her way to the hospital Kate stopped in a nearby town and bought the first outfit she saw—a white full skirt and a peacock-blue peasant blouse. At least she told herself the only reason for the impulsive purchase was because she didn't have time to be more discriminating. But as she went into the dressing room to change, she began to wonder.

The pants and blouse that had seen her through the storm were totally unsalvageable, and she didn't have the time—or the spirit, at this point—to go home and sort through the rubble for her own clothes. But as she looked at her reflection in the dressing-room mirror, she was amazed at the transformation.

The shoulders and bodice of the blouse were filled in with cotton netting from just above her bra to the neckline, which closed with criss-crossed ties and gave a more than provocative view of the beginning of her décolletage. The soft cotton material caressed the shape of her breasts and hugged her waist with smocking and wide elastic, and the brilliant blue improved her complexion enormously, deemphasizing the hollow circles under her eyes and adding flecks of light to her irises. The full skirt floated gently over her hips and outlined the shape of her thighs, falling in abundant caressing folds to the middle of her calves. The effect was delicate and sensuous, and it surprised Kate but did not entirely displease her. She rarely wore skirts, thinking them too frivolous and unprofessional looking, preferring the comfort and maneuverability of less feminine pants and blazers. She tried not to think about why, today, she would want to look feminine, and buttoned her lab coat over her new outfit as she left the store.

Her patients were divided between two local hospitals, one of which was fifty miles away, and she spent more time than she had intended to with each patient, as well as conferring with her colleagues and listening to more stories than she wanted to about the effects of the storm in neighboring towns. It was after lunch when she arrived back at the clinic to find the situation there much more controlled than she had expected.

Her secretary had canceled all but the most urgent regular appointments that day to make room for followup checks on the injuries she had treated last night. She wasn't very surprised to notice that most people had better things to do today than visit the doctor, and by three o'clock she placed the last file on her secretary's desk. "The insurance companies are going to go berserk," she said. "What have we heard on federal disaster assistance?"

"The governor flew in this morning. We probably won't get the exact figures for a couple of days."

Kate nodded soberly, thinking about the lives that had been destroyed, the years of working and building that no amount of money could replace. She started to go back to her office, then paused, gesturing to the account ledger. "What insurance doesn't cover," she suggested, "just write off, okay?"

"I like your style, Dr. Larimer."

Kate looked up at the male voice to see Dr. Brandon approaching. He looked rested and well-groomed, and she met his smile with a slightly self-deprecating smile of her own. "I never promised you we'd make a profit," she said, and gestured him toward her office. "Fortunately for you, we haven't signed any agreements yet. Now's your chance to back out."

"I think it may be too late." He touched her back lightly at the door of her office, allowing her to precede him, and his eyes were warm and relaxed. "I've grown rather fond of this place."

Their meeting went quickly, because Kate knew Jeff had a long drive back and did not want him to get a late start. She explained the technicalities of the junior partnership she was offering, and he found the terms satisfactory—although she was offering him a slightly smaller salary than what he was making now as a staff surgeon at a large metropolitan hospital. He explained to her in his easy, clear-eyed way that he was looking for a change in life-style as well as a chance at private practice, and since he didn't have a family to support, now seemed the perfect time to make the move. Kate once again thought how lucky she was to have found him.

"The practice is growing," she assured him, "along with the town. Don't think a little thing like this storm is going to get us down. And once the hospital is built, I expect we'll have call for more physicians. For now, we'll get you on staff at County General, which is where we admit most of our patients. I'll take you over there and show you around the next time you're in town; I think you'll find their facilities adequate for the kind of work we'll be doing."

They talked for a time longer about procedures and methodologies, and the conversation only confirmed what Kate already knew: their philosophies about medicine and the doctor-patient relationship were in perfect agreement, and she couldn't have found a more compatible partner if she had custom designed him. At four o'clock she reluctantly drew the interview to a close, for she enjoyed Jeff's company and was excited about the plans they were making. It was agreed that they would meet again in two weeks, when he would be down to begin searching for a house, and that he should be ready to join her practice by the end of June.

He clasped her hand warmly as he stood to go. "I've waited a long time for an opportunity like this, Kate," he said sincerely. "I think I'm going to be happy here."

For a moment Kate couldn't believe she had actually done it. The commitment she had just made to this man was going to change her life, and she waited for the panic, the regret, the second thoughts. None came. There was nothing but confidence in her tone as she sealed their bargain with her own handclasp. "We're going to be good together, Jeff."

They both laughed as she realized that her statement had sounded like anything except a business deal, and Jeff winked at her as he turned to go. "And our children will have blond hair. I'll be in touch before I come back down. You'll let me know how Mr. Kensington progresses, won't you?"

Mr. Kensington was the patient on whom he had done emergency surgery in her examining room. "Yes, I will." Her eyes were still dancing warmly as he picked up his raincoat and opened the door. "I'll see you in two weeks. Drive carefully."

When he was gone, Kate leaned against her desk and thought about what she had done. It was incredible what the past twenty-four hours had brought. If anyone had told her that in such a brief time she would survive a natural disaster, treat over one hundred patients—including assisting at an ether-anesthetized surgery and setting her father's broken leg—witness her house fall down around her ears and take a virtual stranger into permanent partnership in her practice, she would have replied quite calmly, "Not in this lifetime." She hadn't the stamina, the physical skills or the temperament to deal with such outrageous demands from life. And she was certain that when she looked back on the experience, she would find that another woman had taken over her body, for very little in her behavior of late reminded her of anything that was Kate Larimer.

The day had been a busy one, and it was only half over. Fortifying herself for the worst, Kate left her office to inspect the damage to her own house.

It was a sad sight. Kate had never considered herself a sentimental person, but standing in the street, looking at the caved-in roof, the scattered glass, the one shingle hanging forlornly by a corner on the front window, Kate felt a low sinking in her stomach. She had loved that house. It wasn't large or pretentious or architecturally original; it wasn't very old or very valuable, and she had only lived in it for five years, but it was hers. She had decorated every inch of it herself, lavishing her spare time and her creative instincts on hanging wallpaper and building window seats, choosing handmade rugs and original art, shopping antique stores and galleries for just the right accessories. Until this very minute she had never realized how much of herself had been invested in a place to live, and it hurt her, deep inside, to see it so desecrated.

But worse had happened to her in the past day, and she squared her shoulders and took a breath as she made her way carefully up the littered walk and through the front door.

The first thing that struck her was how much worse it looked through the clear eyes of reason than it had last night in the blur of panic. It wasn't just the dining room's bay window that was broken, but two of the living room windows, as well. Beams and plaster littered the floor; a broken water pipe hung wantonly from the ceiling. Pictures had been thrown from the walls, and crushed bric-a-brac was scattered everywhere. The west wall bowed inward from the weight of a tree that had fallen on the roof, and a magnificent crack ran the length of the ceiling as far as she could see. The second thing she realized was that she would have to find some other place to spend the night.

The enormity of the cleanup task that lay before her was overwhelming, and she could only deal with a small portion at a time. The first thing she had to do was board up the windows against more inclement weather. She stripped off her lab coat and tossed it over a broken chair, then went to the storage shed in search of tools, giving the tire of her crushed car a disgruntled kick as she passed.

As was typical of the random damage caused by tornadoes, her small aluminum storage shed was untouched, while her house, her car, even the chain-link fence that bordered her backyard, were in shambles. Inside the shed she found some scraps of lumber she had collected over the years and dragged them to the house, returning for the stepladder and a hammer and nails. She set up the stepladder outside the dining room first and went immediately to work covering the hole that used to be the window.

That was where Kevin found her fifteen minutes later. "You have pretty legs, Katie," he drawled from beneath her.

Kate was certain the light skipping rhythm of her heart was from no more than surprise, and she replied without turning, "That's very adolescent, Dawson." She banged in another nail. "Standing under a ladder just to look up a girl's skirt."

"I am not standing under the ladder," he protested. "I'm standing beside it. And..." He grinned as she glanced at him. "I can't see all the way up your skirt. Just enough to tell you have pretty legs."

Kate positioned another nail and dropped it as she drew back the hammer. "Then make yourself useful and hand me that nail. What are you doing here, anyway?"

"I've been here a couple of times today. I thought you'd need some help getting your things together. Now, come on down from there. You're making me nervous."

She turned on the ladder and saw he was extending his arm to her. She also noticed that he had shaved and changed clothes and was no longer wearing a sling. A collarless knit shirt was tucked into stylishly loose-fitting white pants; he wore black suspenders and white sneakers. The placket buttons of his shirt were undone at the throat, and the elasticized waistband of the high-fashion pants emphasized his lean, lazy form. He looked tanned and healthy and as sexy as a television commercial, and under the circumstances Kate should have resented his expensive good looks. Instead, she found him enormously and unaccountably appealing.

"Why aren't you wearing your sling?" she asked.

"Your dad said I should try to use my fingers, and I couldn't very well do that with my arm bound up. Are you coming down or not?"

She could hardly argue with her father's prescription, as much as she might have liked to. So she merely replied, with as little ill grace as possible, "If you rip out my stitches, I'll make you put them back in yourself."

"Yes, ma'am. But if you don't get off that ladder, I'm going to be forced to volunteer to do the job myself, and that wouldn't be very good for either my shoulder or my ego. I'm not exactly an expert with nails," he confessed, and Kate grinned in spite of herself.

She glanced at her boarding job and decided it would hold for now. She backed carefully down the ladder, Kevin's hand, light upon her waist, guiding her. "I'll have to find some more lumber tomorrow," she said, absently nudging a narrow piece of plywood away with her toe, "to fix the other windows."

"Easier said than done," Kevin pointed out. "The early birds got the lumber today, sweetie. It's going to be hard scrounging up a toothpick around here for the next couple of weeks."

Kevin's hand was still light and protective on her back as she picked her way back into the house over shattered glass and broken shelves toward the living room. Once there, she stopped, letting the full impact of it sweep over her, just once more. Despair was heavy and gripping.

"Oh, Kevin," she said softly, "just look at this."

His hand came up to caress her neck gently, a warm gesture of caring and support. "I know, Katie," he said simply, quietly. "I'm so sorry."

He could have offered encouragement or platitudes; he could have reminded her how lucky she was to be alive and how less fortunate some of her neighbors were; he could have minimized the damage or made some blithe comment about insurance coverage. Had the positions been reversed, Kate was certain she would have resorted to some of those meaningless tactics to lighten the moment. But Kevin did not. He simply said, "I'm so sorry," and she knew he meant it. He understood, and knowing that he shared the loss with her, in however small a way, strengthened Kate to face it.

She reached up and touched his hand lightly and tried to smile. Then she moved away from him, threading her way through the rubble, compelled to see what could be salvaged.

She moved aside an end table that had been deposited atop a watercolor landscape. The frame was broken, and the canvas was punctured. But even as she reached, with a stab of sadness and anger, for the destroyed painting, her attention was caught by something else. She knelt on the floor and picked up a fragment of hand-painted porcelain. She looked at it for a long time.

It once had been part of a candy dish delicately painted with butterflies and daisies. Artistically speaking, it was no great treasure and might even have been considered tacky by some, but it had been one of her mother's first experiments with a kiln and paint back during what Kate and her father had laughingly referred to as her mother's "sculptress phase." It was the only thing Kate had taken from her parents' house after her mother's death.

Kevin was standing above her, close and comforting. He said, "I remember that. It used to sit on your mom's coffee table, and she always kept it filled with divinity."

Kate subdued a quick flash of tears, and she wasn't certain whether they were prompted by sorrow or grateful wonder for the fact that there was someone in her life who shared her memories, someone who, despite the changes and movements of the years and even this final great devastation, was connected to her and all she had experienced. Kevin had been there, raiding her mother's divinity dish. Kevin had been there after the funeral, when Kate took the dish home with her. And Kevin was here now, saying goodbye.

There was something very, very special in that.

Kevin knelt beside her, his arm going warmly around her shoulders. With his other hand, he took the fragment of porcelain from her and laid it on the table. "Katie," he said gently, "you probably don't want to hear this now, but after you think about it, I think you'll realize that as bad as all this is, there's some good, somehow... I mean, sometimes you have to wipe out the past to get a good grip on the future. Starting over, sometimes, can be the best thing in the world...and the best way to do it is without anything from the past dragging you down. Do you understand what I mean?"

His eyes were so earnest, so caring, that Kate felt another sting of moisture in her own. The truth was she didn't entirely understand what he meant, nor was she inclined to try at this moment, but she was moved by his concern and deeply grateful. She made an attempt to smile, but the corners of her mouth turned down instead of up, and the expression was reluctantly wry. "Philosophy, huh? I'm impressed, but if you don't mind, I'd really rather feel sorry for myself a little while longer."

"I mind," he said firmly, and he grasped her hand and pulled her to her feet. "Come on; let's get out of this cave before the rest of it falls in on us. You're spending the night with me."

She stared at him, and he gave her a half-apologetic grin. "You probably don't want to hear this now, either, but my place is completely untouched. Still no electricity but plenty of hot water for baths and a dry bed to sleep on. Just throw your things in a suitcase and let's go."

She dismissed it without a thought. "Don't be silly, Kevin. I'm not spending the night with you."

"Oh, yeah?" He regarded her patiently. "Just where were you planning to stay?"

She hesitated only a moment. "With my dad, I guess."

"Bad idea." His fingers closed around her arm, and he guided her toward her bedroom. "For one thing, his place isn't secure—the windows are broken, and the door is sagging. For another, he's not there."

She stopped at the entrance to the bedroom, turning to him in shock and suspicion. She hadn't seen her father since morning. "Where is he?" she demanded.

He replied complacently, "With Iris."

Disbelief and confusion registered on her face. "Iris? What's he doing there?"

Kevin assumed thoughtfulness. "Well, considering the shape his leg is in, probably just watching television and sleeping on the couch. But I don't imagine that will last very long once he's up and moving around."

Kate scowled at the implication, not in the least amused. "You have a filthy mind, Dawson."

He only laughed and gave her a gentle shove into the bedroom. "This storm is going to make stranger bedfellows than that, Katie. Where's your suitcase?"

"I'm not going home with you." But it was said absently as she noticed, with great relief, that the damage in this room wasn't too extensive. A sheer paneled curtain was caught haphazardly against a shard of broken glass that protruded from the window, and there was a dark stain on her ceiling from a broken pipe, but otherwise everything seemed to be in shape.

Kevin strode over to the closet and opened the door. "Fear not, fair damsel; your reputation is safe with me. Somehow I suspect the *Victoria Bend Gazette* will have more than enough copy for their next issue without reporting on who Kevin Dawson slept with while he was in town. Besides, it seems to me your choices are limited. So..." He dragged down her overnight bag one-handed from the closet shelf and tossed it on the bed. "Pack. And take enough for a few days. You shouldn't come back here until someone has been in to shore up the roof."

Once again, irritably and absently, Kate started to protest, but then the logic in his offer descended on her. Where else was she to go? The thought of spending another night at the clinic did not appeal to her in the least, and the motel was too far away.

She didn't understand why she should be so reluctant about spending the night at Kevin's house, anyway. She thought about the many times Kevin had stayed at her house until three and four o'clock in the morning, eating her popcorn, watching her television and tying up her telephone. Or the marathon Monopoly sessions in which he rooked her father while Kate fell asleep on the couch, waking at dawn to find the two of them still at it. She had never worried about what people would say then. And if she had begun her determined effort to kick Kevin out at midnight, it had been through a sense of impatience, not propriety. Why should this be any different?

She said hesitantly, "You have hot water?"

He regarded her with a confident gleam in his eye. "Uh-huh. Gas water heater."

A bath. She couldn't think at that moment of anything she wanted more.

"Well..." Reluctance was evident in her tone. "Maybe just one night."

He drew a sober face. "I think you've made the right decision, Doctor."

She gave him a playful nudge with her fist as she moved past him toward the closet, and he grinned.

"My clothes are wet!" she exclaimed in dismay, running her hand over the neat row of blouses in her closet.

Kevin glanced up at the ceiling. "Water pipe," he observed. He pulled open a bureau drawer and looked inside. "Well, these are dry." He scooped up an armload of lingerie and dumped it into the suitcase, then returned for more.

Kate watched him, laughing. "Well, if I want to change my profession from physician to centerfold, I'll be well dressed." She removed the pile of underwear from her overnight bag and tossed it back into the drawer. "When I was six," she remembered, and the chuckles dissolved into a wistful, sparkling smile, "I decided to run away from home, so I packed my suitcase with every pair of panties I owned and nothing else, reasoning that since my mother always told me to wear clean underwear, I was going to be prepared."

Kevin was watching her as she rearranged the clothing in the drawer, and the smile in his eyes was indulgent and pleasured, and as Kate glanced up at him, she thought she caught a glimpse of something else, something that left her half breathless as he lifted his hand as though to caress her or draw her close and then made her feel silly when all he did was slap her lightly and most irreverently on the backside.

"If that's your way of telling me I pack like a six-year-old, you're on your own. I'm going to see what I can scavenge from the kitchen."

He left her feeling immeasurably lighter than she had when she had come to the house less than an hour ago and absurdly pleased with her decision to stay with him tonight. She didn't want to be alone tonight in some motel room or in the uncomfortable confines of her office, with its nightmarish memories. She wanted to relax in the company of someone who was familiar and comforting, someone who understood what she was feeling because he had lived through it with her, yet who was carefree enough to allow her to escape, for just a short time, from all that was waiting for her. She didn't want to be alone. She wanted to be with Kevin.

She packed her overnight bag with a change of underwear, a nightshirt and her toiletries, hoping that by tomorrow she would be able to find a place to launder her wet clothes. Kevin met her at the door with a sack of groceries salvaged from her cabinets. "We're in luck," he said, gesturing her back toward the kitchen, where another brown paper sack waited. "Some of the stuff in your refrigerator was still cold. I couldn't salvage the milk, but we've got plenty here for dinner, and for breakfast tomorrow."

She chuckled lightly, shaking her head as she went into the kitchen to get the other sack. "You're really into this roughing-it stuff, aren't you?"

"Old Colt would be proud," he agreed cheerfully, and opened the door for her as she struggled through with the grocery sack and her bag.

Kevin had borrowed a car somewhere, and automatically he started toward it. Kate protested firmly, "No way, hotshot. You can barely drive with two good arms, much less one. Whoever loaned you that car should be brought to trial for endangering the public safety, anyway." She gestured him toward her father's car. "I'm driving."

"Coward," he shot back, but made no further argument as he helped her store the packages in the back and got into the passenger seat beside her.

His eyes twinkled as he slid his hand across the back of the seat and grasped a strand of Kate's hair at the nape, tugging gently. "I'm fixing dinner," he announced. "Prepare yourself for an adventure."

"One adventure a year is my limit," she informed him, switching on the ignition. "And last night filled my quota for five years to come."

"Child's play," he scoffed, "compared to a night with Kevin Dawson."

"I'm beginning to think this is a big mistake," Kate grumbled as she put the car in gear.

Kevin laughed softly and rested his hand against the back of her neck in a warm and firm caress. "My dear," he informed her grandly, "you have not yet begun to live. After tonight, you may never be the same."

Kate fixed him with one of her familiar disparaging looks, and he grinned and removed his hand, brushing his knuckle playfully against her chin as he gave an airy command to drive on. Kate struggled to repress a grin of her own as she obeyed, but she couldn't explain the suddenly increased rhythm of her heart as she turned the car toward Kevin's house or the strangely unbidden, dimly exciting notion that he could be right. After tonight, she might never be the same.

Chapter Eight

"Kevin," Kate exclaimed in some wonder, "who did you find to clean your house?"

The transformation from the last time she had been here was remarkable. Dust covers had been removed to reveal gently polished surfaces and clean gray upholstery. The hardwood floors had been swept, though it would take some time to restore the original patina, and the draperies had been tied back and the windows opened to admit a cleansing stream of fresh, wood-scented lake air. Late-afternoon sunlight filled the room with a warm, gentle glow. How refreshing it was, after all she had seen in the past twenty-four hours, to be inside a place that was clean, orderly and undamaged.

"Me," he replied promptly. "I might not have gotten all the cobwebs out of the corners, but I did manage to scatter away some of the dust and put clean sheets on the beds."

Kate was appropriately impressed as she followed him to the kitchen to dispose of the groceries. This from a man who only yesterday couldn't even exert himself to tell someone to make a phone call that would connect his utilities? "My, my," she murmured. "Could it be, Mr. Dawson, that you're learning to take care of yourself?"

He grinned. "Necessity is the mother of invention." He began to unpack the groceries. "You go on and take your bath. I'm doing dinner, remember?"

Kate was only too happy to leave him to it, and she turned toward the guest bedroom and bath. Kevin's last decorator had gone a bit wild with this part of the house, she noticed with a grimace as she entered. The bedroom was a neutral gray-white with chrome-and-mirror accents, and all the furniture seemed to be growing from the walls. Except for a brilliant yellow-and-red geometric mural, the room was sterile and featureless and not at all conducive to restful repose. It reminded Kate of an operating room. The adjoining bath featured a claw-foot tub and wraparound shower curtain in black-and-white stripes; the shiny porcelain fixtures were blood-red and the carpet and wallpaper were black. It was all fairly hideous.

She opted for a shower and shampoo, and despite her tasteless surroundings, enjoyed every moment of it. The hot water was heavenly, and it was wonderful to be able to wash her hair. It felt like days, not hours, since she had been able to shower. She felt a small twinge of guilt for indulging in even so small a luxury, for allowing herself these few short hours of escape when so much waited for her, but under the cleansing spray of the water and the sensual indulgence of Kevin's scented soap, the last shreds of responsibility that tied her to the real world were washed away. She needed this time of peace and quiet away from those who depended on her. She deserved it.

She towel-dried her hair and applied a light dusting of fragranced powder before stepping into fresh underwear and the skirt and blouse she had worn over here. She didn't bother with either a bra or shoes as she left the room in search of Kevin.

There was no response to her call, and when she saw the open patio door, she stepped through it onto a wrap-around deck that overlooked the lake. Kevin waved to her as he spread a blanket on the grass near the shore, and Kate went down the steps to join him.

The sky had cleared into fluffy, picture-book-perfect clouds that broke up the expanse of blue and reflected themselves in the mirror sheen of the lake. A warm, playful breeze tugged Kate's skirt around her calves and molded it to her thighs; the grass was soft and ticklish against her bare feet. The scene was idyllic—trees, sky and grass reflected like a painting in the lake; Kevin, like a hero from a storybook as he spread the plaid blanket on the lawn and began to unpack the picnic basket; the sun caressing his wind-tousled curls and stroking the lean lines of his perfect body. Pausing on the slope of the hill and looking at the picture he made, Kate found it impossible to believe that less than five miles away an entire world had been disarranged and nothing but rubble had been left behind. It was hard to believe anything bad was happening anywhere, so peaceful and isolated was this scene.

"This is what you call fixing dinner?" she teased him lazily. She stroked the back of his neck playfully with a cattail she had plucked before sinking to the blanket beside him, her full skirt billowing around her.

"Count yourself lucky there was no electricity," he replied, removing from the basket a package of cheese, ham and an assortment of condiments pilfered from her refrigerator. "I might have tried to cook."

Kate drew up her legs and wrapped her arms around them, looking out contentedly over the lake. "This is so pretty, isn't it? Hard to believe that only yesterday..."

"Yes," he agreed, and opened a bottle of wine—also rescued from her kitchen. "It seems like another world."

He poured the wine and handed her a glass, and Kate reluctantly straightened her legs and turned to take it. "I really should go back to town," she said, not wanting to. "If something should happen during the night, no one would know where to reach me."

"Your dad knows where to reach you," Kevin corrected firmly. "If anyone needs you, it won't be all that much of big deal to get word to you. But no one is going to need you."

Kate sighed, need warring with duty. "Kevin, I'm a doctor. I can't just abdicate responsibility whenever I feel like it. I should go back to town."

Kevin's eyes held a measure of resolve that looked noticeably out of place on him. "I'm aware of that," he acceded mildly. "Which is why I didn't kidnap you and take you out of the country. But it's not going to hurt you to relax and take care of yourself for one evening."

What a thoughtful thing to say...and Kate found herself peculiarly disinclined to argue with him. Escapism was a powerful temptation; her mind and her body cried out for it. Just for one night to be like Kevin—carefree, irresponsible, independent. And he was right. It wasn't as though she were on another planet. If anything came up, her father could get word to her.

She lifted her glass to him, a relaxed glint of consent coming into her eyes. "You talked me into it, you silver-tongued devil."

His own eyes twinkled as he touched his glass to hers. "A toast. To Katie, my hero."

Playful surprise caused her to lift her eyebrows. "It's an act of heroism to spend the night with you?"

He winked at her. "Better women than you have tried, my dear." And then, as he sipped from his glass, his expression grew serious. "I mean it, Katie. You were great last night. They ought to give medals for what you did in that storm."

Kate remembered a terrified child sobbing into Kevin's shirt, near hysteria and clinging to him like a lifeline, and she had to drop her eyes. "No," she said quietly, "I wasn't great at all. I—never wondered much how I would cope with pressure," she admitted with difficulty. "I just kept hoping, I suppose, that I'd never have to find out. In my profession that kind of self-deception can be dangerous. And last night . . . I almost didn't make it, Kevin." *I wouldn't have made it,* she realized slowly, on an unbidden thought that was as shocking as it was confusing, *without you.*

Kevin's forefinger touched her chin, making her look at him. His eyes were sun-softened velvet, his face golden smooth and quietly sincere. He said, "But you did make it. Not one woman in a million could have handled it the way you did, and the fact that you were just as scared as everyone else only makes it that much more courageous. I've always admired you more than anyone I've ever known," he said simply, "and last night I saw things in you that I'd never even guessed were there."

Kate tried to smile, but a small, questioning flutter in the center of her chest made the gesture seem shy, uncertain. Kevin admired her. Kevin was proud of her. Why should that mean so much to her?

She took a sip of her wine to avoid his eyes. "Things like panic?" she suggested. "Hysteria, incompetence and utter terror?"

He shook his head a little, his face relaxing into a rueful smile as he sat back, bending one knee and resting the hand that held the wineglass loosely across it. "You're still doing it," he commented. "Being too hard on yourself. I thought tonight you were going to lighten up."

"Easier said than done," she returned, but she *was* beginning to relax, far more than she would have thought possible. Kevin made it easy.

She sipped the wine and made an appreciative sound. "I have good taste in wine," she commented, and lifted her glass again, a mischievous spark coming into her eyes. "All right, my turn. A toast—to my hero, Colt Marshall."

He laughed as she clinked her glass to his, and sunlight seemed to scatter from his eyes. "I suppose that's meant as a compliment."

"What else would it be?" She found a secure seat for her wineglass on the grass and reached around him, beginning to put together a sandwich.

"I didn't feel much like Colt Marshall last night," he admitted.

"Well, you certainly acted like him." She got a flash of Kevin rushing through live wires toward a car that was leaking gasoline, and it was all she could do to repress a shudder. She supposed she would never get over being angry with him when she thought about that—the chances he had taken. And yet she was puzzled, too, because none of Kevin's behavior last night had seemed to belong to him at all.

"Did I?" He seemed very thoughtful. "I didn't mean to."

Kate paused in the process of spreading mustard on a slice of pumpernickel, looking at him. It had always been difficult to resolve the image Kevin portrayed on television with the man he really was; what was disconcerting now was to discover how much more difficult it was to resolve the man she was seeing now with the image she had always had of him. He had changed. She wondered if she would ever be able to think of him in the old familiar way again—as her careless, carefree, self-indulgent and basically worthless Kevin.

Her brow knotted a little both from the glare of the lowering sun and the difficulty of her confession. "I guess," she said slowly, "I saw parts of you I had never known before, either."

His eyes were very clear. "Or maybe parts you never wanted to see before." And then, before she could analyze what seemed to her a very unsettling notion, he shrugged and put aside his own glass, taking from her the jar of pickles she had been struggling to open. "That's the whole thing with acting, you know—people have a preconceived idea of what they want to see, and giving them what they expect is easy. It's stepping out of character, sometimes, that's hard...both for the actor and the audience."

Kate wondered whether he had been stepping out of character last night or merely extending the role. She had an uneasy feeling that it was the former, and he was right—it was hard to accept. It was hard to believe that all these years she had only seen from him what she wanted to see, that she had never really known him at all.

She said, reaching for the pickle jar, "Wait, you're going to hurt your arm. Give me that."

He winced a little with the effort, but the lid came off with a final twist. He returned the jar to her.

Kate said, by way of neutralizing the conversation and therefore dismissing what she did not understand, "It's amazing, the things stress brings out. People do and say things they never would dream of otherwise—they act like different people altogether. But as soon as the crisis passes, everything is back to normal."

"I don't know." Kevin took the mustard knife from her and began to ply his own bread with the thick brown mixture. "I read a script last year—by accident, really. Somebody told my agent it was a disaster film, and Carl was trying to talk me into going big screen—anyway, it turned out to be some sort of psychological drama about the aftereffects of a disaster. I don't remember much of it, except that it was about this group of people who had survived a plane crash and how, even though they were alive, their lives were changed forever, and that they would never be the same again. Whatever the crisis brought out—whether it was courage or weakness or fear of failure—was permanently imprinted, because in that one moment of stress each one of them had to take an honest look at themselves, and they had to live with what they found there, forever. No more hiding behind images and defense systems. Weird film, but I can't help thinking there's a grain of truth there."

Kate paused in the process of lifting her sandwich to her lips, fascinated. "And your character? What did he do?"

Kevin's brow wrinkled, remembering. "Committed suicide, I think."

Kate's eyes widened, impressed. She had never thought of Kevin in a serious dramatic role before. "But Kevin, what a great part for you! Why didn't you take it?"

He shrugged, building a mammoth sandwich out of ham and cheese and pickles. "Not quite the image for Colt Marshall fans, was it? I suppose I figured, why mess with a good thing? Also," he admitted with disarming honesty, "it was hard. I wasn't sure I was up to the challenge, and I didn't want to ruin the film."

Kate took a bite of her sandwich, thinking about what he had said, thinking about a lot of things. She wondered what the aftereffects of the disaster, psychological as well as physical, would be on the people of Victoria Bend. She wondered if she would ever feel the same about herself again . . . or about Kevin. Six months from now, when the scars had faded and the town had been rebuilt, when wounds were healed and life resumed its normal, easy pace, would she still be tensing at the sight of thunderclouds, freezing with fear at the prospect of an emergency? Would her heart stop every time she heard an emergency broadcast test or when the civil defense siren, tested regularly every Wednesday at noon, went off? Or would she discover new strength, new confidence, in having faced the worst and met the challenge?

Except for residual fear and shock, Kate didn't feel very much changed inside. Perhaps, in time, as the memory faded and the effects of stress passed, she would find that she felt and thought and dealt with life just as she always had. She would once again be secure in her comfortable little world, relying on consistency and routine for her strength. But somehow she doubted it. Deep inside she believed, as Kevin had suggested, that none of them would ever be quite the same after this.

And then she laughed softly with the sudden thought that had come to her. "Kevin, do you realize what we just did?"

He slapped a top slice of pumpernickel on his sandwich and glanced up. "What's that?"

"We just had an intelligent, intellectually stimulating conversation all by ourselves. I don't think that's ever happened before."

He grinned at her, opening a bag of potato chips. "Stay tuned, babe. Coming up, I dazzle the masses with my brilliant interpretation of the theory of relativity."

They ate in companionable silence for a time, enjoying the dubious gastronomic pleasures of potato chips and white wine, ham and cheese on pumpernickel with chocolate cookies. And then Kevin said, "I've been on the phone most of the day from the mayor's office. We're speeding up construction on the hospital. The building should be ready by the end of the summer, and if you can get your equipment and staff in, there's no reason you shouldn't open the first of September."

Kate stared at him, amazed. "Kevin, that's wonderful! I thought it would take twice as long. How—"

But he seemed immune to her enthusiasm, and as he stared out over the lake, his face looked very sober, almost grim. "I feel bad about it, Katie. If we had had the hospital last night— If only I'd gotten it done sooner."

She was confused. "What do you mean? It wasn't your fault. No one could have known we'd be the target of a disaster. The plans for the hospital weren't even drawn up until last year."

"That's what I mean." His tone was curt, and he tossed a crumpled napkin into the picnic basket with a gesture of restrained frustration. "It all should have been done sooner. This town has needed a hospital for a long time; I should have seen that it got one. I should have pushed construction ahead; I should have stayed on top of it. There was something I could have done."

How strange, how very strange, to hear words like that coming from Kevin, who, as far as Kate knew, paid only the vaguest of attentions to where his money came from or where it went and whose only concern with charitable activities was to sign his name at the bottom of the endowment papers. She said gently, studying him, "Making sure this town got a hospital was not your responsibility, Kevin. It was a nice thing you did, but no one ever expected it of you, or demanded it."

But he shook his head slowly and fixed his eyes on the changing colors of the lake. "I should have made it my responsibility. And that's exactly what I'm going to do now."

She felt a swell of tenderness for him that was deep and intense and pure. She wanted to slip her arms around him and hold him in warmth and affection; she wanted to kiss him and touch him and explore him. There was so much of Kevin she didn't know, so much she was just beginning to learn. The discoveries were gently thrilling, sweetly exciting. She savored each one.

The sun was beginning to set, casting brilliant ribbons of color over the lake. Kate leaned back on her elbows, her knees bent slightly, letting the long folds of her skirt drape between her legs, relaxed and content. "It's funny, isn't it?" she commented after a time, nodding toward the red-gold sunset, "how something so awful could leave such beautiful colors in its wake. I don't think I've ever seen a prettier sunset."

"Maybe it's the company," Kevin teased, and Kate chuckled. But she noticed the way his eyes traveled over the shape of her legs, outlined by the white skirt, and she thought with a small and almost unrecognizable glow of pleasure, *Yes, maybe it is.*

Kevin reached forward to refill her wineglass, and Kate lifted a hand in protest, already feeling a little sleepy. "No, I'm so tired, and I haven't eaten much today. It'll make me drunk."

"Wouldn't hurt you a bit," Kevin decided, and poured the last of the wine into her glass.

Kate, listening to the rustle of the breeze in the grass and the gentle lap of waves against the shore, was disinclined to argue with him. Kevin sat beside her, close but not touching, one long leg stretched beside hers, the other drawn up as a casual prop for his forearm. Together they sipped wine and watched the sunset change from magenta to golden violet to dusky blue.

"It will be dark soon," Kate said reluctantly, not moving. "We should go in while we can still see the way back to the house."

"Plenty of time," Kevin replied. "It's nice out here."

"Let's take a walk," Kate decided suddenly, gathering her energies for the undertaking. "If I don't move soon, I'm going to fall asleep right here."

"And what a tragedy that would be." Kevin's tone was lazily sardonic, and he groaned as she got to her feet and extended her hand to him.

"Especially," she retorted, "since you would leave me here all night on the wet ground and I'd probably catch pneumonia."

His hand closed warmly over hers, and he made her apply some strength to pulling him up. But once beside her, he slipped his arm easily around her waist, and she found herself doing the same, looping her thumb into the tab of his waistband where the elastic gave way to a stylish cotton belt. They walked companionably together in the soft grass at the edge of the shore, her head against his shoulder, his arm strong and warm around her waist. She noticed with dim surprise what an easy, natural rhythm they had together, for walking like this with most men was uncomfortable and awkward. But with Kevin it felt natural.

''Do you ever think how strange it is,'' she mused after a time, ''that the two of us have known each other so long?''

''All the time,'' he admitted without hesitation. ''With the kind of life I lead, knowing somebody who's been around for longer than a year is not something you take lightly. Your longevity is one of the two things I like best about you.''

''I'm not exactly sure that was a compliment,'' she murmured, and glanced up at him. ''What's the other?''

His eyes twinkled, and he brushed his chin lightly against the top of her tousled, towel-dried hair. It was a spontaneous gesture of simple affection, but it caused a small flush of pleasure to go through Kate from her head to her toes. ''That you've never lost your cute little Southern drawl,'' he responded immediately, and she made a face at him.

''Which of course,'' she retorted, ''*you* lost along with everything else the minute you left Mississippi.''

He stopped and looked at her. His expression was very serious, and his eyes reflected the colors of the sunset. He said softly, ''Not everything.''

He looked at her, his face bent close to hers and her face lifted to him, and Kate could feel the tingling of her pulse, the catch of breath in her throat as she knew he was going to kiss her. And to be kissed, to kiss him, was what she wanted more than anything in the world right then. *So much, Kevin,* she thought. *So much we have to share, so much yet to discover.*

His eyes went over her face rapidly, lightly and caressingly, and she could feel their movement like a touch. Yet there was question in Kevin's face, and hesitation, and after a moment his lashes obscured his expression, and he looked away. It had all been so quick, so uncertain, that

Kate could almost believe she had imagined it as they started walking again.

But she hadn't imagined it. There was a new hardness to Kevin's muscles beneath her hand, and a new and unconsciously sensual languor to his touch upon her waist. The grass beneath her feet was losing the heat of the sun, and the shadows were lengthening in gold and green patches. Only a shimmering spot of silver remained reflective on the lake's surface, in a distant corner. And between Kevin and Kate a new awareness tingled, something hesitant and exciting, strange and uncertain. Something was changing between them, and each of them welcomed it; each of them was afraid of it. Neither was willing to take that first step to acknowledge it.

After a while, Kevin said casually, "My last marriage broke up because of you; did you know that?"

She glanced at him, startled. "What?"

He looked sheepish and shook his head a little. "Well, not because of you exactly. I shouldn't have said that. But she was jealous—crazy jealous, if you know what I mean—and I guess I talked about you too often or made too many comparisons. Anyway, our last argument was about you." His eyes glinted with easy mischief as he slanted a glance toward her. "How does it feel to be the evil other woman?"

Kate did not think it was in the least funny. Her head was spinning with a thousand confused emotions. Kevin had talked about her, had made comparisons; even then she had never been far from his mind. What was she supposed to think? How was she supposed to feel? She began uncertainly. "Kevin, I—"

He laughed and squeezed her waist, his fingers spreading down to caress the side of her hip in easy affection. "Don't look so stricken, Katie. You know how it was with me and marriage. Easy come, easy go." And then his tone grew thoughtful as he added, "My trouble was, I never loved any of them. Oh, I was *in* love, if you know the difference, but it was never anything permanent. I guess I always knew that, and almost from the wedding day I was looking for ways to get out. But I was never unfaithful while I was married." His voice was serious, and he looked at her as though it were important that she know that. "Not once."

Kate shook her head slowly, uncertain what to say. "Kevin, don't you think that's rather sad? I mean, broken promises, failed commitments..."

"I think it's very sad," he emphasized without hesitance. "But," he added reflectively, "I was in my twenties, a kid, really. I made a lot more mistakes than just getting married. I like to think I've grown up—at least in some ways—since then."

Yes, he had grown up. In some ways, at some time when Kate wasn't watching, he had changed. And so had she. At least she had changed enough to see him differently.

They walked in silence for a while, watching the sun evaporate into mystical blue twilight, inhaling the fresh woodsy scent of the approaching evening. Kevin said softly, looking out over the lake, "God, it's beautiful here. I don't know why I ever left."

"To become rich and famous, of course."

"Well," he agreed modestly, "there's that." Then, without any warning at all, without the slightest change of tone or expression to indicate the mischief that was coming, he invited lazily, "So tell me about these fantasies of yours, Katie dear."

She looked at him sharply, accusingly. "You promised!"

His eyes were dancing. "I'm a consummate liar, darlin'; you know that. It's the nature of the business."

With a growl of mock rage, she broke away from him, running toward the shelter of a weeping willow tree. That proved to be a mistake, for she became entangled in the long, leafy fronds, and in three strides he was upon her, swinging her around with one arm around her waist. For a half-moment they stood there, her hands braced against his shoulders and his arm holding her tightly around the waist, laughing into one another's eyes. And then, as the most natural thing in the world, Kate's arms lifted and looped around his neck. Their lips met.

It was sweet, so sweet. Unlike the desperate, fear-based passion that had consumed them last night, they explored each other now with leisure and wonder and infinite delight. He tasted of sunshine and wine; he filled her with warmth and sensual pleasure. She took a deep, luxurious breath, filling herself with the wonder of him, the scent of him, the strength of him. She parted her lips for him, inviting him inside.

Her heart beat heavily, strongly, as Kevin's tongue explored the shape and texture of the velvety flesh of her inner lips, played over her teeth, mated briefly with the tip of her own. Light, teasing, arousing, they explored each other with joy and welcome, discovering and savoring. Kate's hands cupped his head, her fingers buried in the thick luxury of his hair. Her tongue traced the shape of his lips, as his did hers, darting playfully inside and retreating with butterfly grace to taste the flesh around his mouth again. *Ah, Kevin,* she thought dizzily, helplessly. *At last.* She could feel his breath, shallow and heated, upon her face and his pleasure, as though it were a tangible thing, joining with her own. One of his hands spread warmly over her back, holding her near; the other lightly guarded her waist. He bent to drink more deeply of her.

With a surge of power that was intense and swift and breathtaking, his tongue invaded her mouth, demanding and drawing from her. Kate's heart lurched hard against her rib cage, once, and then scattered into a heavy, rapid rhythm that pumped heat and weakness through her muscles, heaviness through her veins. His fingers were tight and strong against her back, pressing her close to the hardness of his thighs and abdomen. She gave to him as he demanded, helpless against the onslaught of sensations he evoked. Her pulses hammered; her head spun. There was nothing but Kevin, infusing her with heat and weakness that spread like a flush from the surface of her skin to the core of her womb. He made her anxious; he made her helpless.

How long, she wondered, how long had she wanted him without knowing it? When had it begun to change between them? How could she have fought it for so long? But at that moment it hardly mattered, for it seemed as though she had wanted him forever, and all her life had been no more than waiting for this moment.

His mouth bent to her neck, darting flames against her throat and her ear and the hollow of her collarbone. Her hands drifted down over the heated cords of his neck, along his shoulders and the shape of his back, touching him, memorizing him, filling herself with him. She was a composite of sensations and needs and suspended wanting, and Kevin was the life force that gave her breath.

His hand caressed the shape of her waist and moved upward to cup her breast, a warm, heavy pressure that expanded her pores with electric awareness. His lips touched her throat, nibbled gently at her ear, infusing her with a shudder of pleasure. Lightly his fingers spread over her breast, and weakness grew from his touch, flowing deep inside her. She tilted her head back and drew a long, moist breath that was a silent moan of pleasure. *Oh, Kevin,* she thought. *How long we've waited for this.* She was trembling, and a golden yellow haze obscured reason. She knew only that she wanted him, and she wanted all of him.

She felt then the struggle begin within him as he wrapped his arms around her and held her close, his face against her neck. His breath was hot and taut with the effort he made to steady it, and he turned a gentle kiss upon the side of her face. She felt his heartbeat, fast and strong against her chest. And then, helpless against the instincts she could not control, she turned her face to his.

Their kiss was deep and raw and urgent. They clung to each other as though afraid of being swept away by the unfamiliar tide of passion into separate destinies. They clung to each other as though to the only right and true thing in a desperately spinning world. Kate's hand moved restlessly on his back and his neck and through his hair, wanting to press him closer, and closer still. Then her trembling, unsteady fingers moved down across his waist and the shape of his hip between their bodies, to rest lightly on the heat and hardness of him that pressed against her.

He moaned softly deep within his throat, and he pulled his lips away from hers. She could feel the fan of his breath on her heated face and the male strength beneath her hand, and she opened her eyes to the haze of passion that blurred his flushed, damp face. His eyes were dark, and though he tried to smile, there was an intensity in his eyes that seemed to singe her very soul.

"Katie," he said huskily, "if that's a question, the answer is yes." His breathing was unsteady, and the smile faltered. His eyes moved over her face, seeking her own answers. "I do want you."

Yet there was doubt and uncertainty, and even as he spoke, he started to move away.

Kate's hand slipped away from him, resting against his waist, and all that she felt was naked on her countenance. She whispered, "That wasn't the question."

On his face she saw hesitation, questioning joy and disbelief. And then he drew her slowly into his arms. His hand stroked her hair; his lips touched her face. Then, moving lightly to cup her chin, he kissed her lips, gently and with restraint. She was terrified, in that single moment, that he would say no, that for all of this, he still didn't understand. But he only smiled and lifted a forefinger to lightly trace the shape of her cheekbone. His eyes were still afire with need. He murmured a little breathlessly, "I wonder what Colt Marshall would do now?"

"Break his vow?" Kate suggested, and lifted her arms to his neck, drawing him gently down onto the ground with her.

In many ways, over the years, Kate had been Kevin's superior, his guide and his teacher. But in this, the mystical art of love, he was her master. Kate was accustomed to being in charge, to taking the lead and calling the shots. But here, for the first time with Kevin, she found herself in a position of helpless surrender, receiving instead of giving, letting him take her strength and infuse her with magic.

The soft grass was their bed, the pale green enclosure of willow leaves their canopy. In this secret, peaceful place they lay together and lost themselves in each other, in the wondrous touch of lips and hands, the whisper of breaths and the fever that built between them with slow, exquisite certainty. He kissed her lightly, delicately, on her face and her throat and the thin material that covered her breasts. As her demand rose, so did his, and he returned to her mouth with a searing heat that controlled passion even as it fueled it. Her hand slipped beneath his shirt, exploring muscle and sinew, hard ribs and the light dusting of hair on his chest. She pushed the material up, anxious for his skin against hers, and he straightened, impatiently tugging the garment over his head and then removing her blouse.

He lay against her for a moment, the wonderful sensation of firm, heated flesh against flesh, his hardness against her softness. Then he bent his head, his mouth covered her breast and she lost herself to whirling clouds of pleasure and need.

His hand slipped beneath her skirt, pushing the material up, stroking the length of her leg. And with each movement the yearning inside her increased, tightening and flaring, until she thought she would cry out from the intensity of it. His mouth moistened and suckled, lips and teeth and tongue teasing, nibbling, stimulating unbearably, and his hand moved upward, caressing the shape of her hip, spreading across her abdomen. She lost her breath to the wonder he was creating within her, to the spreading ache that wanted to absorb him, to draw him into her. She strained toward him. A sound of half pleasure and half pain escaped her as he gathered her close, holding her, his breath, his heartbeat, mingling with hers, becoming part of her.

With trembling hands, she stroked the damp flesh of his face and his hair. Through a haze she saw his eyes, pupils enormous, alive with fire. He kissed her face; he inhaled deeply of the fragrance of her neck. For a moment his arm tightened about her so intensely it was painful, and yet she held him just as strongly, bursting with need for him. He whispered something, a ragged, desperate sound that might have been "Oh, Katie, are you sure?"

But her answer was in her kiss, in her movements, as the frenzy overtook them both, blinding her and driving him. The remainder of their clothes were discarded, and she felt his thighs, strong and hard between hers, his mouth on hers, his lips whispering words she could not understand. She moved against him, her hands greedily exploring the length of his shoulders, his back, his buttocks. Her tongue tasted salt on his face and his throat; her leg bent to caress his hip and stretched to stroke his lean, muscled calf. And then his fingers slipped beneath her hips gently, bringing her to him. With a single low, long, sliding thrust, he buried himself deep within her.

How strange it felt to have him inside her, stretching her, filling her. Unconsciously, she made a sound of startlement and wonder, and immediately his hand came up to stroke her face, soothing her, caressing her. She opened her eyes to his face, so familiar, so gentle, and yet so strange, so wonderfully strange, flushed with pleasure and softened with need, his eyes deep and slightly unfocused, drowsy with the sensations that flowed between them. Kevin. Her Kevin. Joining with her in this most exclusive act of intimacy, showing her pleasure, opening her to him in the final, most meaningful way a man can communicate with a woman. There was disbelief, there was wonder, there was even, in that moment, a little fear. And then he began to move within her, his hand upon her face, his lips brushing hers and caressing

her, his body drawing from her the very rhythm of life.
Kevin. Hers.

Had Kate been of a rational mind, she would have
known not to expect too much from the first joining of
unfamiliar lovers. She had known awkwardness before,
the clumsiness and anxiety that comes as two bodies, as
well as two minds and personalities, try to become accustomed to pleasing each other. There was never magic
the first time, she knew that.

But with Kevin it was different, and perhaps she had
known that all along, too. Though intimacy was strange
to them, closeness was not, and it was as though all years
that had gone before had only been in preparation for
this moment and sharing what only the two of them
could give one another. They joined together perfectly,
their rhythms instinctive; they blended together as though
they had never been separate. And through the beauty
that dazzled her, the intensity that blinded her, Kate
thought dizzily and deeply and yet so distantly she was
hardly even aware of it, *Oh, Kevin, it was you all along.
How could I not have known it was you?*

They moved with sweet, slow, sensual breaths, drawing each moment to its finest extension, savoring and
letting the passion build to its finest dimension. There
were colors, dusky and golden, and soft rustling breaths
of breeze and whispers. There was heated, slippery flesh
and straining muscles and long, trembling breaths of
stillness as they strained to capture and hold forever the
wonder of what they shared. And then the urgency grew;
his thrusts became deeper and more powerful, and Kate's
consciousness receded to a pinpoint of desire focused
upon Kevin as she rose to meet him, grasping for him,
gripping him and crying out in a single explosive moment that came too quickly but lasted forever. Pleas-

ure—simple, blinding, mindless. More than physical, it was a great bursting wave of emotions unrecognized, needs too long unfulfilled, a mystical joining of something deep within her with something deep inside him, and it would leave her changed forever.

In drifting spirals of wonder and joy she clung to him, her soul reverberating with him. And she felt his muscles tremble as with one deep, final thrust, he gathered her close and released himself inside her. She held him; he held her. They were together, as one, and for the longest time that was all that mattered.

Chapter Nine

Morning came in, soft and gray, drifting over the twisted pewter-colored sheets of Kevin's bed like a heavy fog. Kate awoke reluctantly and found that Kevin was not beside her. She was glad.

The sound of the shower running in the other room revealed the whereabouts of her lover. She turned over slowly, drawing the sheet more surely around her stiff and overused body, and focused soberly on the ceiling. She had a few moments of privacy in which to resign the unprecedented excesses of the night with the demands of the morning, and then she had to face Kevin.

In the languorous afterglow of lovemaking, they had returned to the house the night before, and Kate had been too stunned and drained with pleasure to give much thought to the consequences of what they had done. And almost as though to forestall the return of reason he could surely sense coming, Kevin had begun to make love to her again. The path to passion was familiar now, easy to follow, and she was eager to explore the new dimensions of sensuality Kevin taught so expertly. They did not talk. Except for whispered words of ecstasy and satisfaction, they had said nothing to one another since the moment they fell to the grass beneath the willow tree. Kate had fallen asleep in Kevin's arms in a state of glowing exhaustion, and not once had it occurred to her what she would be facing this morning.

Many of her anxieties were expected and did not deserve dwelling upon. Kevin Dawson, the legendary lover, had made another score. The last thing she had ever expected to be, or wanted to be, was one of his conquests, and she cringed to imagine what he was thinking now. He would be cavalier and sophisticated, just another night in a long string of nights, no sooner over than forgotten. Worse yet, she had practically begged him to make love to her. She had come on to him like a sex-starved escapee from a prison farm, and there was no conceivable way she could place blame upon him. She might have felt better if she could have.

But none of those things was what really worried her. For almost thirty years she had known Kevin; she had joked with him, looked down upon him, teased him, scolded him, fought with him, despaired of him. Whatever affection had existed in their relationship had been of a perverse sort, each of them bringing out the worst in the other. But she had allowed Kevin to share with her an intimacy only a very few had known before him; she had given to him something that, while it might be relatively meaningless to him, was very important to Kate. Closeness, most especially the physical kind, did not come easily to Kate, and she did not take the act of love lightly. Emotions, as well as sensations, were invariably involved.

And that was the worst part. More than simple physical satisfaction had been involved last night. Everything was changed; everything was confused. She did not even know how she was supposed to feel, much less how to deal with those feelings.

She heard Kevin come in from the bathroom, and she had a brief and childish impulse to close her eyes and pretend to be asleep. Deliberately scolding herself for a coward, she turned her eyes slowly to meet him.

His hair was wet and tousled, his body glistening in places from shower steam. A large black bath towel was wound around his hips and trailed on one side to his calf, which was slick and molded with damp dark hair. His smile, for just a moment, seemed almost as shy as she felt, but his tone was gentle as he said, "Hi, sweetie."

She returned his smile, fleetingly, but found she couldn't look at him. She had to clear her throat before replying, "Hi."

There was a hesitation, and then he said, in a voice that sounded surprisingly casual, "It's almost eight. You have office hours today, don't you?"

"Umm...yes." She struggled to sit up, dragging the sheet with her to cover her nakedness. She was perfectly aware of what a silly, girlish gesture that was. The one thing she had never been shy about was her body; one could not have viewed as many naked humans as she had and maintained any sense of false modesty about her own physical appearance. But everything was different today. She hardly knew herself anymore.

She could feel Kevin's hesitation above her, and when she ventured a glance at him, she was surprised by what she saw. A dozen unreadable emotions played across his eyes, though he kept his expression carefully casual. There was debate there and the same kind of uncertainty Kate felt, and she was confused, because there was none of the nonchalant, easygoing morning-after attitude she had expected. And then he seemed to come to some sort of decision; he sat down on the bed beside her and smiled, reaching forward to tuck a spiky strand of hair behind her ear.

"In case you're wondering," he teased gently, "it was worth breaking my vow for."

She tried to match his casual tone. "I'm flattered."

That did not seem to be what he wanted to hear. There was a faltering of the smile in his eyes, just briefly, and then he cupped his hand lightly on the side of her face. He smelled of spicy soap and warmth, and her eyes were drawn, without volition, to the flex of his long bicep, the damp tangle of hair under his arm. She found that for some reason uncomfortably sexy, and she moved her eyes away restlessly.

Looking at her with gentle intensity, he said, "Are you okay this morning?"

"Sure." She returned a false smile. "The sex was great, if that's what you mean."

The light died slowly from his eyes, and his hand left her face. "No," he said quietly, "that's not what I mean. But I'm glad to hear it, anyway. Always nice to know I haven't lost my touch."

He got up and walked toward the closet, and Kate thought tightly, *Damn*. She didn't know whether she was angry with herself or with Kevin and thought it was a little of both. She had handled that clumsily, and she wasn't used to being clumsy. But what did he expect from her? Why was he making it so difficult?

Kevin loosened the towel and let it drop to the floor, revealing to her taut white buttocks and lean runner's thighs. She swallowed hard as she looked at him and wondered what he would say, what he would do, if she opened her arms to him and called him softly back to bed. And then she was appalled at herself for even thinking such a thing. She was in enough turmoil as it was.

He took a light cotton shirt from the closet and pulled it on, turning to face her as he buttoned it. He was easy in his nakedness, and Kate was fascinated for a moment by the male beauty of him, his unself-conscious grace. And then she noticed he was using only one hand to button his shirt, and she felt a stab of guilt. His shoulder pained him this morning, as naturally it would after the uncalled-for exercise of last night. She thought briefly and wryly that as a physician she should have warned him against engaging in sexual activity for a few days, and then she had to close her eyes, a wave of bleakness and despair overcoming her. *Oh, Kate, what have you gotten yourself into?*

Kevin said coolly and rather dryly, "You don't have to be embarrassed, Kate. I can imagine what a shock it must have been to go to bed with Colt Marshall and wake up with Kevin Dawson."

Her eyes snapped open in an immediate flare of anger and horror, and for a moment she could only look at him, churning with insult. Though she knew her best course was not to dignify the outrageous statement with a reply, she couldn't seem to help herself. She said lowly, her eyes darkening, "That was uncalled for, Kevin."

"Was it?" His tone was mild, but his eyes, too, were churning as he fastened the last button at mid-chest. "Then will you kindly tell me why you keep looking at me as though we've just committed a felony?"

"I'm not!" But even with the instinctive, angry defense she knew he was right. Guilt and uncertainty were gnawing at her defenses, making her afraid, leaving her vulnerable and at a loss. She retaliated by withdrawing from him, and the last thing she wanted to do was withdraw.

Raw emotion flared between them, and it was hard to accept that she had hurt him for no other reason than that she was afraid. She hadn't meant to hurt him. But she didn't know what he expected of her.

"Kevin, I'm sorry. I know..." She floundered for the right words and came up, of course, with exactly the wrong ones. "That this is not what you are used to from women the morning after...." She saw a swift flash of something in his eyes—it might have been disgust, or it might have been pain. She hastened to try to make amends. "What I mean is...this is an awkward situation, I know, but let's try to be mature about it."

"Let's not." His voice was smooth as he crossed to the bureau in search of underwear. He wore small, sexy briefs, she remembered from last night, and she was annoyed and embarrassed to be dwelling on such a thing. "I think our ideas of maturity might be too different at this point."

She moved her eyes away as he bent to step into his briefs. "Oh, yes?" Her voice was brittle. Damn, how had it come to this? How could they be arguing with such cold carelessness after what they had shared? She felt absurdly as though she were going to cry, and that made her only angrier. "In what way?"

"Your idea of being mature, I think," he replied coolly, "is to be blasé and sophisticated and try to get yourself out of my bed with as little embarrassment as possible. I'd prefer a bit more honesty myself."

She turned her eyes on him in speechless astonishment as he moved back to the closet. She—blasé and sophisticated? That was his role. But everything was turned upside down this morning; nothing in her entire world made sense, and she had no reply. His alternative was unthinkable. How could she be honest when she didn't know what the truth of the situation was?

She had never seen Kevin like this, stiff and angry and far more in control than he had any right to be, talking to her about honesty and maturity in precise, clipped sentences that made her feel like a thwarted child who didn't know what she wanted. Maybe he was right. Maybe she had gone to bed with a stranger. Not Colt Marshall but Kevin . . . a Kevin she had never known.

She wanted to curl her arms around her pillow and bury her face in it and give in to a slowly creeping misery she didn't understand. She wanted Kevin to come and hold her and comfort her and somehow make things, if not the way they used to be, then at least right between them. She was angry at herself for being a woman and victim of irrational needs, and she was angry at herself for being human and confused. She wanted to turn back the clock three days and pretend Kevin had never strolled back into her life, to erase the storm that had molded them together and made her vulnerable, to save herself from the mistake of last night. If it was a mistake.

But she could not, of course, do any of those things. She simply sat there, staring at the opposite wall, waiting for Kevin to get dressed and leave the room so that she could do the same. But when she heard his footsteps cross the carpeted floor, he was moving toward her, not away from her. She looked up to find him standing above her, dressed in dark cotton trousers and the white shirt, looking sad and gentle and resigned. He held a wine-colored velour robe, and he handed it to her.

"Here," he said. "You go ahead and shower and I'll see what I can do about breakfast."

He started to turn, then hesitated. "Katie," he said softly, "we have to talk about it... but I know you need some time. I just wanted you to know I'm not sorry." Then, in the most casual of tones he added, "Don't leave without me, okay? I need a ride into town."

Kate showered and dressed with dogged rapidity, wanting only to be away from Kevin and back into her own familiar world where, hopefully, she would have breathing space to assess the events of the past eighteen hours—but where, more likely, she would find a way to put the entire problem out of her mind. Kevin made instant coffee with hot tap water—under normal circumstances they both would have laughed and sparred wits over that—and they ate dry sweet rolls without tasting either. Kate dropped Kevin off at her house to pick up his car, and very little was said between them on the trip. He murmured something polite about seeing her later, and Kate was still finding it difficult to meet his eyes. She was glad to get to the routine insanity of her office.

Kate had more than enough to keep her busy that day. She made rounds at the hospital and dismissed two patients, then met with the administrator and chief of surgery to discuss Jeff Brandon's admission to the staff. She saw patients all morning—most of whom needed nothing more than reassurance and tranquilizers and a friendly ear to whom to tell their problems—and used the lunch break to try to find someone to begin making repairs to her house. And Kevin was never off her mind.

She hated the way she had acted this morning, and she couldn't believe it was she who had behaved like such a child. Even if last night had been no more than an accident of chemistry, she had still known Kevin longer than she had known anyone in her life except her relatives. Only a fool would abandon such a friendship because of one night of indiscretion. She had been so concerned because everything was changed between them, yet she had gone out of her way to make the change permanent and tempered with anger. No man deserved to be treated the way she had treated Kevin after the night they had spent together. She couldn't believe that in this, the most dramatic aspect of their long relationship, she had failed him so.

They had been so good together. It was that, perhaps, that bothered her the most. They shouldn't have been, but they were. None of the dictates of logic prepared her for the fact that she and Kevin should get along better in bed than they ever had out of it. She was not a superstitious person; she did not believe in karmic relationships or heaven-made love affairs or that there was only one man in all the world for every woman. She knew perfectly well that sexual compatibility did not necessarily have anything to do with emotional involvement. But she could not deny the fact that with Kevin there had been magic.

And when she thought about him now, her heart beat faster, and her skin flushed. She remembered long, smooth muscles and his face, softened with adoration, his eyes, brilliant and dark and alive with passion. She remembered him, and she felt weak and wanting, absurdly happy and disconcertingly sad. Her mood swings peaked and dropped. She wanted desperately to see him again; she was afraid of what would happen when she did. Kate was no fool, although she was acting like one now. She knew what was wrong with her. She was in love with Kevin Dawson.

It was absurd, of course. There was no future to it, no basis in reality; it was a temporary mental aberration brought on by stress and incredible chemical attraction.

It was thrilling, and it was distressing, and the best thing for her would be to put it out of her mind and get on with her life. Only, of course, she couldn't.

Kate had tried every contractor, handyman and remodeler in three counties; absolutely none was available. She hung up the phone with a force that jarred the bell and an imaginative oath that was loud enough to be heard by Iris in the lab. The older woman poked her head in the door curiously. "Are you all right, Doctor?"

Kate ran an impatient hand through her hair, disgruntled and embarrassed. Displays of temper were not her style, either, especially during office hours. She was annoyed with herself and remembered now why she so infrequently had lovers. The entire experience was upsetting to her equilibrium in ways she could not afford.

"I'm just having trouble getting someone to come in and look at my house," she said apologetically. "Like everyone else in town, I guess." And then she looked up, trying to keep her expression neutral. "I understand Daddy stayed with you last night."

"Well, I had the extra bedroom," she confessed, "and with the shape his house was in . . ." Was that a trace of color Kate saw tinging Iris's soft, fifty-year-old cheeks? She added, a little anxiously, "You don't mind, do you?"

Kate almost smiled. Iris was obviously concerned about her boss's opinion of her reputation, which was both amusing and endearing. She wished she had Iris's problems.

"Don't be silly," she answered easily. "I appreciate it, as a matter of fact. If you think Dad's house is bad, you should see the shape mine is in." And then, realizing she had left herself wide open for an inquiry about where she had spent the night, Kate hurried on. "How's Dad's leg? Any swelling?"

"I told him to stay off it today, but you know him." Iris made a face. "He's got some sixteen-year-old kid chauffeuring him around. He keeps saying he has things to do."

Kate could well imagine. Her father was an important citizen in this town, and he wouldn't be able to sit by and let the crisis take its course without his help. "I'm sure our esteemed mayor and city council are finding plenty for him to do," she agreed dryly. "See if you can get hold of him, will you, and ask him to come by. I'd like to check the cast."

Iris nodded. "We've got a couple of patients waiting. Are you ready?"

Kate took a final sip of her cold coffee and pushed herself to her feet with an effort. There had never been a day when she did not enjoy the work, when she did not look forward to seeing patients and doing what she was best at. Today her mind was in a thousand other places, and her body wanted to follow. "Get them set up. I'll be right in."

In the afternoon, Kate treated a dog bite, an infant she had helped deliver who was now ready for his first DPT shot and a young wife who thought she was pregnant. Things were getting back to normal.

When she came back into her office, thinking vaguely about going out to her house and seeing what she could do on her own, Kevin was waiting for her.

Her pulses leaped, and she felt a quick tightening in the pit of her stomach. She tried to tell herself it was only from anxiety but knew it wasn't. It was joy.

He was lounging on her sofa, one ankle crossed on his knee, his arm stretched across the back of the sofa. His hair was slightly tousled, his gaze lazy and relaxed. The white shirt was parted from throat to mid-chest and revealed a tantalizing triangle of smooth golden skin and dark chest hair, and the black pants were molded to his thighs. He looked sleek and continental and primally sexual.

"Kevin. What are you doing here?"

"I came to see you" was his simple reply.

She crossed quickly to her desk, and she could feel his eyes following her. She found herself grasping for shreds of her composure like motes of dust in the wind. She said, "Did you want me to check your shoulder? Are you feeling okay?"

His expression was composed, his eyes steady and tolerant. "No, I'm fine."

She sat down behind her desk, aware of the feeling of security and power that seemed to give her. She could look at him now with no more than a slightly increased rhythm to the thumping of her heart, and when she folded her hands atop her desk, they hardly felt damp at all. She said, in an almost normal tone of voice, "I thought you would be gone by now."

He lifted a questioning eyebrow. "Oh? Gone where?"

"It's Wednesday," she reminded him. "Didn't you have a party to go to?"

He looked only momentarily puzzled; then he shrugged. "I guess I'm going to miss it, aren't I?"

"I guess so." It was an inane statement, accompanied by a weak smile, and Kate glanced down at her hands briefly.

She took a breath, determined not to let the silence grow uncomfortable. She was the one who had wanted to talk about being mature; it was time she started acting like it. She sat back in the chair and returned her gaze to him. This time her smile was more natural, and so was her tone as she asked, "So, what did you want to see me about?"

"I've given you some time," he replied simply. "Now I think we should talk."

With a sigh, Kate let go of her last defenses. "Yes," she agreed quietly, and met his gaze, "I guess we should."

She got up and closed the door, then returned to her desk, but leaning against it now, not sitting behind it. This wasn't going to be easy—none of it was easy—but she and Kevin had known each other too long to start hiding from each other now. She didn't know what to say to him; she didn't even know what she wanted to say. But she had to try.

"Kevin," she began with difficulty, "I'm sorry I acted so stupid this morning. I guess you know I'm not... Well, I'm not used to waking up in strange men's beds, and I didn't handle it very well." She tried to smile. "I guess I'm not as sophisticated as I look."

"I'm not exactly a stranger," he reminded her.

She nodded. "I think that's the problem," she admitted softly.

He released a breath, lifting his arm to rub the back of his neck in a weary, tense gesture. His eyes wandered away, then back. "Katie," he said at last, gently, "I don't know what you're thinking—but I didn't plan it. After all these years, I wouldn't do anything to deliberately hurt you. You know that, don't you?"

She smiled, reluctantly and rather ruefully. "Kevin, don't try to placate me. There's nothing wrong with my memory. I seduced you, not the other way around."

He looked at her intently. "Then why...?" But he stopped himself, shaking his head curtly. "No, I'm not going to ask you that. I do understand, Katie, as much as I can," he told her earnestly, simply. "Knowing you as well as I do, how can I not understand how hard this is for you? I just . . . don't want you to make it any harder on yourself than you have to."

He drew another deep breath as though for courage, and he looked at her steadily. "Look, I'm not going to ask you any hard questions or tell you anything you don't want to hear. I just want you to know that you've been a part of my life for too long for me to let you go now. If you're ashamed of what happened, that's okay. I understand." That seemed to be difficult for him to say. "I know how your mind works. And if you want to forget it, we can try that, too. If you want to go on the way we always have and . . . never let sex be a part of our relationship again, we can do that. I won't like it, but I can live with it." His eyes were dark, his expression sober. "I can live with anything except the way you looked at me this morning."

Kate felt a twist of pain that was tempered by a tenderness so acute her throat felt moistened by it. She wanted to step over to him and take him in her arms, to hold him and be held by him, and she wanted it so badly that she had to tense her muscles to keep from taking the first step. She loved him, in that moment, with heartbreaking simplicity. And it took all her willpower to keep from telling him so.

But words of emotion would only complicate an already unbearably complicated situation. For Kevin, commitments were easy and temporary, as spontaneous as his own good nature. Kate was more sensible. And she had only her good sense to rely upon now, for both their sakes.

She braced her palms against the top of her desk, curling her fingers around the edge. Her arms tensed in an unconscious display of the emotions that were warring within her. She said, as honestly as possible, "Kevin, I never meant to hurt you, either. I—the truth is, everything has been so upside down in the past couple of days I don't even know what to think, or how to feel anymore. I know—" she had to drop her eyes briefly "—that you've had a lot more experience in this sort of thing than I have, and I'm making a big deal out of nothing, but it's the way I am." Now she looked at him. "Things changed last night—inside me as well as between us. And even though I wanted it . . . I still wasn't prepared, I suppose, for what it would mean. And now I'm having trouble dealing with it. I'm sorry."

His eyes went over her face, examining her, it seemed, for truths behind the words. Whether he found them or not, she could not tell, because there was a question in his eyes, and caution. "Does it have to be a bad thing, these changes?"

"I don't know," she answered simply. Inside her, questions were building, anxious and uncertain. What did *he* want? Did he want to be her lover or just her friend? Did he want to go back to the way things were, or would he be disappointed, even angry, if she suggested it? Was he sorry now? Had last night meant anything to him besides the inconveniences of redefining their relationship now?

But she asked none of those questions, mostly because she was not sure what she wanted the answers to be.

He said softly, "It was good between us. It wasn't just an accident."

"No." Her throat was tight, her voice barely a whisper. Of that much she was sure. "It wasn't an accident. It was good."

There seemed to be a measure of relief in his expression, the softest of sighs, as though he had been holding his breath. He still watched her searchingly, intently, yet there was restraint in him, as though he were holding back something from her, just as she was from him. "Does it bother you, then, all this experience of mine you keep talking about? Do you think I'm just seeing you as a one-night stand—is that it?"

"No." Although that was it, at least in part. "Not exactly."

"Because it was a big deal to me, too, Katie," he said with quiet, inarguable force. "How could you think it wouldn't be?"

She closed her eyes, briefly and helplessly, against the new onslaught of confusion that just kept building with every word he spoke, every moment he stayed. How she wanted to touch him. How tempting it was to explore this barest of beginnings to their new relationship, and how dangerous.

She said softly, "I don't know, Kevin. I just don't know."

There was silence, long and suspended and aching with things unsaid. And then he got up and came over to her; he lightly touched her face with his hand, tilting it upward to look at him. "All right, Katie," he said gently. "I promised no pressure. I don't want to complicate your life, and I know you have to think everything out to its smallest common denominator." He smiled a little, coaxing a faint reciprocal smile from her.

And then his eyes grew serious, looking into hers, so dark and so intense that she caught her breath. His fingers stroked her cheek lightly, warmly, making her turn her face slightly to the caress. He said softly, "But while you're thinking, maybe you should know that I—"

They heard the brief knock on the door, and Kate sprang away from him just as her secretary opened it. The other woman looked a bit harried and rather awed—which was not unusual in the presence of Kevin Dawson. She said, "Excuse me, Dr. Larimer, but there are some people here—reporters looking for Mr. Dawson. One of them is from—"

Kevin muttered a short, foul curse and turned away. "I've got to get out of here," he said. "I've been trying to duck those guys all day."

Kate's heart was pounding, and her skin was warm, a retrograde reaction to Kevin's touch and the barely suggested promise of the moment that was so abruptly shattered. But her expression was calm and composed and perfectly in control as she nodded to her secretary. "Please tell them that this is a medical facility, not a celebrity lounge," she said coolly. "If any of them need a doctor's attention, we'll be happy to see them. Otherwise, please ask them to leave."

Her secretary left, looking suitably impressed, and Kevin turned to her with a gentle spark of admiration in his eyes. "You're really something, aren't you? Always on top of things."

Kate's returned smile was half uncertain, half wry. "Most of the time."

He looked at her for a moment longer, his expression soft and unsure and poised in expectancy. Both of them waited for what would come next; neither of them knew what it should be. And then he lowered his eyes; he reached into his pocket and took out a key, placing it on her desk. "Listen, I'm going back to the house. You still need a place to stay and—well ..." He looked at her. "Separate beds are okay with me, if that's what you want."

Kate glanced at the key and then at him, but he didn't give her a chance to say anything. "I've got to go," he said quickly, moving toward the door. "Before we all end up on the cover of *People*. I'll see you later, Katie." It wasn't a question or a promise, just a casual statement of fact. And then he was gone.

Chapter Ten

At four o'clock, Kate's father came in. She had seen her last patient of the day and could no longer avoid the necessity of making a decision about where she was going to spend the night. Her eyes repeatedly strayed to the key on her desk, but she didn't pick it up. She listed over and over in her mind all the excellent reasons why she should go anyplace else but Kevin's house tonight.

She was extraordinarily glad for the distraction of her father's visit. She made a great business out of checking his cast, asking after his health, giving him advice. He tolerated her with cynical amusement. She asked a multitude of questions about the progress of the city council, the damage estimates and disaster aid, and he obliged her with answers. She inquired after the state of his house, and he replied that he had gotten his windows fixed. He asked if she had a place to stay, and she answered something unintelligible, turning to file away a chart.

He watched her for a moment with easy, alert patience, then said, "All right, Katie, out with it. You didn't send for me to play doctor or to discuss the weather or the state of the municipal government. What's on your pretty little mind?"

Kate closed the file drawer with a soft release of breath and turned to face him slowly. She said simply, "I slept with Kevin last night."

His expression was blank, and she hastened to clarify. "What I mean is, you already know I was staying at his house, but what I mean is, we—made love."

He looked completely unimpressed. "Since you don't usually make it a habit to keep me informed of the comings and goings of your sex life, I assume there's more?"

"What more could there be?" she exclaimed, exasperated. "Isn't that bad enough?"

He arched his brows questioningly. "You want me to avenge your honor?"

Kate closed her eyes briefly, restraining impatience. Men. She'd never understand them. "Forget it," she said shortly, and made a great show of pulling out her desk chair, sitting down and opening her drawer, pretending to look for something.

Jason Larimer leaned back against the sofa, carefully lifting his injured leg to rest on the coffee table, and relaxed. He smiled at her. "All right, Katie, I didn't mean to tease. What's upsetting you?"

"No wonder you and Kevin get along so well," she muttered, not glancing at him. "You're just alike."

"That's highly significant."

"I doubt it."

He was thoughtful for a moment, assessing her gently. "What's the problem, Katie?" he insisted. "Tell me about it."

She was on the verge of retorting that if she knew what the problem was she wouldn't need to talk to him about it, and then she realized that was precisely why she had wanted to talk to her father. She needed a chance to put her own feelings into words, if she could.

She closed the drawer slowly, linked her hands atop her desk and looked at him with hopelessness and confusion in her eyes. "The problem is," she admitted, "I don't regret it. And I should. I'm not an impulsive person—you know that—but this has changed everything between Kevin and me, and I'm completely thrown off balance. And," she confessed regretfully, "I'm not handling it very well, I'm afraid."

"What's there to handle?" he inquired simply. "If you ask me, this is long overdue."

She stared at him, but her father was unmistakably serious. "How can you say that?" she demanded incredulously. "Until two days ago Kevin and I barely tolerated each other."

"Now that's not true," he pointed out. "Kevin has always been fond of you."

Kate dismissed that as irrelevant. "But *I* wasn't fond of *him*," she insisted. "I didn't even like him very much. We certainly never thought of each other sexually."

"Didn't you?" her father interrupted mildly. And as she formed an instinctive denial, he lifted a hand for silence. "Now, just wait, Katie, and think about this for a minute. Maybe you didn't notice—maybe even Kevin didn't notice—but if you had been a dispassionate observer like myself, it might have occurred to you that all these years you've been sparring with each other, a great percentage of your quips were sexual in nature. Old Freud knew his business, my girl, and if he were alive today, no doubt he'd make the same observation I'm making—you've been sublimating, both of you. And it's been going on almost since the time you reached puberty."

The notion was almost too incredible to consider. Kate tried to think back on her relationship with Kevin over the years, to the careless remarks tossed back and forth about each other's sex lives, to the teasing insinuations and invitations that, she was certain, had meant nothing. Nothing at all except they were two adults who knew each other too well to be coy. Her father's suggestion that those innocent thrusts and parries had only been a disguise for real sexual attraction was ridiculous. She was almost sure of it.

She felt confusion begin to swamp her again, and she could only counter with "That's not the point. The fact is, I never intended to get involved with Kevin."

"You've *been* involved with him," Jason corrected definitively, "for quite some time."

He was determined to make this as difficult for Kate as possible. "No," she said firmly. "Until yesterday I didn't care if I never saw him again."

"And now?"

"And now," she admitted, with difficulty, "I care. A lot."

The smile that lit her father's eyes looked suspiciously like gentle satisfaction. "That is not a bad thing, Katie. To care for someone else."

"But don't you see?" she insisted, a little desperately now. "It never should have happened. It was just . . . the stress of the storm, the old cliché of two people thrown together in the dark. It can't be real—or permanent. All it's doing is upsetting my life and confusing me and making me miserable."

Her father looked at her thoughtfully for a long time. "Well, if that's the case," he decided at last, "I don't see the problem at all. You made a mistake; you forget it and move on and make sure it doesn't happen again. There's nothing very complicated about that."

A rational assessment except for one thing: It didn't feel like a mistake to Kate. And for that reason it *was* complicated. "It's not that easy." She sighed unhappily. "On the one hand, everything is changed. On the other hand, nothing has. I know that. A week ago all Kevin did was get on my nerves. A week from now, maybe, or a month, I'm going to wake up and find that I still don't like him. After all, I've known him for years, and it just doesn't make sense that in two days he could suddenly turn into the kind of person I could... well, take seriously. It was just the storm, and just because we were lovers is no reason for me to feel like I'm—"

"In love with him?" her father suggested perceptively, and Kate colored uncomfortably. The words sounded foolish when applied to Kevin and her, embarrassing and laughably inappropriate. But she couldn't deny them, and the fact made her miserable.

"All right, Katie." Using both hands to guide his leg to the floor, her father sat up straight and looked at her frankly. "I'll tell you this one thing, and then you're on your own. Sometimes, it's true, a crisis will draw two people together who have nothing at all in common except the crisis. But sometimes it takes moments of stress to strip away the veneers and pretenses and let us see the truth about ourselves and each other. Sometimes..." And his smile now was a little introverted, tender and reminiscent, as though he were not exactly talking about Kate and Kevin at all. "It takes something like that storm to give us the courage to recognize what's been there all along."

Abruptly, he looked embarrassed, impatient with himself, and Kate was peculiarly convinced he had been thinking about himself and not her. But before she had a chance to question, he said firmly, "My advice, dear girl, is to give yourself a chance. Stop trying to make sense out of something that can't be measured in the lab.

And stop being so hard on poor Kevin. My guess is..."
He chuckled as he reached for his crutch. "The boy has
no idea what he's gotten himself into. He deserves all the
support he can get."

That made Kate smile as she got up to help her father.
And after all the turmoil she had been through over what
was, after all, a simple biologic function, it felt good to
smile.

She was in much better spirits after having talked to her
father, although she couldn't say exactly why. He had
had nothing helpful to offer whatsoever; in fact, if she
made an effort to try to understand what he had said, she
would only be more confused than ever, but his matter-
of-fact attitude had allowed her to put things a bit more
in perspective.

It wasn't until after he had gone that Kate realized she
had forgotten to ask him whether or not he had room for
a houseguest for a few days. Impatient with herself for
having allowed intangibles to overshadow more prag-
matic matters, however briefly, she decided to simply
surprise her father with her presence. She might even fix
him dinner. First, however, she had to stop by her house
and try to rescue some of her clothes.

The sight that greeted Kate as she pulled up to the curb
outside the remains of her house was simply astonish-
ing. Three pickup trucks and at least a dozen workmen
filled her front lawn. A tow truck was tugging her
crushed car down the driveway, while a chain saw nois-
ily reduced to firewood the tree that had been resting on
top of it. Another chain saw was busy on the tree that had
gone through the roof, and the sounds of busy hammering and shouted orders added to the cacophony.

Kate got out of the car slowly, dodging two-by-fours
and squares of Sheetrock that were being carried up the

walk, her eyes wide with amazement. She spotted one man in denim overalls and a green eye-shield cap who looked more authoritative than the others, and she approached him, moving carefully around sawhorses and generators.

"Excuse me."

He looked at her.

"Who *are* you?"

He returned, "Who are you?"

"I'm Dr. Larimer," she replied in undisguised distress, "and this is my house you're tearing down!"

"Ain't tearing down," he answered implacably. "We're putting it back together." Then he shouted, "Joe! Hey! You make sure that roof's got some support before you go ripping into the walls!"

She tugged at his arm, protesting, "But I didn't order this! I tried everyone and—"

Impatiently he dug in his pocket and came up with a work order. He scanned it efficiently. "This is two-eighty Applewood, ain't it? You're Kate Larimer?" She nodded to both questions, and he stuffed the order back into his pocket smugly. "You got any problems, talk to Mr. Dawson. We got work to do, lady."

Kevin. Of course. She could have searched until next spring for someone to do the job; she could have wheedled, cajoled and demanded until she was breathless, but Kevin's specialty was moving mountains. She had never thought of asking him, but he had thought of doing it. And something sweet and lovely and light began to sing through her veins as she looked around at the miracle he had wrought, not because of what he had done but simply because he had thought of doing it. For her.

She tugged on the man's arm again, shouting over the sound of the chain saw, "Can I go inside?"

He looked at her blankly, mouthing the word "What?"

"I need some things...." But he obviously couldn't hear her over the racket. She made an impatient gesture, shouted, "Never mind!" and picked her way through the rubble into the front door.

It was like negotiating an obstacle course, and it quickly became apparent that this was the last trip she would be able to make here for several days. Everything she owned had either been wrapped in heavy-duty plastic or swept away into the trash pile, and she knew that this was her only chance to salvage what she could. Blithely, she stuffed as many clothes and toiletries as possible into two suitcases and left with a cheerful backward wave to the scowling foreman.

She never made the conscious decision to turn toward Kevin's house instead of her father's; she simply did it. And having done it, the solution to her quandary became amazingly simple. She was in love. It might be no more than chemical reaction, stress-induced hysteria or the aftermath of sexual intimacy, but it was definitely there, and there was no point in arguing with what her body told her was true. This state of physical and emotional euphoria had come upon Kate too rarely—if ever—for her to turn her back on it now. It might not be permanent or destiny-changing or even right, but her only course was to enjoy it while she could. After all, love was not supposed to make sense.

KEVIN'S BORROWED CAR was out front when Kate arrived at his house, but there was no answer to her knock. She let herself in, and her heart was tripping with a light patter of excitement, perhaps even trepidation, as she called his name. There was no answer, and she was puzzled until she went to the picture window and looked out. Kevin was sitting on the gentle hill that looked out over the lake, absently tossing pebbles into the water.

A warm and secret thrill went through her as she watched him, solitary and lost in thought, the picture of romance on this soft spring evening. A gentle breeze ruffled his curls and caressed the light material of his shirt as low sunlight danced across his skin. His eyes were narrowed slightly upon the horizon, giving his profile a brooding, slightly Byronic look. Kate wondered if he was thinking about her.

Of course he was thinking about her. After her unprecedented behavior of the past twenty-four hours, what else would he be thinking about? On a ripple of tenderness and chagrin, she moved toward the door to join him, and then she stopped, a wave of unexpected shyness prickling her. She still didn't know what she would say to him. And she wasn't as confident as she would have liked to have been that he would welcome her just then.

She turned back into the house, needing a bit more time before she faced Kevin again, and she took her bags into the guest room to unpack. Kevin had invited her to use his house while hers was under construction; of that much she was certain. Everything else was still unresolved between them.

She discovered, to her delight, that Kevin had electricity. She took a load of laundry to his utility room and dumped it in the washer, thinking all the while how comfortable she felt in Kevin's house and how rare it was that despite the strain that had developed between them since last night, she had never felt as at ease with anyone as she did with Kevin. She helped herself to a shower and then put on the maroon robe Kevin had loaned her this morning. A faint scent of Kevin clung to it, and inhaling, Kate felt a warm and contented thrill.

In the kitchen she found a crumpled package of instant soup mix on the counter and a cup with a bit of broth left in it—obviously the remnants of Kevin's dinner. She thought he must be desperate indeed to have forced down such a culinary disaster and have called it dinner, and that made her smile. She heated water for her own cup of soup and then went back into the living room, sitting on the demisofa that faced the picture window, sipping her soup and watching Kevin.

It was full twilight when he began to climb the hill back to the house. Kate had switched on a small lamp beside the sofa and sat waiting for him, a wonderful, calm anticipation filling her now that she was actually here. It had never been complicated at all. She wanted to be with Kevin. Now she was with Kevin. It felt good, and for as long as that good feeling lasted, she would not fight it.

Kevin must have seen the light as he approached, for when he slid open the door and stepped inside, there was no surprise on his face, just a carefully controlled question mixed with anticipation, much like what she was feeling. He closed the door behind him with a click and said, "Katie."

She smiled at him. "I'm moving in. Although—" her brow quirked with amused uncertainty "—the way you got those men to working on my house, I'm beginning to wonder how much I'm welcome. The way they're going, they'll have it done in record time. Maybe that's a hint."

Kevin came toward her, his eyes alight with quick awareness but his stance still cautious and unsure. "I'll tell them to take longer coffee breaks," he assured her, "if it means you'll stay longer."

Kate said simply, "Thanks, Kevin, for taking care of that for me. No one else could have done it."

He shrugged, a little self-consciously. "Like you said, it's amazing how fast people will jump for a celebrity. You've got to use what you've got."

"Did I say that?"

"Words to that effect."

He stopped only a few feet before her, and unspoken questions hummed between them with static alertness. His eyes were busy on her face, his body taut and suspended, and she could feel uncertainty emanating from him, the same kind of uncertainty she had felt only a few moments before but strangely felt no longer.

At last, he said softly, "Well, Katie. What now?"

Her voice was mild and steady as she replied. "Your choices are: A—watch television; B—play cards; C—tell ghost stories; D—take off your clothes and lie down on the floor."

His eyes sparked with immediate relaxed surprise, just as she had known they would. "Why, Dr. Larimer," he exclaimed in a soft and exaggerated Southern drawl, "your boldness finds me completely at a loss! Whatever can you have in mind?"

"I owe you a massage, remember?" she responded promptly.

He looked at her with feigned consideration, though his eyes were bright with pleasure and amusement. "Are you any good?"

"Top of my class in Massage 101."

He gave her another moment of thoughtful hesitation. "In that case," he decided finally, "my choice is D."

"Wise decision, Mr. Dawson." She stood up and began to drag the cushions off the sofa and onto the floor,

deliberately refusing to let her eyes stray to the move
ment his fingers were making with the buttons of his shir
or to the way his eyes were watching hers. "Lie dowr
there when you're finished," she instructed, and wen
into the kitchen.

When she returned, he was sitting on the cushions or
the floor, tugging off his shoes. His chest was bare, hi
shoulders, marred only by the white patch of bandage
near his left collarbone, gleaming goldenly in the lamp
light. His lines were beautiful, sleek and taut and lean
and Kate was surprised that with all her clinical detach
ment toward the human body, she could become so
aroused by merely the sight of Kevin's.

He glanced up at her suspiciously. "What is that?"

She held up the bottle of olive oil for his inspection
"For lack of anything better—salad oil."

"I'm not sure I like the idea of being basted like a tur
key," he objected warily.

She laughed. "You're going to love it." Then, looking
at him meaningfully, she added, "I meant *everything*
Mr. Dawson."

His grin was fleeting and shy and deliberately endear
ing as he got to his feet, his fingers moving to the buttor
of his pants. "You still intimidate me, Dr. Larimer."

She watched as he unzipped his pants and slid then
down over his hips with movements that were curiously
erotic, and Kate's pulse speeded slightly as she followed
the lines of tanned muscled thighs and hard masculine
calves. He left on his underwear, and Kate teased him
gently, "Shy?"

"Always have been," he assured her blithely, and
lowered himself with easy grace to lie facedown on the
sofa cushions. "There's the reason you've never seen me
as a pinup centerfold."

Kate knelt beside him and poured a bit of the oil into her hand, warming it between her palms. His shoulders were tense beneath her hands, and Kate could well imagine why. For all her bravado, Kate had never been a sexually aggressive person, and her sudden change of personality had caught him off guard. Only with Kevin would she have dared it. Kevin, whom she knew so well and with whom she had always been so comfortable.... Kevin, who was coaxing her each day into new discoveries not only about him but about herself.

Her oiled hands glided gently over the hard musculature of his back, using special care near his injured shoulder. "If this position is uncomfortable for you," she said, "just tell me."

"It's uncomfortable," he admitted, his voice muffled by the pillows, "but not the way you mean."

She smiled a little and warmed more oil in her hands. She worked his biceps, stretching his arm out as she moved her hand down over the long, strong lines of his forearm, giving attention to each separate finger. His hands were wonderful, she noticed for not the first time, strong but uncallused, the fingers lean and graceful and artistically shaped, like the rest of him. She resisted the urge to kiss those fingers, to draw each tip into her mouth, tasting them and caressing them.

Kate tucked the folds of the robe between her legs and straddled his hips, returning to work with more energy on his neck and shoulders. She noted with satisfaction that the hard muscles beneath her hands had become pliant and relaxed, and he moaned drowsily. "Katie, this is wonderful. Why didn't I ever talk you into doing this for me before?"

She chuckled softly, moving her hands in long, firm strokes from his waist to his neck. ''Probably because you didn't think of it.''

He sighed and shifted his head slightly. His eyes were closed. ''You're a magician,'' he murmured. ''I think I'm going to fall asleep.''

Kate smiled and moved downward, sliding her fingers with firm, smooth kneading motions over his thighs and his calves, and at last with concentrated attention on his feet. He moaned again, drowsy with pleasure, and Kate felt a languorous contentment that matched his own, enjoying the sensation of his planes and curves beneath her fingers, warm slippery flesh and pliant, responsive muscles.

She felt his soft catch of breath as she slipped her fingers beneath the elastic of his briefs and slowly tugged downward, over his thighs and off his legs. Her own heart began to pound with his awareness as she positioned herself near his ankles and moved her hands upward over his oiled and naked flesh. The muscles that once had been supple grew strong with a different type of tension as her fingers shaped his calves and whispered against his inner thighs. Memorizing by touch alone, she moved with gentle massaging motions over his taut buttocks, the spareness of his waist, the gradual flare of his back and his shoulders. She could feel his breathing, and it echoed her own. His skin was warm and gleaming beneath her hands, and her fingers registered the smooth sensation of the sheathed muscles of his back, the slight roughness of hair on his legs, the strength of bone and tendon of his feet. She loved touching him, knowing him, discovering him. Each succeeding moment was a new delight to be stored against the time of emptiness she knew would come.

She moved to sit beside him, her hand curling slightly around his waist. She whispered, "Turn over, Kevin."

He complied, slowly. His eyes were dark and brilliant with alert anticipation, his body strong and demanding in its arousal. And yet he made no move except to stroke her fingers lightly with his own, allowing her to set her own pace and explore her own pleasures. He smiled faintly, and his voice was husky. "Would this, perchance, be one of your fantasies?"

She stifled a throaty laugh and shook her head, moving her legs to rest on either side of his knees, supporting her weight on her heels. "I don't even dream this good."

"Don't be shocked," he murmured, and closed his eyes with a soft release of breath as her oiled hands moved against his chest, "but this has always been one of mine."

She explored the texture of soft hair and defined muscles on his chest with the pressure of her palms and then the caress of her fingers. She saw his face tighten with pleasure as her fingertips traced the shape of his dark, flat nipples and then moved downward, whirling the light pattern of hair on his chest. She watched the play of emotions on his face, exquisite pleasure bordering near pain, as she discovered with growing wonder and shimmering delight his most responsive areas, and a deep possessive joy filled her, simply for the pleasure she was giving him. By allowing her the freedom to give, he pleasured her, and she loved him, simply and intensely, for understanding that.

Her own heart was pounding with need and expectancy when at last she slid upward to straddle his thighs. Her fingertips smoothed his face, tracing the firm, masculine angles there. His eyes opened, heavy with desire and alive with an inner fire, and his hand lifted to tug at the sash of her robe. The heavy material parted, and his large, warm hand moved against her naked abdomen, curled around her waist, urged her gently downward.

They kissed with lightly darting tongues and gently nibbling lips, tasting and promising and building upon pleasures to come. Urgency was a warm, demanding flow released in steady measures, something too exquisite to be unleashed at once. When Kate lifted her face, Kevin smiled and lightly, adoringly, traced the shape of her moist, parted lips with his fingertip. Then he lifted his hand to the shoulder of her robe, and she straightened her arms, allowing him to tug the garment off and discard it on the floor.

He cupped her breasts with his hands, and lifting himself a little, brought his mouth to cover one breast, his hand imitating the massaging, drawing motions of his lips and tongue upon the other. Rippling waves of mindless pleasure went through Kate; her body grew weak and fluid beneath the caresses of his hands and his lips, molding itself to him. A gentle pressure of his fingers against her hips positioned her against him, a heated, demanding hardness between her thighs. She was breathless and aching when he moved his hands beneath her arms, bringing her forward to meet his kiss, and when she felt him slide inside her, the joining was effortless, natural, an emptiness being filled, a blending of entities too long separate.

He kissed her long and deeply, holding her to him with his hand encircling the back of her neck, giving full rein to a passion that had been too long restrained. And then, slowly, he encouraged her to straighten, watching her with eyes that were bold and gentle and alert to her every sensation.

Kate gasped as he sank deep into her, deeper than he had ever been before. He soothed her with gentle stroking motions on her back and her arms, whispered caresses, worshiped her with brilliant, hypnotic eyes. Kate had never imagined it could be like this. She had never known what it could be to look into her lover's eyes and share the emotions, the urgency, the delight, just as thoroughly as they shared the physical sensations they were creating within each other. Never had there been such openness, such complete and thorough knowledge, such uninhibited sharing. They learned of each other wordlessly, gave to each other selflessly, and when the pinnacle of desire was reached and surpassed, the bond that was forged between them was more than physical. Much more.

Low-level electricity still pulsed through Kate as she lay against Kevin, one leg thrown over his hip, her hand curved around his waist, her cheek against the steady, powerful beat of his heart. Her veins felt stripped and washed, her muscles liquid, her mind a composite of floating colors and languorous dizziness. She felt filled with him, her very essence inundated with him, and all she could think was *Kevin*... And every time she thought it, she was swept afresh with a surge of contentment and wonder that was too intense to define, even to herself.

Kevin's hand moved lazily through her hair, his breath gradually calming, his heartbeat resuming a more or less normal pace beneath her ear. His skin was warm and sticky against hers, rich with the scent and texture of their lovemaking. There had never been anything more wonderful than lying here with him, savoring what they had shared.

And then he lifted his face slightly, urging her to look at him. She turned her face to his, and he was smiling, his eyes filled with the glow of all she felt, his face content and relaxed. He kissed her lips lightly and then lay back down again, his hand resuming its gentle, stroking play in her hair. Kate rested her head against his shoulder, and she could see his smile still lingered, absent and tender, and his eyes were warm with it. "Ah, Katie," he said softly, looking at her quietly and caressingly. "I do love you."

Chapter Eleven

Everything within Kate stilled. She lay against Kevin and didn't move or breathe or hardly even think for what seemed like a very long time. It was, in fact, only the space of a few heartbeats.

"I love you." She heard the words, and she felt such a conglomerate of swift, complex and hopelessly entangled emotions that for a moment she could not even defend herself against them. First there was joy, simple and pure, the kind of joy any woman would feel to hear those words as she lay in the arms of a man with whom she had just made such beautiful and intensely satisfying love. And then there was anger, because he didn't mean them, and such words were too powerful to be uttered in vain. And then sadness, because he did not know, could not know, what until this very moment she had not known herself—how long she had waited to hear those words from someone and know they were real. And guilt, because he was only voicing what she felt in that glowing aftermath of emotional sharing and physical satisfaction. And finally, understanding, because she knew that Kevin, in his simple straightforward way of looking at life, did mean it at the moment and cared enough about her to want her to hear it. I love you because I love making love with you and feel good about myself and you and life in general and want you to feel good, too.

She smiled and lifted her face to brush a gentle kiss across his jawline. "Kevin," she said softly, "what a sweet thing to say."

She saw the cautious expectancy in his eyes change to confusion, almost anxiety, and he looked as though he would say something. Knowing only that she did not want to hear it, Kate sat up quickly, tugging at his hand. "I need a shower," she announced brightly. "Care to join me?"

For a moment longer, hesitance and uncertainty lingered in his eyes, then relaxed gradually into a more familiar expression. "Only if you carry me," he murmured, and then laughed as Kate slapped him smartly on the thigh and leaped to her feet.

He made a playful swipe for her ankle, missed, and Kate ducked away from him, initiating a lighthearted chase toward the bathroom. Only when she stood within the circle of his arms beneath the gentle spray of the shower did she realize that her heart was pounding furiously, as though from a narrow escape.

Beneath the warm cascade of water, they discovered a new dimension to sensuality that had little to do with classic arousal. They soaped each other's bodies and tasted the clean, fresh water on each other's skin; they smiled into each other's eyes and let the rhythmic pulse of the water soothe them. It was not foreplay, but something infinitely more satisfying and bonding.

Afterward, Kevin teased her about the oversized football jersey and knee socks she chose to wear to bed, and they made popcorn and ate it in bed, watching television. This, too, was the unfolding of a wonderful new level in their relationship, only it wasn't really new, just dimly amazing. There had never been another man in Kate's life with whom she could be this comfortable— before, during or after lovemaking. With Kevin there were no pretenses. Everything was natural. There were no demands, no expectations, no unfulfilled needs. They were comfortable together. She could sit with Kevin and munch popcorn and watch television and talk casually just as she had done so many times before. The only difference was that they shared a bed and that beneath the covers Kevin was naked.

She drifted to sleep in the middle of the late news, curled into the crook of his arm, thinking what a special thing they had discovered by accident and hoping it would last a little while longer.

In her dream she heard the wind and felt the lash of the cold rain against her face. She saw buildings explode, pieces of her town, her life, all that was familiar, sucked in and whisked away by the forces of nature. She tried to scream, to run away, to call out warnings, to do something to stop it, but she was mute and paralyzed. She could hear the thudding of her heart, loud and fast, and the roaring gasp of her breath. Then she was running through a dark and treacherous landscape littered with corpses and echoing the agonized screams of her friends and family. Bloodied hands reached for her, terrified voices called out to her, begging for help, but she could only shake her head helplessly, sobbing, pleading with them to understand. There was nothing she could do.

And then there was another voice, a more familiar voice, shouting her name. There was desperation in the call, and yet strength, and she knew if only she could reach it, everything would be all right. She saw Kevin in the distance, holding out his arms to her, calling to her, and with a ragged sob of relief she ran toward him. But too late. Even as she ran, he was moving away. Something huge and monstrous had him in its grip and was tearing him away from her. He was growing smaller and smaller on the screen of her vision, calling to her, reaching out to her, disappearing...

"Katie! Katie, love, stop."

Kate awoke with a start, gasping and sweating. Kevin was holding her shoulders, shaking her gently, his face above her a dim blur in the darkness. Instinctively, she pressed herself against him, releasing a long shudder that was half a sob, and he held her tightly, murmuring something soothing and unintelligible into her hair. Her heart wouldn't stop pounding, and she was shaking all over. It felt so good to feel him solid and warm around her, holding her. Safe.

"God, it was awful." The words came bubbling out, hoarsely and unsteadily, as she struggled to get hold of herself. "Nightmare... about the storm. I felt so helpless. I was so scared. You were there, but I couldn't reach you."

"I'm here now." He tightened his arms, showing her his strength, and his face nuzzled hers reassuringly. There was a soft bristle on his cheek, which she found wonderfully comforting. She lay against him, listening to the pounding of her heart trying to regulate itself, trying to push away the childish terrors of the dream, which clung to her like cobwebs.

"I feel silly," she murmured at last.

"I've always thought you were silly." There was an indulgent smile in his voice that coaxed confidence from her, and she stirred against him, slightly, reluctantly.

"I shouldn't be lying against your shoulder," she said. "I'm hurting you."

"You're not," he assured her softly. "It's the other shoulder. Feeling steadier now?"

She nodded but made no further move to leave the protective circle of his arms. Her fist clenched slightly and instinctively against his chest as recalled terror crept over her again. She kept her eyes wide open, certain she would not sleep again. "I guess you were right," she whispered. "It doesn't go away. The crisis is over, but the aftermath stays with us."

He threaded his fingers through her hair, pushing it away from her face. "I guess we were all changed inside by living through what we did. In ways we may not even know yet."

She tried to smile, summoning courage. "I hope I don't have to go into therapy."

He chuckled softly, kissing her temple. "You, Ms Rock of Gibraltar? Not a chance."

She wished she could tell him how wonderful it was to lie in his arms just now. To awake from a heart-stopping nightmare and have someone to turn to, someone to hold and comfort her, someone who cared and understood. She thought there must be no greater contentment in the world, and she snuggled closer to him.

"Do you have them?" she questioned, holding on to him. "Nightmares?"

"No, hardly ever. That's because I don't internalize very much. And during the storm I dealt with every fear known to man right out front—there's not very much left over to work through in my dreams. You had other things to deal with while it was happening, but me—I had nothing to do but be terrified."

"You never let on," she murmured. "I never knew you were scared, except that one time when I asked you. And then I didn't believe you."

"I thought I was going to die," he said simply, and she lifted her face to look at him. His expression was quiet and open in the dim shadows of the night, and his tone was sober. "When I knew what was happening—when you pulled me away from the window and we were lying on the floor—you know how they say your life passes before your eyes? It really does. I thought of things I hadn't remembered in years, silly, unimportant things. Like the time you told me I could catch a bird by putting salt on its tail and I spent three hours tracking a blue jay with a salt shaker." Her laugh was choked and a little smothered, but encouraged, he continued. "And the time I put peanut butter in your sneakers the morning of the cheerleader tryouts."

Her head jerked up. "*You* did that?"

He nodded. "Probably to get you back for the blue jay." Now his voice softened. "And the time you and I rode our bikes out to the lake and spent the afternoon collecting flora and fauna for our science project. You probably don't even remember it, but it's one of those childhood things that just stayed with me for some reason. The day was so beautiful. I can't even describe how beautiful it was. All silver and gold, about three weeks into autumn. And you...you were so smart and so pretty. You were wearing jeans and a fuzzy pink sweater, and your hair was long then, corn-silk yellow, and you wore it in a braid down past your shoulders, and every time the sun would hit it, I would have to stare and wonder what it felt like to touch."

He smiled then. She could feel his smile against the top of her head. "Maybe that was the day I first fell in love with you," he said huskily. "I know it was the day I decided I wanted to have a house here and spend the rest of my life having days like that one." Then, pulling himself out of the reverie, his hand traversed the length of her arm, lightly, bracingly. "But things didn't exactly work out that way, did they?"

Kate was silent, struggling with a lump of moisture in her throat. She did not remember that day. Kevin and she had spent so many afternoons together during their childhood that none was much different from the others in her memory. But Kevin remembered. Kevin recalled one of the most precious days of his childhood, and she had been a part of it. When he thought he was living his last moments, *that* was what he had turned to, one afternoon at the lake with her. And he said he had fallen in love with her then. It was impossible, of course. Kevin's relationship with her had been little short of antagonistic throughout their lives, hadn't it? She wished he would stop talking about love. It made things so much more complicated than they already were.

In a moment, she managed, trying to move him onto a more neutral subject, "I think things worked out fine. You've got your house on the lake and half the rest of the world besides."

He chuckled softly. "Yeah, I guess."

"What's your house like in L.A.?" Now it was comfortable, talking with him like this in the dark.

He thought for a moment, as though it were hard for him to remember. "Well, I have a round bed with mirrors on the ceiling. I don't sleep in it, though. I caught a glimpse of myself waking up one morning, and it put me off mirrors for a long time."

She laughed, and his fingers tightened on her waist affectionately. "That's funny; I never thought about that before. Why don't you come back with me this time?"

Once again he trod the very edges of dangerous ground. She dismissed his invitation with a mild "And just what would my patients do while I'm off playing Hollywood? Wait for a more convenient time to get sick?"

He seemed surprised. "You never take a vacation?"

She shook her head against his shoulder. "I'm too possessive. You know that."

"Well..." Now there was an odd tone to his voice that he tried to disguise with nonchalance. "Maybe when your friend Brandon comes, you'll have more time. At least he'll be good for something."

She lifted her face to him, trying to scrutinize his expression in the dark. "Kevin..." she said softly, half amused, half incredulous. "You *are* jealous."

He didn't hesitate a moment. "Of course I am."

Kate found that difficult to digest. The concept was both ridiculous and exciting, embarrassing and gratifying. That Kevin Dawson would have cause to be jealous of any man—and over *her*. It strained the limits of her imagination.

She demanded, still peering at him, "Why?"

"Because he's perfect for you," Kevin replied with simple, disarming honesty. "And because it's so damn obvious even I can see it."

This was even more difficult for Kate to absorb. He wasn't kidding. He saw Jeff Brandon as a threat, but one did not feel threatened unless one first felt possessive.

And then, as though to forcefully lighten the mood, he added, "Of course I have one advantage over Brandon already." She glanced at him again, half expecting some lewd comment, but he only grinned. "*I* know you wear wool socks to bed. And I don't mind." His hand drifted down the length of her nightshirt, which had ridden up to her waist, and rested warmly and affectionately on her bare hip. "How many men can you say that about?"

Kate chuckled, wrapping her arm more securely about his bare waist. But she was thinking, *Yes, indeed, how many?* She had never felt comfortable enough with anyone to be herself like this in bed. Anyone but Kevin.

She inquired, in the same vein, "Do you always sleep in the nude?"

"No. Usually I wear pajama bottoms." He glanced down at her, a teasing spark in his eyes. "Black silk, to be precise, as you would know if you ever read the fan magazines."

Again she laughed into his chest, wondering how long it had been since she had ever felt this good with anyone. It was almost worth having a nightmare for, to awake and be comforted like this. His hand was comfortable and secure on her bare bottom, his chest a warm pillow. She wanted to stay like this forever.

He kissed her hair again, lightly, and used his forefinger to trace the shape of her lingering smile. He inquired gently, "Do you want to make love again, Katie, or do you want to try to go back to sleep?"

No one had ever asked her that in precisely that way before. Granted, her experience was not enormous, but it struck Kate as incredibly loving, the way he asked. As though it were a shared experience, never to be demanded by one partner or the other. As though if she said yes, he would enjoy it, but if she said no, he wouldn't mind.

She didn't realize that her arm tightened around his waist in a fractional, adoring pressure as she answered softly, "No. I'd really like you to just hold me for a while. We don't have to talk anymore. I just like lying like this."

"So do I," he whispered, and stroked her hair, tenderly, one more time.

They stayed that way, not talking, just holding each other, until Kate fell asleep.

THE NEXT AFTERNOON, Kate had only afternoon office hours, though she still wanted to make rounds at the hospital. If Kevin's phone had been connected, she would have been more than tempted to simply call in her orders at the hospital and spend more time with Kevin. But then she decided it was just as well. She had no intention of letting this love affair disrupt her routine, and it was best not to get too attached to Kevin and the time they spent together. They shared an idyll, something that only the most bizarre of times and circumstances could have created, but no rational person would believe for a moment that it could last. And Kate was very rational.

They made oatmeal and toast and took it out to the deck that overlooked the lake, breakfasting in the sunshine and lazy morning companionability. ''Doesn't it make you feel strange,'' Kate inquired after a time, gazing out over the brilliant serenity of water and spring-blooming shrubs, ''to be enjoying all this while there's a whole world out there going crazy? I mean, there are a million things I should be doing. Everyone else in this town is frantically trying to put the pieces of their lives back together, but I'm sitting here looking at the lake and pretending like nothing else matters.''

''It doesn't make me feel a bit strange,'' Kevin answered. They were sitting side by side in redwood deck chairs, and he reached across and held her hand, letting their entwined fingers swing lightly between the chairs. ''There's always a world going crazy out there, Katie. The trick is to keep your world halfway sane.''

That was a typical Kevin remark, at the same time both reassuring and disturbing. Reassuring because for the first time in many days he had said something that didn't surprise her and disturbing because it only illuminated once again the chasm of personality differences that separated them. Kate could never adopt such a relaxed, self-centered attitude toward life and the people who surrounded her. And she had never approved of it in Kevin.

"What about your folks?" she said. "I thought you were on your way to see them."

He shrugged, gazing at the lake. "I call them every day. I'm going to wait till the shoulder heals until I go down there, though. You know Mom; she makes such a big-budget production out of everything, and she'd drive me crazy, fussing over me. If she doesn't know, that's one less thing I have to worry about."

Kate glanced at him in amusement. "One less thing? What else, pray tell, do you have to worry about?"

He gave her a relaxed grin, stretching his legs out before him. He was wearing only a pair of dark running shorts, and Kate couldn't help admiring the shape of his legs. Long and tanned, with each muscle and tendon perfectly defined, they were the epitome of relaxed masculine strength.

"Oh, the usual things," he replied. His thumb caressed a light circular pattern on the underside of her wrist. "Going bald, getting fat..." And he glanced at her through lashes that concealed his expression. "Growing old without having any babies."

That surprised her, and in such a deep, undefined way that the only way she knew how to respond was with a joke. "I don't know how to tell you this, Mr. Dawson," she teased, "but recent medical research has revealed that due to uncertain anatomical details, the chances are very slim that you will ever give birth."

He smiled, but his eyes were serious. There was no mistaking that. "Don't you ever think about it, Katie?" he inquired gently. "Didn't you ever once, while you were busy doing your doctor thing and devoting your life to the service of others, think about having children of your own, a family of your own? Didn't you leave any room in your life for yourself?"

She was uncomfortable, far more uncomfortable than she would have been if Kevin had asked that question a week ago. She could actually feel her throat tighten and her heart begin to speed as though in preparation for a battle she didn't want to fight. And it all was absurd, of course. Kevin's question was motivated by idle curiosity, nothing more. He wasn't by any stretch of the imagination suggesting that he and she . . .

She replied, not looking at him. "Of course I have. I want a family of my own very much. Just because I happen to be a doctor doesn't mean I gave up being a woman, and most of my male counterparts have families. That's never been a conflict."

"But?" he prompted.

She lifted a shoulder, very uncomfortable now. He was waiting for her to say, as she had said only a few days ago, that she hadn't found the right man. For some reason, those words wouldn't come today. "But I'm thirty-four years old . . ."

"So am I. Don't you think it's time we started to get serious about this thing?"

Her heart was beating very fast now. It was as though she could read his mind, and against all dictates of logic, knew exactly what he meant. Or perhaps it was the way he used the word *we*. Or the way his fingers tightened, almost imperceptibly, on hers. She cast around frantically for some reply, and what she came up with was what a mere week ago would have been the only possible answer. When she said it now, it sounded heartless, deliberately cruel and plainly stupid. "Well, I don't think you've got anything to worry about," she said brightly. "There must be at least a half-million women in this country alone who'd love to have your baby."

The words hung, naked and unforgivable, in the still morning air. She felt him stiffen, and reciprocally, her cheeks scorched. She started to pull her hand away and get up, but his fingers closed tightly, not even allowing her that escape. And when she looked at him, for it would have been cowardly to do anything else, his face was not hurt and angry as she had expected. It was very calm, and his eyes were filled with patience.

He said quietly, "I've had the feeling we haven't been communicating since last night, when I told you I love you. Now I'm sure of it."

She simply looked at him, helpless and miserable.

He swung his legs over the side of the chair so that he was facing her. He held her hand, lightly now, between both of his, and he looked at her soberly. "You didn't believe me, did you?"

"Kevin, I..." She swallowed hard. Honesty had always been so easy between them, a mere second nature. Why was it suddenly so difficult? *Oh, Kate, how could you have screwed things up so badly?* "Kevin, I believe that you meant it." She had to lower her eyes briefly, but that was the coward's way out. She looked at him again. "I—I believe that you feel good about us, and so do I, and it feels like being in love...but let's not get carried away. It's only—"

"No, it's not." His tone was sharp, though his expression was still placid, and she could feel tension radiating from him, in every inch of him. "I know what you're thinking. It's that I've said it lots of times before, and I have, but—"

"Kevin, you don't have to—"

"No, let me get through this." His eyes were dark, and she noticed that the tiny little lines radiating toward his temples were tight. His fingers were hard on hers now, an unconscious pressure that refused to let her go. He took a breath.

"The reason," he explained in careful, measured tones, "I've said it so often before is because of you. Because I've loved you so long I can't even remember when it started and everyone else . . . was just because I knew I couldn't have you. I can't believe you never guessed it. Katie, I've *worshiped* you from the time we were teenagers. It took me ten years to realize that what I thought was an adolescent crush was really a grown-up, very adult love. And another ten years of waiting, hoping you'd realize the same thing . . . and learning to live without you."

She couldn't keep the shock out of her eyes or the disbelief that permeated every cell of her body. She couldn't sort out the emotions that coursed through her in neverending waves. Was joy one of them? Was horror another? Hope, amazement, dread, pain?

He took another short, tense breath. "I don't know how to explain it any better. "When you came to me . . . when we made love . . ."

Then she managed a single, strangulated syllable, not knowing what to say or even what she wanted to say, only that she had to say something. "Please . . ."

Suddenly he took her fingers and brought them to his chest. His heartbeat was strong and rapid beneath her hand, pulsing with the same frightened intensity as was her own. His voice was a little breathless now. "Feel that,

Katie. I'm scared to death. This is the hardest thing I've ever done. Just let me finish, okay?''

She nodded, mutely, and blinked back an inexplicable sting of moisture in her eyes. *Oh, Kevin, what do you want from me? What do you want me to say? What do I want to say?*

"I wish there were some way I could make you believe me," he said, and he let her fingers drop to his thigh, where they curled beneath the shelter of his hand like something broken and hurting. "I can't prove it in bed . . . it's so much more than that. I can't prove it with words—I just don't know the right ones. But, Katie, you're the only woman I've ever loved, and I've loved you forever. You're the only one who makes me feel right about myself and makes me want to be better than myself. You take me *out* of myself, but that's only part of it. I only know that I want to be with you for the rest of my life," he finished simply. The gaze that held hers was brave and quiet, and it went through Kate's soul like an arrow. "All right. Now you can say whatever it is you feel you have to say."

But she couldn't, not just then. She leaned her head back against the chair, and all she could think was that she, too, wanted it to be like this between them for the rest of her life. She had never known a greater contentment, a surer happiness, a more certain feel of rightness about anything, as she had known with Kevin these past days. She wished then with all her might that it could be real, and permanent, and she struggled to remember all the reasons it could not be.

Kevin said he loved her. He said he had loved her forever. But how could that be possible?

At last she had to look at him. One of them had to be sensible. For the first time in her life, Kate wished desperately it did not have to be her.

"Kevin," she said with difficulty. Her voice sounded broken and weak. "I don't know...what to say." She looked at him helplessly, willing him to understand. "These last few days—you seem so different. You've changed since the storm. I hardly know you anymore."

And he smiled, shaking his head slowly, almost seeming to relax. "No, Katie, I haven't changed. And neither have you. You're still smarter than I am, and stronger and braver and more in control of your life. I'm still irresponsible and shallow and careless and all those things you've always detested about me, though I'm trying to do better." He looked at her with such simple confidence in his eyes that everything within her ached to believe him. "The only reason these past few days have seemed different is because for the first time you and I were being real with each other. We were letting things happen that should have happened a long time ago. Can't you see that? We stopped playing the games and hiding behind the roles and just let ourselves be ourselves. And if that's what you mean about the storm changing everything, then maybe you're right. If we turned to each other and found only what had been there all along, what can be bad about that?"

Kate didn't know. She only knew that it was impossible between them, but she wanted it to be possible so desperately that she couldn't think of the reasons why. *Give it a chance, Kate. For once in your life, give it a chance.*

And he must have seen the doubt in her eyes, the hope and the yearning, for he seized the moment, not by pushing his case but by backing away from it. He knew

Kate too well to try any other form of approach; that was why he had always been able to manipulate her so easily.

He glanced at his watch. "If you want to make rounds, you'd better get started." And then he smiled at her gently. "I know you need time to think. We'll talk when you get home, okay?"

He knew she would agree. No matter what her decision, he knew she would return and face him with it. He also knew that by giving her this time alone, he was showing his trust in her. Because, deep down inside, he knew she was feeling the same things he did. He was just allowing her time to realize it.

That wasn't manipulation, Kate realized slowly. It was caring.

She smiled at him, though it hurt a little to smile through all the turmoil inside her. She got up and then leaned down and kissed him gently on the lips. She wondered if she knew how much she wanted to be able to tell him what he wanted to hear. She wondered if, by this evening, she would.

"I'll see you about four, okay?" she said, a little thickly.

He linked his fingers through hers and held them for just a moment before letting her go. His eyes were deep and clear. "I'll be here."

Chapter Twelve

Afterward, Kate would wonder how she could have ever been confused at all, how she could have made so complex something that was, after all, painfully simple. She usually was so much more on top of things than this. Her only excuse was that the business of being in love was very new to her. Emotionally inexperienced as she was, she had few defenses against what was happening to her.

She made her rounds in somewhat of a daze, feeling almost as though she should apologize to her patients for being their doctor. She kept thinking, *Why couldn't Kevin be right? You must know he's right deep in your heart. You've never felt like this before. We were meant for each other; we always have been. It had nothing to do with the storm throwing us together, and it's not going to disappear tomorrow, not if both of us remember how good this is and want it to last. It wouldn't be easy, but it could work out. Why couldn't it?*

And then she picked up a national newspaper in the lobby of the hospital, and she knew why.

The front page teaser read "*Code Zero*—Fact Stranger than Fiction."

Standing there in the lobby, she flipped the pages to the entertainment section. There was a picture of Kevin—a press-release photo, larger than life—and a sidebar of downtown Victoria Bend after the storm. The headline read "Colt Marshall: Real-Life Hero" and was subtitled, "Kevin Dawson Risks Life to Save Woman from Flaming Car."

She read only a few lines. "During the tornado that recently devastated the small town of Victoria Bend, Mississippi, residents were fortunate to have on hand a television star who lives his role. Kevin Dawson, of *Code Zero* fame, was visiting his hometown when..."

Kate closed the newspaper and walked slowly to her car. Her mind was calm, her decision certain. The excited, hopeful yearning had settled into a dull, aching lump in her chest, and everything was suddenly very clear.

She did not really think that Kevin had planted the story or used the tragic misfortune of others to further his own publicity—although the thought did occur to her briefly. She was certain that not even Kevin would stoop so low to seek to profit from something like this. It was simply that seeing Kevin's face featured in a story in which a hundred other dramas played equally important roles brought everything into abrupt and clear perspective for Kate. It was more than the differences in their life-styles, their values and their outlooks on life that had kept her and Kevin apart all these years. It was that, to their very cores, they were different *people*, and they had never—even during the past few days of passion and insight—connected on any except the most superficial levels. When it came right down to it, they simply had nothing in common.

That was, perhaps, an oversimplification, a cliché, but it was undeniably true. She had known it all along, and she had ignored it for no other reason than that she

wanted to prolong the good feeling she had fabricated for
herself out of the sexual attraction and easy rapport she
and Kevin had discovered together. It made her angry
that such a stupid thing, such a mundane thing, could
stand between her and the kind of happiness she had
known these past few days. *They had nothing in common.* It was a trite barrier that kept her away from love
but a very powerful one. And perhaps what hurt Kate the
most was that she did not seem to be able to rise above it.

There was a car parked in front of Kevin's house when
she arrived, a black Continental with a hired driver. *So,*
she thought as she got out of her own car and walked
slowly up the drive, *the world has caught up with us at
last.* It was amazing how little it took to bring down the
house of cards.

She heard the voices before she opened the door. Kevin's was terse and angry; another man's was soothing and
complacent. She paused for a moment, and with a kind
of weary amazement, all she could think was that nothing in her life seemed to be happening in half measures
lately. She had come to say a goodbye that would most
probably break her heart, and from the sound of things,
she was about to walk in on a fistfight.

Kevin was nervously pacing back and forth in front of
the fireplace when she came in; his adversary, a plump,
balding man in an expensive suit, was lounging on the
sofa, looking at ease and unconcerned. As Kate closed
the door, Kevin whirled on the other man and demanded furiously, "How did you let it happen; that's
what I want to know!" He was holding a folded newspaper clenched in his fist, and to punctuate his point, he
threw it at the sofa. Sheets of newsprint floated harm-
lessly to the floor. "Damn it, Carl, I told you on the
phone—"

"Precisely the point, my boy." The other man had a British accent and seemed completely unruffled by what was apparently only another temper tantrum from the star. "I haven't been able to reach you by phone for days. What was I to do but to use my best judgment? And we'll get mileage out of this, old chap, never you fear—"

"I don't want mileage!" Kevin shouted, and took a step toward him. Physical violence was undoubtedly in the offing, but at that moment he noticed Kate for the first time.

For a half second he looked disconcerted, and the effort he made to resolve anger with welcome was painfully obvious. In the end, however, the best he could manage was a terse "Kate, do you know my agent? Carl Cason. Carl, this is Kate Larimer."

The other man got to his feet and murmured a polite greeting, which was drowned out by Kevin's grating "Good God, Katie, did you see this?" He gestured furiously to the newspaper scattered on the floor. "They make me sound like I'm at death's door! My mom's going to be having a freaking fit! How the hell could you do something like this?" he demanded, turning on Carl again. "I told you all publicity had to be cleared through me."

Carl resumed his seat, untroubled. "Interesting point, your mother," he said mildly. "As I've been trying to bring up since the moment I arrived, your family has been quite concerned since the story broke, and as you were, ah, incommunicado, it has been left to me to deal with the frantic mumsy and daddy. In the end, the best I could do to placate them was to promise to deliver you safe and sound on their doorstep by nine this evening, and if we want to make that plane, we'd best hurry."

Kevin stared at him.

"Works out quiet well, actually," continued Carl smoothly, and Kate was torn between an instant dislike and an instinctive admiration for the man's composure under stress. "A few days in Flordia, recuperating under mumsy's doting care—good human-interest angle there—and then we hit the talk-show circuit. We've got *Donahue* on the twelfth, and—"

Kevin exploded. "I'm not doing talk shows! Not about this, not now! Damn it, Carl, when are you going to get it through your head that this was not a publicity stunt I dreamed up for the benefit of Colt Marshall?"

Carl arched a delicate eyebrow and moved gracefully toward the bar, finding a bottle of well-aged Scotch in the cabinet. "Perhaps not, but it is better than anything *I* could have dreamed up, I must admit." He examined the label on the bottle, seemed satisfied and twisted the cap, pouring a measure into a glass. "And no matter what your personal feelings, old friend, we *will* take advantage of it. You know the rules of the game. You've got an obligation to the studio as well as to a hungry audience eager to hang on your every word. This is news, my boy, real news." And he met Kevin's eyes with a quiet force that even Kate could not imitate. "Best to handle it our own way, I think, than to let the reporters write their own stories. If you ever want to have any input into how the rest of the world views what happened here, you'd best begin now. Otherwise, the rags are going to build an image so bloody heroic even *you* won't be able to fill it. Don't you agree?"

Kate could see the debate on Kevin's face. Anger, disillusionment, rebellion—and acceptance. He had wanted to keep this private; she understood that. He had always been so concerned about being forced to live up to Colt Marshall's image; he knew that if he didn't tell the story in his own way, things would become much more complicated later on.

But there was more. Kevin was not accustomed to taking his life into his own hands. He never had to make decisions like this on his own. The only thing he knew was how to take the path of least resistance, and even though it went against his personal instincts, he had never had any choice. His life was not his own.

She saw resolution fade slowly into resignation, and when he looked at her, there was helplessness mixed with distress in his face. "Damn," he said softly. He was begging her to understand, though why he thought she wouldn't, Kate couldn't imagine. "I have to see my folks. They'll be going crazy."

Carl glanced at his watch. "You've about twenty minutes to pack, mate. Hell of a drive to the airport."

The sound of his voice seemed to push Kevin right back to the edge of temper again. Forcefully, he restrained it. "Wait in the car, Carl."

Carl had one more tactical weapon, and that was to know when he'd pushed as far as he could. He glanced at Kevin, took his glass of Scotch and strolled toward the door. "Fine notion, as a matter of fact. I've some calls to make."

When he was gone, Kate and Kevin looked at each other for a long time. Kate had not moved from her position just inside the threshold.

Kevin smiled at her faintly. "Well, dear," he drawled, with a forced attempt at levity, "how was *your* day?"

Kate said gently, trying to make it easier for him, "We knew it wasn't going to last forever, Kevin."

He deliberately chose to misunderstand her. He came forward swiftly and grasped her hands. "Come with me,

Kate," he urged energetically. "Mom and Dad would love to see you, and we could have a real vacation—"

She shook her head sadly. "You know that's impossible, Kevin."

He searched her eyes, saw the truth there and ignored it. "I'll be back in a couple of days," he assured her. "We can—"

"No, you won't, Kevin," she said simply. "You've got things to do."

He released her hands slowly and turned his face away. His breath came through his teeth in a long, low hiss. And then he said, staring at the opposite wall, "I don't suppose this is a good time to continue our conversation from this morning."

Oh, Kevin, please don't. Don't make it so hard . . . on yourself . . . on me. . . . She began quietly, "Kevin—"

He turned back to her quickly, forcefully. "Listen, Kate, I know what you're going to say. I've been thinking about it all day. You're thinking that our life-styles get in the way, that you have a practice here and I have a career in Los Angeles and that we'd never have any time together. But I've never interfered with your work, Katie, have I?" he insisted earnestly. "I know that what you have is much more than a job, and I respect that. I know I'd have to be the one to make the sacrifices, and I'm willing to do that. These things can be worked out, Katie, if you'd just give us a chance."

She shook her head slowly, sadly. "It's not that, Kevin, and I think you know it."

He looked at her, his expression numb and arrested, almost breathless. The look on his face reminded her of the way she had felt in the grip of her nightmare: staring into the face of approaching doom and being unable to run forward or backward, being unable to do anything except to stand rooted to the spot and let it happen. Watching him tore Kate's heart in two.

He said at last, hoarsely, "I want to marry you Katie. I want it to be forever. You know that's the way it was meant to be."

"No." It was barely a whisper, and she had to clear her throat, grasping for strength. "Kevin, please understand. We went through something earth-shattering together, and I suppose we'll always feel closer to each other because of that. But that's all it was." Determinedly, doggedly, she went on. Every word she spoke was like a dagger through her own heart, but she had to say it. It was true. "Bizarre things happened to both of us that night. You became a hero, and I...fell in love. But it was like Queen for a Day, you know? It's nice while it lasts, but when it's over, it's over. What we've had these past couple of days was good, but now it's time to get back to the basics again. And the basics are that you and I don't really have a place in each other's lives. We never did."

He looked at her for the longest time, and in rapid sequence denial, desperation, hurt, pleading and determination rushed across his eyes. He made a move as though to take her in his arms, and Kate stepped away. If he touched her now, she would crumble, and she couldn't afford to do that. She couldn't prolong the agony, for either of them.

His hands went into his pockets, and she saw them bunch into fists through the material. His face was tight, and his eyes were dark. He said lowly, "Damn it, Katie, I've spent half my life loving you. I'm not going to just walk away from you now."

"You have no choice." How calm her voice was, how steady her gaze. Inside, a thousand battles were being fought and lost. "You see, Kevin," she said simply, "I don't love you. I'm sorry, but that's one thing that hasn't changed."

And just as abruptly as it had begun, the new and tenuous wonder they had discovered on the night of the storm was ended. She stayed just long enough to see the slow agony of something beautiful and untouched within Kevin's eyes begin to die, and then she turned and walked away. She was crying before she even reached the car.

SHE CRIED A LOT in those next weeks. She couldn't understand why. She cried for no reason at all, and she cried for every reason in the world. She moved in with her father for the two weeks it took to remodel her house, but he didn't help a bit. He merely looked at her with a faint mixture of pity and tolerance in his eyes and said nothing. It was obvious he thought she had done the wrong thing.

Kate was just as certain she had done the right thing. What other choice could there have been? Could Kevin have actually thought she would *marry* him? Even if they had only remained part-time lovers, they would have ended up hurting each other eventually; it was best to end it neatly and quickly, as she had done. Kevin would get over it; he had admitted himself that he had a notoriously short attention span. He would be fine. Kate wished she could be as certain about herself.

It was stupid. There had been nothing between them except sex, a few brief and wonderful encounters that meant nothing except what she had allowed them to mean in her own mind. An entire lifetime couldn't change in a matter of days. Kevin had meant nothing to her before, and he meant nothing now. They why did it hurt so much?

She kept expecting him to call. Throughout their long relationship the one thing she could always count on from Kevin was persistence. Scarcely a week had gone by in their lives when she hadn't heard from him in one form or another. But he didn't call.

He did talk shows, which she didn't watch. He was on magazine covers, which she didn't buy. Everywhere she turned, she heard the name of Victoria Bend's real-life hero, but she didn't listen. She couldn't bear to listen.

At first she was angry. How dare he put her in such a situation, anyway. Was he crazy? Did he think she was another one of his Hollywood airheads who would follow him around like a besotted puppy, worshiping at the shrine of Colt Marshall? What kind of future could he have possibly imagined for them? She had an entire town filled with people who depended on her for their very lives; he had a grueling schedule in one of the most demanding industries in the world. And conflicting responsibilities were only one of their problems. What could he have been thinking of?

That was the problem, of course. He hadn't been thinking. Kevin never thought of anything much beyond his own instant gratification, and that left Kate to play the heavy. And she was angry.

Yet she still thought about it, in a half-daydreaming, half-masochistic fashion, imagining what would have happened if she had said yes. Imagining that there were no conflicts and no schedules and no responsibilities and she and Kevin could have lived forever the idyllic days and nights they had known after the storm. Those were self-destructive and futile fantasies, she knew, but in some perverted way they seemed to help her get through the night.

In June, Jeff Brandon moved to town and took up his place in her practice with a minimum of strain and transition. At first she had been panicked, certain that the stress of the storm, which had caused her to make such a drastic mistake with Kevin, had also influenced her judgment in hiring Jeff. It was with enormous relief that she found only her heart had been affected that night and not her professional good sense. Jeff was as easygoing and efficient as she remembered him; her patients loved him, and every day he more than justified her trust in him.

The town slowly showed signs of righting itself. With incredible energy, shopkeepers and residents set to rebuilding bigger and better than before. The hospital went up with astounding rapidity. Kate passed it every day, stopped to watch the work and thought of Kevin.

She moved back into her house and started to cry again. Somehow, without her foreknowledge, Kevin had given orders to duplicate every piece of furniture and every replaceable knick-knack that had been damaged in the storm, down to the smallest detail. Except for a few original pieces of art and personal mementoes, everything was exactly as it had been. Kevin had always loved her house, and he had given it back to her exactly as he remembered it.

She started to call him then. She stopped only because she didn't know what to say.

She had never known it was possible to miss anyone so much. She tried to think back over the years and discover whether this much time had ever before passed between Kevin's visits or phone calls. Though she was certain that with his busy schedule he must have been away from Victoria Bend for much longer periods than this, she couldn't recall a single one. She kept thinking that one day he would show up on her doorstep, invite himself in and settle down to raid her refrigerator and drive her to distraction with his annoying habits and that everything would be back to normal. And then it made her sad, because she wasn't sure what normal was for the two of them anymore or if she even wanted things to be normal again. She only knew that she wanted to be with him.

By August she gave up waiting for him, expecting him, wishing for him. She was busier than she had ever been, organizing the hospital, orienting Jeff, assembling a staff. As the town was recovering from the aftermath of the storm, so was she. By inches and degrees her shattered emotional equilibrium was repairing itself, and soon everything would be just as it had been before the disaster struck. All it took was time.

She still had nightmares occasionally and awoke gasping, reaching for Kevin. No one was there to comfort her. And she never turned on her television set anymore between the hours of eight and nine on Monday evenings. But other than that, everything was back to normal. She hardly thought of Kevin at all anymore.

IT WAS THE FIRST OF SEPTEMBER, and the hospital dedication ceremony was less than a week away. Kevin Dawson had been invited to officiate and had respectfully declined, due, ostensibly, to a scheduling conflict. Though everyone made understanding noises, there was some confusion and some hurt feelings among the townspeople. Kevin had never denied them anything before, and for the first time they were being forced to realize Kevin did not belong to them.

The impact of Kevin's decision not to return to Victoria Bend for the ceremony affected Kate on multiple lev-

els, many of them so deep she had yet to recognize them.
She didn't understand. Kevin had cared deeply about the
hospital; she was certain of that. She remembered the
look on his face that afternoon by the lake when he told
her construction had been speeded up. It had become a
personal project for him then; it had been the first of his
many philanthropic gestures in which he had taken an
active part. And he must have known how his sudden
absence would hurt the townspeople with whom he had
always been so close. Was it possible he was turning into
one of those celebrity snobs Kate had always accused him
of being? Or was there something more?

She only knew that on some deep and unconfessed
level she had been holding on to hope for this moment.
She had been certain that no matter what else happened,
she would see Kevin again. And she had counted on seeing him at this ceremony. She couldn't fool herself anymore. Kevin wasn't coming back. Not ever. She had to let
him go.

Again she was angry. Had he cared so little for her that
he could forget about her just like that? Disregarding all
those stirring words of love, how could he let a twenty-
year friendship dissolve overnight? Was he really that
shallow, that thoughtless, or was he just living up to what
she expected of him?

A forlornness settled over her that was much like the
mourning period after the death of someone close. How
empty her life seemed without him. How painful it was
to realize how close she had come to happiness and to
know that she had been the one who willfully threw it
away. She was thirty-four years old, and life was moving
too quickly for her. At one time her patients, friends,
neighbors and family had been enough for her. But Jeff
was taking on more and more of her patient load, and as

childish as it was, it hurt Kate's feelings somewhat to see how easily those she had always assumed could not survive without her accepted a stranger as their primary provider of medical care. Her father never seemed to have time for her anymore, and Victoria Bend, which she had always loved for its steady, placid nature, seemed strangely lacking in challenges. She was lonely.

KATE AND JEFF SAW their last patient early one afternoon and lingered in Kate's office, discussing final plans for the hospital opening over a cup of coffee.

"Well, I've got to hand it to you, Dr. Katherine Larimer," Jeff pronounced with satisfaction, draining the last of his coffee and leaning back in his chair. "You have single-handedly organized and staffed an entire hospital, and I wouldn't have believed it if I hadn't seen it with my own eyes. You're one hell of a woman."

"Am I?" Kate's surprise was genuine, but her smile was weak. The past months had been a blur of activity for her without real purpose or goal, just something to keep her hands busy so her mind didn't have to think. She supposed one day she would look back and be amazed by what she had accomplished, but at the present it didn't feel like any more than doing her job. "Maybe they'll dedicate a wing to me."

"I wouldn't be a bit surprised."

"Well, I guess that's it, then." Kate closed the folder on the last of the yet-to-be-done requisitions. "Now all we need are patients."

"We'll have them," Jeff assured her. "Nature, unfortunately, has a way of taking care of details like that."

"I hope the first one is obstetrics. I can't think of a better way to christen a hospital than with a birth."

"Very possible. Mrs. Daniels is due in three weeks."

Kate laughed. "We may have to fight over who gets to deliver her."

"How about a team effort?" Jeff suggested, eyes twinkling.

"These things usually are," Kate agreed. She straightened the folders and started to get up to put them away. She wasn't particularly anxious to go home, but she didn't want to keep Jeff any longer than she had to. She had discovered in her few months of working with him that he was something of a homebody; he liked working in his yard and on his house, and unlike so many other of her colleagues, never sought excuses to extend office hours into social ones. He was perfect for the small-town life.

He surprised her by saying, "Have you got a minute, Kate?"

"Sure." She sat down again, giving him her full attention. "What's on your mind?"

"I realize that the past months have been really hectic around here," he said, "but now that the hospital is off the ground and we're ready to settle into a routine, there's something I've been wanting to ask you."

She nodded, waiting. But there was no way she could have been prepared for what he said next.

"How do you feel about fraternization between employees?"

At first she didn't understand what he meant. Then she thought, with a faint twinge of disturbance, that he might be interested in Rose, her twenty-year-old secretary. But the last thing she wanted was to become involved in his personal affairs, so all she could say was "Well, actually, I've never felt anything about it. There's never been any reason to."

He smiled. "In that case, do you mind if we form a policy now?"

She tried to be open-minded. "No, I suppose not. What's your opinion?"

By now he could see that she wasn't following him, and the fact registered with gentle amusement in his eyes. "I'm all for it," he confessed. "Would you have dinner with me tonight?"

Kate couldn't hide her surprise, and he laughed softly. "In case you're wondering, my intentions are strictly honorable." And his expression sobered a bit, in a way that made Kate's heart skip a beat. "You can't really say you didn't see this coming, can you, Kate?"

Kate didn't know why she was so incredulous. Since the first moment they had met, the conclusion had been obvious. Within twenty-four hours after having first laid eyes on him, they had been jokingly discussing marriage. That they should become socially, as well as professionally, involved was only logical. Still, she felt compelled to point out, "Jeff, I know the social life in Victoria Bend leaves a great deal to be desired, but there are plenty of eligible young women who would love to go out with you. I'm sorry I didn't think of it before, but of course I'll introduce you—"

"I know all about the eligible young girls, and I've already met my share of them, thank you. It just so happens that I'd rather go out with you right now. We *are* a good team, Kate," he said simply. "Do you have any objections to finding out whether we could be more than that?"

Objections? She would be foolish to object. If she hadn't been so wrapped up in feeling sorry for herself because of Kevin, she would have seen the obvious so much sooner. She needed meaning to her life, and purpose. She needed to expand her horizons, move outside herself, begin to think about having a family. Jeff, whom she liked and respected, the perfect partner with her, shared her interests and her goals. In addition, he was pleasant and attractive and easy to get along with. There was no reason in the world why the two of them shouldn't explore the possibilities in their relationship. Jeff was perfect for her; even Kevin had said so. He could be the most perfect thing that had ever happened to her.

She looked at him, and thought about it. And then she said gently, consideringly, "There's no point to it, Jeff. It would never work."

Only the faintest flicker of surprise registered in his eyes, and she suspected he understood exactly what she meant. Still he asked simply, "Why not?"

She smiled faintly. "I think... because we're too perfect for each other. There are no surprises, no challenges, nothing to fight about." She looked at him helplessly. "Do you understand what I mean?"

He shook his head, but there was a smile in his eyes. "I think you mean that you'd rather have someone who's exactly wrong for you."

Kate answered softly, "Maybe I would."

He got up and came around her desk. Kate stood to meet him. He touched her arms lightly, and his eyes were warm. There was no awkwardness as Kate rested her hands against his chest and they kissed.

His lips were soft and warm and pleasant. His kiss was thorough and leisurely and enjoyable. But that was all it was. Just a kiss.

When they parted, they both knew, and they both smiled. Jeff said gently, "Do fireworks ever happen the first time?"

Kate's smile began to fade, and it was a struggle to maintain it. Unexpectedly, her eyes misted over. She replied, with a strange hoarseness to her voice, "Sometimes."

He looked at her without reprimand or demand. "At this point in my life, Kate," he said simply, "I'm not sure how much I care about the fireworks. I think it's more important to find security, compatibility and permanence." He smiled. "I'm getting too old for surprises."

Kate felt a wave of sadness that was inexplicably mixed with something else—wonder, because until this moment she had never realized what it was she really wanted. She said softly, "Funny. I used to think the same thing."

And then she stepped away from him, a hundred half-formed thoughts bombarding her. She was suddenly seized by the urge to be moving, to be alone, to try to sort through what her mind was trying to tell her. She looked at Jeff, smiling with a brightness that was half relief, half questioning happiness. "Jeff, thank you," she said sincerely. "For caring, for wanting me. But we both know nothing is happening between us. We're great business partners and a perfect medical team, but to try to make it into anything more would make us both uncomfortable. And it's good that we found out now."

He looked at her for a moment, and then one corner of his mouth turned down in a wry admission of the truth. "Well—" he sighed "—it was a good idea."

She smiled and leaned forward and brushed his cheek with a kiss. "Yes, it was." She turned to go.

"Dinner is still open," he called after her, but Kate was hurriedly gathering up her purse and her bag. She felt suddenly almost breathless with the need to examine the things that were just beginning to occur to her.

"Thanks," she returned on her way out the door. "Another time." She paused with a wave and a grin. "My treat!"

Without thinking about it, she drove toward her father's house. Things were beginning to make sense to her, and she was not at all certain she liked the picture that was forming. It was an exciting picture, to be sure, thrilling and hopeful but disturbing nonetheless. She needed someone to talk to. And because she couldn't talk to Kevin, her father would have to do.

She had been so certain that what had developed between her and Kevin had been nothing more than the result of the crisis they had survived during the storm. But Jeff had been with her during the storm, too. He had, figuratively if not literally, saved her life. She had looked up from a state of near panic, and he had been there, calm and controlled, and he had seen her through it. He had actually given her more technical support than Kevin had. She had depended on Jeff more during those nightmarish hours than she had Kevin. She would never forget that horrid stretch of makeshift surgery; no two people could share something like that and remain unchanged.

But when fear and shock had overtaken her, it had not been Jeff's strong chest against which she had broken down and sobbed. It had not been Jeff in whose arms she felt safe enough to sleep. She had not fallen in love with Jeff.

By all rights she should have. Jeff was attractive, articulate, intelligent, good-natured. They had everything in common, up to and including an office and a practice. He had stood by her side through the most demanding crisis in her life, and she had let him share the most protected part of her life—her patients. But he had no place in her heart, because Kevin was already there. He always had been.

The most astounding part was that it had taken Kate this long to realize it. It still made no sense—she still didn't know how to deal with it—but the truth was undeniable. She had loved Kevin long before the storm brought them together. And she loved him still.

Her father didn't answer her first ring, but Kate was persistent. She saw his car in the driveway and knew he was home. She was about to use her key when she heard his disgruntled voice on the other side of the door. He flung it open with a scowl on his face.

He looked as though he had just flung on his clothes, which Kate found peculiar for the middle of the afternoon. His belt was unbuckled, his shirt was unbuttoned, and his hair was rumpled. She was about to comment on his appearance when the scowl on his face faded to resignation and he opened the door wider. "Come in," he said.

And then he did the most startling thing. He turned and called over his shoulder, "Honey, it's Kate. Come on out."

Shock was the mildest of words to describe what Kate felt as Iris, her employee, part-time mother and long-time friend, came out of the bedroom, wearing only Jason Larimer's robe. Of the two women, Iris seemed the more composed, although she was far from comfortable in the situation, it was obvious. Kate felt her face go every shade from white to scarlet, and she couldn't say a word.

Her father looked at her with dry and distant amusement. "If it makes you feel any better," he said, "we're getting married."

He extended his hand for Iris, and she came forward, wrapping her fingers around his in an age-old lover's gesture. The worry on her face was softened momentarily by tenderness as she glanced at Jason, and then she looked at Kate. "Kate," she said, "I hope you're not too upset."

Kate sank to the nearest chair.

Jason cast an amused glance at Iris. "What did I tell you? She never suspected a thing."

The two of them sat on the sofa across from Kate, her father looking wearily expectant, Iris looking nervous. And all Kate could manage was "Why did you keep it such a secret?"

Her father laughed broadly. "Secret! Little girl, everybody in town knows but you! We were beginning to think we'd have to send you an engraved invitation to the wedding before you'd catch on. You can be so blind sometimes, Katie."

Kevin's voice, eyes sparkling tolerantly. "You're so blind sometimes, Katie." He had known even then. Perhaps because he saw with his heart and not just his eyes.

Iris said quickly, "Kate, it's my fault, I'm afraid. I was afraid you wouldn't approve, and I thought we should approach you slowly."

Kate's eyes grew wide. "Approve?" She was having enough trouble just adjusting to this, much less deciding whether she approved. "Why wouldn't I?"

Iris and Jason shared a glance that was so filled with relief and affection that if ever there had been any doubts on Kate's part, they were erased. And now that the truth had a chance to sink in, Kate discovered that she *did* approve, wholeheartedly. If she had ever considered matchmaking for her father—which of course she hadn't—Iris would have been the woman she would have chosen. Her earliest memories were of the two of them as a team; Iris had almost been part of the family all these years. It was just that she had never pictured the two of them romantically, and adjusting to changes was not something Kate did well—as she had proved with Kevin.

Puzzled, she said, "But how long... I mean, when did this start?"

Iris smiled. "You know how it was, Kate. Your father and I have been together so long it's difficult to say exactly when we fell in love. We just sort of grew to love each other."

"After your mother died," Jason added, "especially in these last few years, since I retired, Iris and I have been seeing each other differently, I suppose. Only we were both too comfortable," he added ruefully, "or maybe just too damn cussed, to do anything about it." And he sobered. "Until the night of the storm and we realized how close we came to losing each other. Life's too short, Katie. I made up my mind then not to waste any more of it."

He looked at Iris, and Iris returned softly, her eyes only on his, "So did I."

"You told me one time," Kate murmured, half to herself, "that the storm didn't really change anything; it just made us see more clearly what was already there."

Her father returned his attention to Kate. "Did I? Then I was right."

"Daddy, what would you say if I told you I was marrying Jeff Brandon?"

Iris looked shocked; Jason's brows drew together in a piercing glare. "I'd say you were a damn fool."

Kate couldn't help grinning as she got up from the chair. New discoveries, insane hopes and absurd desires were bounding and buoying inside her until she felt as if she could fly. "That's what I thought you'd say."

She swept over to the sofa and embraced them both swiftly. "Congratulations, you two. I couldn't be happier."

She was at the door before her startled father thought to ask, "Wait a minute—what did you come here for?"

"Just some advice to the lovelorn," she called back. "Thanks for giving it to me."

She closed the door behind her, and Iris looked at Jason curiously. "What do you suppose she meant by that?"

He looked worried. "I don't know."

Iris's brows came together thoughtfully. "You don't think she was serious about Dr. Brandon, do you?"

Jason looked at the woman who had brought him love again after so many years, and he came to a decision. "I'll tell you one thing," he said firmly. "I'm not interested in taking that chance. It's about time somebody put a stop to this nonsense. It might as well be me."

He reached for the telephone.

Chapter Thirteen

"Will somebody get me wardrobe?" Kevin shouted. "How many times do I have to ask?"

Wearily, the director rose and crossed over to him. "What's the problem now, Kevin?"

Kevin turned to him, snapping, "You tell me! Just look at this shirt!" He wore a denim jacket embroidered on the back with a brilliant multicolored eagle and beneath it a screen-print T-shirt with a red abstract design. It was the design he seemed to be objecting to. "What the hell is this supposed to be, anyway?" He gestured furiously. "It looks like a damn spaghetti stain." He stripped off the jacket—at five hundred dollars a shot, he went through approximately two of them a week—and let it drop to the ground. Then he peeled off the shirt and threw it in the director's face.

"All right, babe. Hey, no problem," the other man soothed. He balled up the shirt and thrust it at a passing technician. "So we get you another shirt." Then, at the top of his lungs, he yelled, "Wardrobe!"

"And another thing," Kevin continued shortly. He picked up a copy of the script and gave it a contemptuous thump with his fist. "Who writes this damn dialogue? Why don't the women on this show ever get to say anything besides 'Oh, Colt, I don't know what I'd do without you'? Real women don't talk like that!''

His female guest star gave him a grateful look, but the director only patted his shoulder. "That's why they call it fantasy, babe," he explained patiently, and Kevin thrust the script at him.

"Fix it," he advised darkly, and turned on his heel and stalked away.

In passing, someone slipped a black shirt over his arms; someone else scurried to drape his jacket over his shoulders like a cape. Kevin walked faster.

A canopy had been set up on the lot to protect a wet bar and a couple of chairs from the glare of the noon sun, and it was there Kevin found Carl waiting for him. "It's about time you got here," he greeted him ungraciously. "I called you over an hour ago." He took a club soda from the ice bucket and popped the cap.

"My feet are like wings *sahib*," Carl replied lazily, but his expression was alert. He didn't make house calls to the set except in case of emergency. This emergency of Kevin's had been building for weeks. Perhaps months.

He settled back in a chair with something more potent than a club soda and watched Kevin dispassionately. The network's highest-paid star had lost about ten pounds over the summer; the cameras loved it, but Kevin thought it made him look sick. For a while after returning from Mississippi, Carl had worried that his most lucrative client might indeed be ill—or trying to make himself so—but after a while he had straightened up, started working out and getting some sun. He looked fine on camera. The weight loss made him look tougher. The scar on his shoulder had worked out well, too; Kevin had been right—they had written it in as a bullet wound and written the season opener around it. It was only off camera that it became obvious things weren't so fine with Kevin Dawson.

"Notice you're keeping up the temper tantrums," Carl commented, sipping his drink. "That's fine, old chap, just fine. Make them think you're dissatisfied. Then we'll strike for a bigger contract next year."

Kevin watched the bubbles dance as he poured the club soda into a glass. He said mildly, "I'm glad you brought that up." He took his glass, strolled over to a chair and settled down. He looked Carl straight in the eyes. He said, "I want out."

Carl was impassive. "Out of what?"

"Out of this show."

"Impossible." Carl waved a languid hand, as though the concept did not even merit serious rebuttal.

But Kevin's eyes were steady, the set of his jaw firm. Carl had a moment to reflect that Kevin looked calmer at that moment than he had seen him in months, and that worried him. "My contract is up with this season," Kevin said without qualification. "I'm not going to renew."

Absolutely nothing registered on Carl's face. He was a pro. "Would it trouble you too much if one inquired why?"

Kevin looked down into his glass for a moment, took a sip and then met Carl's eyes again. There was nothing in his expression but calm resolve. "I've outgrown it," he said simply.

Carl drank from his glass without ever losing eye contact with Kevin. "It will take a bit more than that, dear boy."

If there ever had been a doubt that this was a spur of the moment decision, a threat or another one of Kevin's recent and inexplicable lapses into temperamental behavior, it was erased by Kevin's next words. This was obviously something about which Kevin had thought long and hard; it occurred to Carl to notice that this was, in fact, the first time since he had known him that Kevin had seemed sure about anything.

"The image has worn out," he explained. "I don't have room in my life for the schedule anymore; too many important things are falling by the wayside. I'm not the same person who developed Colt Marshall, and I don't believe in him anymore." He shrugged, then smiled. "Didn't you ever wake up one morning, Carl, and realize that you hate what you do?"

Carl's gaze was steady. "Every day." He lifted his glass again. It was almost empty. "Now, assuming that this peculiar madness still possesses you when it comes time to actually renegotiate your contract, what is it, exactly, that you plan to do? Retire to the Bahamas and weave baskets? Dogsled in Alaska? Or perhaps settle down with your doctor friend in Victory, Mississippi, and make babies?"

Kevin's eyes grew very hard, like fired glass. It was an amazing thing to see. Kevin had always been such a placid, malleable personality, but lately—most especially when one happened to mention that unfortunate little burg in Mississippi—he acquired characteristics that made even Carl hesitate. He had never realized before that beneath all the fuss and feathers there might be a force to be reckoned with in Kevin Dawson.

Kevin said coldly, "It's Victoria Bend." And he looked as though he might say something else, something both he and Carl would regret, and both men tensed for it. Then Kevin stood abruptly and paced back over to the bar. His movements were tight and his voice, when he spoke, very restrained. "Right now, I want to start doing films. And I want to look at some good parts. None of this hackneyed fluff, either. I want something solid.''

Carl lifted a mild eyebrow. ''Was it a mere year ago I was begging you to expand your horizons? You told me then, if I recall, that you weren't interested. 'Not ready,' I believe, was the term you used.''

Kevin turned, bracing his arms against the bar. His eyes were still very cold. ''Well, I'm ready now. If acting is the only thing I can do, I may as well do it right. What about that new Morgan property? Everyone in this town has seen it but me.''

Carl dismissed it out of hand. ''Not for you, matie. The male lead is a psychotic; murders his wife and children. Your fans would commit mass suicide were they to see you play a role like that.''

''It sounds like a challenge,'' Kevin insisted stubbornly. ''It's exactly what I want a chance at.''

Carl was getting worried. ''Now, look here, my friend—''

''Mr. Dawson, there you are!'' A young man ran up, panting. Kevin looked at him impatiently. ''There's a phone call for you in your dressing room. It sounds urgent.''

Kevin scowled and turned back to Carl. ''Take a message. Now, you listen to me, Carl—''

''But it's long distance! A Dr. Larimer—''

Kevin felt his heart stop, and when it started beating again, he thought his head would explode. He took two steps toward his dressing room and then turned back to Carl. ''Get me that script,'' he commanded, and then he ran.

Kevin burst into the trailer, flinging the door open so hard that it bounced on its hinges and then slammed itself closed with a bang. His palms were so slippery that he almost dropped the receiver as he snatched it up, and his heart was pounding so loudly in his ears that he was certain he wouldn't be able to hear the voice on the other end. After all this time, all this waiting.

"Katie?" he said breathlessly into the phone, and his disappointment was so acute it twisted in his stomach with a physical pain when he heard the reply.

"So," Jason Larimer said with a low chuckle, "that answers one question, anyway."

Kevin had to sit down. He felt foolish and hurt and bitterly disillusioned. He should have known. Katie was no silly romantic given to sudden changes of heart. She had said she didn't want him. No, she had said she didn't love him. She knew her own mind, her own feelings. She wouldn't change.

And how long was he going to nurture this insane dream that one day she would?

"Hello, Dr. Larimer. How are you doing?" It was an effort to make his voice sound normal. His throat hurt, as though with the tightness of tears. That made him feel like a child, and he was impatient with himself.

"A lot better than you, it sounds like," Jason responded. "I'm getting married."

"Are you?" This time Kevin was able to force a modicum of genuine joy into his voice. He was pleased; he only wished it were he saying those words and not the man on the other end of the telephone. "To Iris? Well, its about damn time. Congratulations!"

Again Jason chuckled. "We never had you fooled for a moment, did we, boy? I always did say you had a lot more sense than Katie ever gave you credit for."

Kevin's throat tightened again at the mention of her name, and he couldn't prevent the next words, half muttered and unhappy. "Not necessarily." Then, quickly, he changed the subject. "When's the date? Am I invited?"

"I'll let you know. And of course you're invited. Not," he added shrewdly, "that I'd hold up the party waiting for you to show up. I hear you've gotten a bit too busy for us hometown folks lately."

Kevin sighed, running a hand through his hair in a gesture that was half nervous, half weary. "Listen, if you mean about the hospital dedication, I'm really sorry about the schedule conflict, but—"

"Don't give me that bull, son," Jason said shortly. "You can try it on anybody else, but I know you too well. And you're forgetting that I've been on the mayor's planning committee since day one and I have access to certain information other people might not bother to investigate... like the fact that you haven't been too busy to give every detail of this hospital project your personal attention, from cost control to safety inspection. Am I right? If it hadn't been for you pulling strings, we wouldn't have had this building up until this time next year, and if a man can take time out of his busy schedule to personally sift through that much red tape, why, I would say that man's schedule has to be pretty flexible, wouldn't you?"

Kevin uncomfortably shrugged out of his jacket. The air conditioner was broken again, and it was hot and sticky inside the trailer. "Look," he said, "that was different."

"Damn right it was," Jason declared adamantly. "For the first time in your life you didn't let your lackeys do everything for you. I've got to point out that that doesn't sound much like the Kevin Dawson I once knew. What's gotten into you, I wonder."

Kevin leaned back in the squeaky swivel chair, his expression fading into a sort of embarrassment. "Damned if I know. Maybe I grew up a little when I wasn't looking, hmm?"

"Could very well be," Jason agreed soberly. "But somehow it doesn't seem very grown-up to me to refuse to come to the dedication ceremony when you've worked so hard to get the hospital on its feet."

"No," Kevin admitted quietly, tired of glib denials and self-deceptions. "That's just cowardice."

"And that," Jason said in the same quiet tone, "is what I called about."

Kevin tried to smile. "You should have reversed the charges. That's a subject that could take the rest of the day to explore."

"No it won't. Because I've got one thing to say regarding your cowardice: it doesn't suit you anymore. You've changed, Kevin," he said simply. "And you don't even realize how much yet. You're still playing the same games, but you're in a different arena. How long," he asked, "were you going to wait before you went after Katie with the same kind of energy you used to get this hospital built?"

Kevin's heart started pounding again, tightly and heavily. "It's not the same thing. Katie's not the kind of woman who can be chased. She doesn't want me."

"How do you know that?"

"She told me so."

"And you believe that?"

Did he? Six months had passed. He, Kevin Dawson, whose reputation was second to none, who had his pick of any of the starlets of Hollywood, had not been with another woman. He hadn't been tempted, not even for consolation. Always before, women, relationships, affection, had been a mirror to his ego, a balm to his confidence, a method of reassurance and a substitute for stability. He didn't need such placebos anymore; he didn't even think of them. Because in Kate he had found his real stability; nothing would ever change that, and nothing would ever be the same because of it.

Kevin said, a little gruffly, "I'm not sure it matters what I think."

"Oh, it doesn't, does it?" Jason's voice was sarcastic. "Well, maybe you'd better think again. Katie's a fine woman," he continued in a milder tone, "smart as a whip and strong enough for any two men, and I'm proud to have her as a daughter. The only trouble with her is that she's gotten too used to bossing people around. She's been doing it to you all your life, hasn't she? Maybe it's time you showed her you can think for yourself."

Kevin ran a hand impatiently through his hair, then underneath his collar, which was not buttoned but nonetheless felt too tight. "Come on, the day of the caveman has passed. I can't make Katie do anything she doesn't want to. I certainly can't make her..." He had to swallow before he said the words. "Love me."

"But," Jason advised gently, "you might give her a little help in making some hard decisions. And you might also like to know that Dr. Jeff Brandon hasn't exactly been sitting on his hands since you've been gone. And Katie's talking about marriage."

Kevin tensed, then forcefully relaxed. He knew the ploy for exactly what it was; no one was going to incite him to jealousy long-distance over a woman who wasn't even interested in him. And if Brandon was who Katie wanted, that was who she should have. He would be better for her anyway. They were perfect for each other. He opened his mouth to say exactly that, but what came out was, negligently, "Listen, put my name back on the roster for the dedication ceremony, will you? I think I see a break in my schedule coming up."

Jason was chuckling when Kevin hung up the phone, and Kevin sat there for a long time, frowning thoughtfully. Jason was right about one thing. He wasn't a coward anymore, and refusing to return to the town he loved and to which he had poured so much energy was a childish act of defiance that did not suit him any longer. He was only ashamed that it had taken him this long—and the interference of another person—to realize it.

He did not have to see Katie, of course. At least not on a personal basis. He had no intention of interfering in her life. Katie had always made the right decisions, and there was nothing he could about that.

He would leave her alone, he decided firmly. It would be better all around.

Like hell it would.

The absent scowl on his face turned into something fierce, and a surge of adrenaline went through him that was second only to the one he had felt on the night of the storm. His fists bunched as he sprang to his feet, and he didn't look back as he strode out the door.

KATE RETURNED THE TELEPHONE to its cradle without dialing. *This is insane,* she thought, and then sank to the sofa, wrapping her arms around herself tightly as though to prevent herself from trying such an action again or to protect the curious happiness that threatened to give way to logic.

If Kevin had wanted to talk to her, he would have called. Who was she to just call up and say, "Kevin I've changed my mind. If you don't mind dropping everything, completely rearranging your life and falling in love with me again, I'd like to give us a chance."

She glanced at the telephone again. It was stupid. She knew Kevin. By now he was probably with some other woman, telling her the same sweet things he had told Kate, swearing undying loyalty and perhaps even proposing marriage.

But everything in Kate rebelled at that. Kevin hadn't been lying to her. Instinctively, she had known that all along. What was between them was different than what had been between him and someone else. It was stronger, and it was deeper; it had lasted over twenty years. When he had said he had loved her, she had known it was true; perhaps the only true thing about their entire relationship. The only thing that had kept her from seizing that gift that was meant only for her was her own cowardice.

If he had found another woman, Kate decided fiercely, she would fight for him. Because nothing any other woman could give him was as strong as what she and Kevin had together.

Her hand was on the telephone again when she stopped and backed away worriedly. Then why hadn't he called?

Because, Doctor, you lied to him. You told him you didn't love him. How was he supposed to fight that? How she must have hurt him, after he had opened his heart to her, by rejecting his feelings so coldly and so effortlessly. Had she said merely, "It can't work out," or "There are too many problems," he might have been able to challenge her. But she had said, "I don't love you," and there were no words more final, no goodbye more complete.

But I lied....

Love. What a euphemestic term for something as complete, as abiding, as all encompassing as what she felt for Kevin. He was a part of her. The good parts and the bad parts, the best and the worst of her; he had been with her forever. It was familiarity, and it was mystery; it was challenge and companionability, a mirror of contrasts.

For years she had fought it by seeing only the worst in Kevin, by convincing herself that no matter what else he was, Kevin Dawson was not a person she could like or respect. She had set up that distance between them because she knew the danger to her emotions should she ever let him get close, should she ever acknowledge to herself what was really between them. Then the storm had come and wiped away all facades, and she was forced to see the parts of Kevin she had hidden from before, just as he was forced to let her see them. And what had remained was the love, deep and untouched, that had always bound them together.

"We grew into love," Iris had said.

"It's the way we were always meant to be," Kevin had said.

That was the hardest thing of all, to discover love that had been hidden and fallow for all those years and to recognize it for what it was, to accept it without question. Kevin had been able to do that. Iris and Kate's father had been able to do it. But Kate had been afraid.

But she wasn't any longer. If the disaster through which they all had lived had done nothing else for Kate, it had shown her strength. It had proved to her that she possessed capabilities she'd never guessed she had before. It had shown her courage she never knew she had. She picked up the telephone.

Kevin was not at home; his housekeeper said he was at the studio. With much effort, Kate finally got the number but his private line was busy. When she tried again ten minutes later, someone told her he had left for the day.

No, he hadn't gone home. He was out of town, and no one knew when he would be back.

Kate sat for a moment, biting her lip in frustration. Then she came to a decision. She would go to California if necessary. These things could be worked out; all it required was a little effort on her part. And she had no intention of letting the rest of her life slip away because she was afraid to try. She picked up the phone again and dialed.

"Jeff," she said a little breathlessly, "are you still free for dinner?"

IT WAS TEN O'CLOCK in the evening when Jeff drove her home. They had gone to a country inn just over the county line, and Jeff assured her dinner had been excellent. Kate had been too excited to eat, and she'd had a lot to say.

His hand was light and protective on her elbow, his manner lightly amused as he walked her to the front door. "So," Kate said with a breath, taking out her key, "it's all settled. You'll handle the office for the next two weeks, and when I get back, we'll discuss rearranging the patient load."

He nodded. Kate had left on both the porch light and the living room lamps, and in the golden illumination his expression was tolerant and indulgent, though still slightly bemused. "Don't worry about a thing."

She started to unlock the door and then turned to him. "Are you sure you don't mind?"

"Would it matter if I did?"

"No," she said, smiling. "I'm afraid it wouldn't."

"In that case, boss, I don't mind." He looked at her for a moment, the smile in his eyes fading to gentle understanding. "You're doing all this so you can run off to your Hollywood playboy, aren't you?"

Kate tilted her head thoughtfully. "What would you say if I were?"

"I'd say you're crazy," he responded flatly.

Kate laughed and leaned forward to brush his cheek with a kiss. "Thanks for everything, Jeff. Good night."

"Good night, Kate. Good luck..." And then he paused. "I think."

Kate was still smiling as she stepped inside and closed the door behind her, placing her purse and keys on the table near the door. She started toward the telephone, intending to try Kevin one more time, and then she stopped. Everything within her stopped.

He was sitting on the sofa, wearing his Colt Marshall costume of bleached-out jeans, battered cowboy boots and embroidered denim jacket. His black shirt was unbuttoned to the chest, his ankles were crossed on her coffee table, and he was sipping a glass of her wine. He looked more tired, sterner and thinner than she remembered. His hair was tousled, and there was a faint bristle on his chin; he was scowling. And he looked so beautiful to her that she actually felt dizzy from looking at him. Happiness and wonder soared through her and left her weak.

She smiled; she couldn't help it. Then she leaned back against the door for support and murmured, "Well, if it isn't Colt Marshall, as I live and breathe."

His brows only drew together more tightly over the bridge of his nose and his eyes were dark and tumultuous. She didn't care. All she could think was *Kevin, Kevin...it's you, it really is.... Thank God...*

He took a short gulp of the wine and demanded, "Did you have a good time?"

It took a long time for Kate to focus on his words, much less what they meant. Her head was spinning. In the end she answered with another question. "How did you get in here?"

"I put the locks on," he replied, glaring at her. "Naturally I have a key."

She wanted to cross the room to him, to gather him in her arms and feel his shape beneath her, to kiss him and hold him and tell him all that was singing and shouting within her. But her heart was pounding so hard she could barely breathe, and her knees were too rubbery to move. Unable to think of anything else that would give her the time to regain her strength, she finally said, "My father is getting married."

"I know." His tone was terse, and his eyes darkened another fraction. He drained the last of the wine. "So, I hear, are you."

She hardly had time to absorb this incredible statement before he was on his feet, slamming the empty wineglass down onto the coffee table with a force that made it tip on end. He stalked over to her, his eyes blazing. "For God's sake, Katie, are you out of your mind?"

Her eyes were wide with confusion and protest, and she began a weak "Kevin—" But he cut her off.

"No, damn it, you just listen to me." He looked as though he would grab her then, but he stopped a few feet before her, his eyes churning, his stance taut. "Maybe I can't stop you from ruining your life, but I can make you listen to me for just this once!"

He took a breath, dragging his fingers through his hair in a gesture of restrained anger and forced control, half turning from her for a second. "Do you know what your problem is?" he demanded, whirling on her again. "Your problem is you're too damn used to being right. I'm used

to your being right. But let me tell you something, Dr.
Katherine Larimer—you were wrong about us!''

She whispered, "I know.''

But he didn't hear her and continued furiously. "You
were so damn sure we were just imagining what happened between us. You had me half convinced that I
didn't know my own feelings. But it wasn't just the
storm; it wasn't just stress, or whatever the hell you
wanted to make me believe. It's been six months, and I've
never stopped loving you. I—"

He paused suddenly, sucking in his breath sharply. He
stared at her. "What did you say?" he breathed.

Her eyes were suddenly blurred, and her voice was
choked. She said, "I said, 'I know.' I was wrong."

He stood there, just looking at her, for the longest
time. The moment was held like a breath, questions and
answers hovering between them in half-suspended
awareness. He even took a half step toward her and then
stopped. This was too important to rush.

His eyes lowered and then lifted to her again. He said
quietly, searching her face, "Katie, I want you to understand something. I know that I'm known for being impulsive, and even headstrong, sometimes. I've made a lot
of mistakes because of it. But you and I... we went
through more than life together. We survived death together, and after living through the kind of destruction I
saw last spring, watching the world literally blown apart,
leaving people's lives in shambles... I haven't looked at
anything in the same way since. Maybe I never will
again.''

He took a breath. "I guess you thought since I could
walk away from it, I could forget about it just as easily.
But I couldn't. I might not have lost anything of material value that night, but I did lose something just as im-

portant—my childhood, I guess. And it was probably about time.

"Things are in a different perspective for me now," he said simply. "I'm not the same man you used to know. The things that used to be important to me don't seem to matter much anymore. I don't care so much about taking the easy way out, and the good times are—well, they're not as good as they used to be." He smiled a little, faintly. "I guess what I'm saying is that I'm not the little kid who used to tag around and pester you for attention anymore. And maybe you won't like the man I've become."

Kate's fists clenched slowly into balls, and it was purely from the effort it took to keep herself from reaching for him. "It didn't occur to you," she said, lifting her chin a little, "that I might have changed, too?" Her voice sounded a little thick, but it was steady. "Maybe the one thing I needed in my life is to learn how to deal with things I can't control. The storm was one of them. You're another. There are a lot of things I still don't know about myself, Kevin, and about life, but I know one thing, and maybe it's the most important one—I want you in my life."

He stood there, looking at her with hesitation and disbelief and cautious hope slowly lightening his eyes. And then he lifted his hands slightly, as though to reach for her, and she walked blindly into his arms.

He held her tightly, burying his face in her hair. She twisted her arms around him until the muscles ached. She could feel his heartbeat and his warmth; she inhaled the scent of dusty denim and Kevin and felt the trickle of tears from her eyes that she couldn't seem to control. She didn't know why she was crying, and she didn't even want to know. She just wanted to hold him.

His fingers threaded shakily through her hair, and she felt his lips lightly brush her temple. He cupped her face and lifted it gently to look at him. His eyes were very sober. "Do you remember you asked me once if I ever had nightmares?"

She nodded.

"I have, for the past six months. Every night. And they were all about losing you."

She pressed her face against his shoulder again. "Oh, Kevin," she whispered. "All these months—why didn't you call me? Why didn't you...?"

His arms tightened, and she felt his inhalation of breath. His voice was husky. "I started to. Every day. I had to make myself stop. I told myself I'd give it six months, to prove you were right." And then he took her shoulders, pushing her a little away. His eyes were dark, almost feverish, but his face was sober.

"Katie," he said, "I have changed in some ways. Maybe you were right about that. No one faces death and remains completely unchanged. I've learned things about myself I never knew before, mostly what I want from life. In some ways I'm stronger, but in other ways I'm still the same." He took a breath, searching her eyes anxiously. "I can't be what I'm not for you. I can't turn into a genius overnight, or be a real hero, or a lot of the other things you want. I can only give you what I am, and maybe that's what you really need."

She smiled through the tears that glimmered on her lashes; the smile seemed to go through her entire body. "Maybe it is," she whispered.

She saw the hope in his eyes, and for a moment he seemed too moved to do anything but hold her arms, looking at her, questioning and uncertain. She reached up and touched his face lightly, unashamed of the slight tremor in her fingers. "Kevin," she said hoarsely, and pain crossed her eyes with the intensity of the statement. "I'm so sorry—for putting you through this, for hurting you this way. For risking everything. But I was afraid, don't you see? Of the challenge, of the change . . . of loving you."

"And now?" It was barely a whisper.

"I'm still afraid," she admitted. "A little. But I can't help loving you."

Their arms closed around each other again, and they kissed. The intensity of his touch, of his lips meeting hers, went through Kate like liquid fire; it made her head roar and her pulse race out of control. Kevin was here. At last. Hers. Certainty and joy swelled between them, but even the kiss could not communicate it all, and when they parted, Kate was breathless with a dozen soaring, pulsating emotions, questions that needed to be asked, words that had to be spoken.

But none of them were appropriate for this moment; none of them could begin to fill the emptiness that had been building inside them both for so long. Without a word, without even a shadow of hesitation or question, their hands linked, and they walked together into the bedroom.

The magic had not faded. If anything, it was more intense, more precious and brilliant for having been so long lost and at last recaptured. Kate trembled as her clothing fell away and his kisses brushed her pliant skin like dewdrops. Her touch was more urgent, more greedy, as her eager hands pushed away his clothing, anxious for the sensation of his flesh against hers, for the familiarity of his scent and his taste. Yet he restrained her with tenderness and patience, holding back the fire that burned in his own eyes, determined to prolong the moment.

Once before they had made love in surprise and discovery, the very newness of it pushing them over the heights. Another time they had discovered sensuality and giving, learning to be comfortable with each other and to derive pleasure from that openness. Tonight their bodies spoke a different message to each other, and it was one more beautiful, more enduring and meaningful, than any that had gone before. Tonight they came together because they belonged together and because it was forever.

Katie felt the soft brush of his muscled legs against hers, the heat of his body that penetrated every cell of her own, and she thought with simple, wonderful, finality, *Mine*. With her fingertips she explored his lean planes and ropy muscles, adoring him, all of him, with a gentle, possessive certainty that opened a new dimension within her. For in that night, in that simple act of giving and sharing, they were no longer two separate identities, but one, just as it always should have been.

His fingers, tender and adoring, memorized her body as though he had never known it before. The touch of his lips aroused her to new heights of pleasure and lulled her into sweet, dizzy anticipation. And when at last they joined, she looked into his eyes, soft and brilliant with adoration, and saw only the man she would always love.

Their rhythm was slow and exquisite, intensifying not only sensation but emotion. The night stretched before them without end, and the moment captured would last forever. He entwined his fingers with hers; her lips played a delicate dance across his face. Their bodies were joined, but it was so much more than that. Their lives, too, were enmeshed with each other, their hearts and their souls inextricably entwined, and for all time.

The passion built, and urgency drove them, yet when satisfaction was reached, there was more, far more, than physical fulfillment. For it was not the end of the journey, only the beginning.

For a long time afterward they lay in each other's arms, stroking and holding each other, listening to the synchronization of their heartbeats. The night was still and benevolent around them. And even their minds, for a time, were stilled.

Kevin propped himself up on one elbow, looking at her. His smile was slow and lazy, and he bent to place a gentle kiss on her forehead. "We've never made love in your bed before," he said.

She caught his fingers, linking them with hers, bringing them up to rub gently against the side of her cheek. "For good reason," she reminded him. "Since I barely had a house when you were here before." And she looked up at him. "Thank you, Kevin," she said sincerely, "for fixing up my house. You got everything," she added a little wondrously, "even to the last detail, perfect."

He smiled and dragged one finger playfully across the bridge of her nose. "I wanted you to think of me while I was gone. That was the only way I could think of to do it. And how could I forget anything about this place? Most of my dreams have centered around it, for longer than you would believe."

She smiled at him. "And so are we going to live here or at your house?"

He gave it very little thought. "Only one of the many problems that lie ahead for us, love. I imagine on that, like everything else, we'll have to learn to compromise."

Her eyes went over him slowly, filling herself with him, just as he did with her. It wasn't happiness that filled her but something deeper, more abiding and deeply certain. For a moment it took her breath away, and all she could do was smile at him.

When she could speak again, the only thing she could think to ask was "Who told you I was getting married?"

A shadow crossed Kevin's face, and he dropped his eyes. She could feel him tense. "Your father. When he called, I thought it was you. And then he told me about Brandon and—it felt like a knife in my chest." He looked at her intensely. "I couldn't let you do it, Katie."

Kate drew a breath, and she was as startled as he when it was released as a laugh. "That interfering old busybody! I'm not marrying Jeff Brandon. I *have* been calling you all day, Kevin," she told him, "but not to talk about Jeff Brandon."

Confusion and uncertainty were rampant on his face. "You called me? But—then why?"

"To propose," Kate answered simply.

His eyes widened, and he drew in his breath. "What?"

"Well," she acceded demurely, "it occurred to me I'd better act fast, while I could still catch you between marriages."

His laugh was soft and weak, and it went through her like a thrill as he drew her into his arms. "Oh, Katie," he murmured, "it can work. I told you it could." And he looked down at her. "With the end of this season, I'm leaving the show," he told her. "We'll have time, then, for each other. I want to start doing films and then study production—and if I do well, I'd like to have a studio here, in Victoria Bend. It's something I've always wanted, always thought about in the back of my mind, and now's the time to go for it."

Kate's eyes were sparkling. "Jeff—the ex-Mr., Dr. Larimer—has agreed to take on more of the patient load, which will free my time, too. I guess—" and she lowered her eyes briefly "—one of the things I had to learn was to let go." Then she looked up at him. "Also, I've arranged to have two weeks off. So if we move fast, we might even have a honeymoon."

They moved into each other's arms again, happiness and laughter bubbling between them in waves too great to be contained. A long time later, Kate murmured against his shoulder, "You didn't answer my question."

He nuzzled her back. "What question?"

She leaned back a little to look at him. "Will you marry me?"

His eyes crinkled with the depths of a tender smile. "I think that was my line."

"I'll answer your question," Kate whispered, "if you'll answer mine."

They looked into each other's eyes for a long time, giving and receiving promises too deep and too binding for words. And then, in unison, they said, "Yes."